The Mazatlan Showdown

Patrick Weill

Weill & Associates

Sharky Cornell appears with permission. All other characters in this book are fictitious. Any resemblance to actual persons, living or dead, is purely coincidental. The Oceanside Port Authority is fictional while the San Diego Lifeguard Service, the San Diego Harbor Police, and the Oceanside Police Department are actual institutions. Humphrey's Concerts by the Bay is real, although it is an outdoor venue at the time of writing. The Marine Room exists as described, while Sammy's, The East End, the San Diego Music Center, and Boca Negra are figments of the author's imagination. Every effort has been made to represent reality where possible but creative liberties have been taken, and no depiction of any action or omission by any person, authority, or organization, real or fictitious, is meant to imply or explicitly refer to any real impropriety committed by that or any other person, authority, or organization. This is a work of fiction.

Copyright © 2023 Patrick Weill. All rights reserved.

Published by Weill & Associates

Version 2.0, October 2023

Ebook ISBN: 978-1-959866-03-9

Print ISBN: 978-1-959866-02-2

Cover design by cover2book.com

Map of San Diego by Bernard Oliver

Dedicated to my family with all my love.

CONTENTS

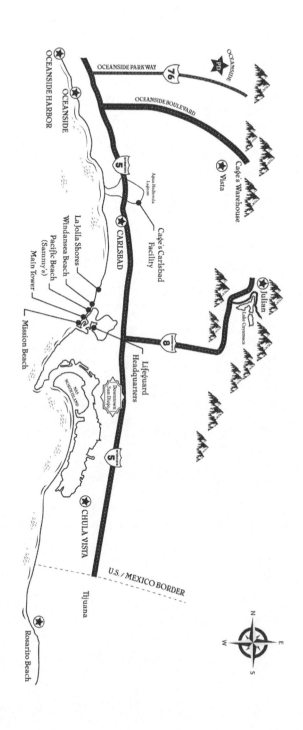

1

GUNSHOT WOUNDS

THIRTY YEARS AGO

L ieutenant Thomas Walker's eyes shot open in the predawn
   darkness with no need for the alarm he'd set the night before.
He scooted toward his wife and snuggled up against her.

"Morning," he whispered.

"Mmmmmm."

He slid his hand over her pregnant belly, kissing her neck, feeling
the warmth of her body, and breathing with her for a time, yet the
important events of the day ahead set him promptly into motion
like a giant fist that scooped him up and shoved him into the
shower.

He went through the battle plan as he bathed: he and Christine
were slated to testify in the court-martial of Lieutenant Trent
Bolton, a fellow naval aviator. But the man would never fly a
fighter plane again. After Walker's testimony, Bolton would be
dishonorably discharged and hopefully sent to prison for several
years.

As he shrugged on his white dress uniform, Walker thought to
fill up the Mustang while Chris was still getting ready. He left the
house and strode across the driveway to his black GT convertible,
scanning the neighborhood, as was his habit. The breaking light of
dawn gave him a clear view of the cars on the street, and the only
vehicle he didn't recognize was a red crew-cab pickup parked three

blocks away. Walker didn't see anyone inside, so he turned back to his black Mustang, slid behind the wheel, started its engine with a roar, and grumbled onto the road in reverse. Without coming to a full stop, he shifted into first and pressed the pedal lightly. The street-legal race car leapt forward. Dropping into second gear, he picked up speed, the cold morning air blowing in through his open windows. Walker wished it were a warmer breeze like the one at Rosarito Beach, where they were planning to take little Jeffrey on his first vacation once he was born and big enough to enjoy it.

A hundred yards from the stop sign at the corner, he glanced up at the rear-view mirror. A jolt of panic rocked his body like a pair of defibrillator paddles. *Fuck!* The big red pickup was approaching fast from behind. As it came alongside on the left, it collided with Walker's car, forcing him to choose between crashing into his neighbor's living room or braking to a stop.

Walker brought the Mustang to an immediate halt and popped the glove box to grab his Glock 17. He then flew out of the car and to the corner, cutting right, looking everywhere for a safe place from which to call Christine. He had to warn her in case his attackers went back to the house, and he suspected they might. The best option was a gas station on the other side of the street, so he sprinted for it, his strong legs pumping as he glanced over his shoulder. Three men emerged from around the corner with pistols leveled. BAM! BAM! BAM!

Despite the bullets snapping past his body, he made it into the restroom, securing the steel door with a heavy sliding bolt as his pursuers' rounds slammed into it, startling him and denting the metal. He hustled to the most defensible corner, flipped open his phone, and gave his wife the short version.

"I'm calling the police," she said.

"It won't do any good," he replied. "This is going to be over in two minutes. Get out of the house immediately. Rent a room where we spent our honeymoon and I'll meet you there if I can."

BOOM! BOOM! BOOM! Fists pounding at the metal door. "Let me in, Walker, or I'll make it even worse!" barked a familiar voice.

Walker's emotions swelled in his chest as he chose what he knew were parting words. What could he say? "You know you're the love of my life."

Christine didn't reply, but she didn't need to. Her muffled sobs told him more than any words could.

He flipped the phone shut and tossed it aside. The pounding on the door had stopped. As seconds stretched into minutes, and minutes into hours, the sound of an engine grew louder, accelerating, approaching. Walker charged into a stall, leapt onto the toilet seat, whirled around, and aimed his pistol at the dark-green door just as it was smashed in with a squealing of twisted metal, creating a gap between the door and its frame.

As the big red pickup backed away, Walker peered over the stall's dividing panel, estimating the width of the gap at a foot and a half. His attackers would have to squeeze themselves through to enter, so that's where he aimed his Glock. He heard three of the pickup's doors clunk shut, but no targets stepped into view, just an army-green frag grenade that came sailing in and clattered to a stop on the floor outside the stall.

The blast tore the dividers out of the wall and hurled Walker to the floor. As he fell, he smashed his head on the toilet with a sickening thunk. He pushed himself up onto his hands and knees, the ringing in his ears drowning out all other sounds, and a strong pair of hands hauled him up to a standing position. He swayed on his feet as he blinked his vision into focus on two men he couldn't identify, and on Trent Bolton, the crook he'd been about to testify against. All three stood out of reach with their pistols leveled.

Bolton's black hair was clipped short in a high and tight, and his chiseled features showed little emotion as he stared down the sights of a Ruger P90, targeting Walker's head. "Any last words?" he asked.

Walker knew better than to waste the final seconds of his life conversing with a drug-addicted criminal. Instead, he closed his eyes in gratitude for all the time he'd spent with Christine, for their intoxicating courtship in Kentucky and the ten sunny years in San Diego that followed. He thought of Jeffrey, the son he'd never get to know; they'd call him Jeff, or maybe "Walker" like him. He wished his boy a long life of good deeds and close friends. The final picture in Lieutenant Walker's imagination was of his lovely wife beaming at him with baby Jeffrey in her arms. Swaddled in a blue blanket with only his little face exposed, the infant cooed and grinned at his father. Walker took the child and held him for a moment. He kissed his son on the forehead with all his love, then handed him back and gazed into Chris's liquid brown eyes.

Bolton's bullet pierced Walker's brain and blew out the back of his head, killing him before he heard the shot.

Present Day

Jeff Walker sat on his surfboard, rising and falling with the swell as he waited for the next set to roll in. He glanced up at the gathering clouds, dark and heavy, blown in by a chilly wind. A storm was coming, but it hadn't yet spoiled the conditions; to the contrary, the waves were double overhead and still breaking cleanly. Out on the horizon, he spotted a parallel formation of wide-faced peaks rushing him like a brigade of charging soldiers, so he dropped to his belly and swiveled into position, paddling toward the shore. Soon a wall of water towered over him then surged up from below. Walker sprang to his feet and tipped forward to look down, free-falling for an exhilarating second.

The board hit with a slap and raced down the face of the wave. At the trough, Walker drove his back foot hard, carving a right bottom turn that sprayed a long rooster tail behind him. Time stood still, the glassy water pitching over his head as he careened through the swirling tube in slow motion. Looking ahead like a motorcycle rider, he saw the eye of the barrel closing up. Walker braced himself for a wipeout, but his good speed and strategic positioning shot him out of the tunnel in a mist as if from a whale's blowhole, just in time. *What a way to start the day!* he thought as he rode the wave all the way in.

Minutes later, he was sitting on a flat boulder in a beach chair under a broad blue umbrella marked with the word "LIFEGUARD" in white letters, scanning his area of responsibility. No one was out in the water, every surfer and swimmer having been sent home by the impending squall. To his right, an older couple held hands on the beach as they gazed out at the angry chop. *Squeezing in a walk before the rain hits*, he supposed, running his fingers through his long blond hair. They smiled and waved, and he returned the friendly gesture.

Walker hadn't seen rain clouds this ominous for years, and the ocean was growing rougher by the second. Even so, he took comfort in the salty, earthy smell and the pleasant sounds of the coast, as his earliest, most treasured memory was building sand castles at Rosarito Beach with his mom. He must have been two or three. The rising tide had toppled the forts they'd made, mother and son splashing each other, beaming and giggling in the sun, reveling in the presence of their favorite person in the world.

A sharp thunderclap jerked him back to the present. Lightning bolts sizzled down from low black clouds as the rain began to pelt his umbrella and dapple the sand around him. When drizzle became deluge, he hopped off the rock and stored everything in the shed, pulled out the "Beach Closed" sign, and placed it at the bottom of the stairs.

He hurried up to the parking lot and swung a leg over his motorcycle, but just as he was about to turn the key, something down in the water caught his eye: a small white yacht racing around the bend at Big Rock, veering much too close to the jagged shore. Its skipper tossed a bag overboard before a second vessel pulled up alongside, a gaudy blue ski boat carrying three men, two of whom stormed aboard the yacht with rifles leveled. They bounded up to the helm station, where the skipper dropped to his knees and put his hands on his head. The gunmen took aim, fired—CRACK CRACK CRACK!—and the skipper fell forward, clutching his stomach. Then they grabbed him by his arms and legs and heaved him off the upper deck into the thrashing sea.

When the ski boat and the small white yacht motored away, heading north, Walker flew down the stairs to the shed, grabbed his radio, pressed to talk, and barked, "Main tower, this is Walker at Windansea!"

A fellow lifeguard's voice came crackling back. "Copy, Walker, this is Paul Johanssen. Go ahead."

"I've got a gunshot victim near Big Rock. The scene is safe and I'm swimming out."

"Roger. I'll send you the rescue boat."

Walker grabbed his buoy and fins and sprinted into the shore wash, diving in. His constant flutter kick and long reaching arms powered him past the surf line despite the opposing waves. Stopping to crane his neck up and out, he treaded water for a second to find a reference point, then put his head back down and gave it everything he had as the rain stung his back like needles. He found the patient floating face down in a scarlet cloud, so he turned the body over and stared into vacant eyes. Dropping his gaze to the man's stomach, Walker saw three stringy holes leaking wispy blood and other fluids. The man wasn't breathing and had no detectable pulse.

He was about to initiate rescue breathing when he detected the approaching rumble of an outboard motor. Whipping his head around, he spotted Tony Park and Mark Thompson heading his way in the surf rescue boat. Park, at the helm, was a giant Asian man and one of Walker's two best friends; Thompson, a rookie, was tall and wiry. Both wore red shorts, white shirts, and windbreakers emblazoned with the words "San Diego Lifeguard."

Park cut the engine and coasted up as Thompson dragged the patient aboard. Walker clambered into the boat and immediately started CPR while Park throttled forward, speeding them back to Mission Bay.

"He's gone!" Park yelled over the engine noise. "Just hang on."

Heavy spray pelted their faces as the boat bounced from crest to crest in the driving rain. Walker grabbed a handrail. He and Thompson held the corpse down so it wouldn't bounce overboard.

Twenty minutes later, they were standing under a covered walkway at the docks with several other members of the lifeguard service. Two emergency medical professionals, one of them an attractive woman, pulled a sheet over the corpse and turned the body over to the Harbor Police. The good-looking paramedic must have felt Walker's eyes on her, since she glanced up to flash him a dazzling smile, then climbed into her ambulance and expertly maneuvered it out of a tight spot, cutting through the flooded parking lot as she drove away.

Park turned to Walker and Thompson. "Johanssen says Lieutenant Molloy won't be back for another couple of hours. Race you guys to the main tower?"

It was a terrible idea. The wind and rain hadn't abated in the slightest, and they were already at lifeguard headquarters, where they were required to be for a debriefing with their supervisor. So it was unquestionably better for them to remain where they were and simply wait, with hot showers and gallons of steaming coffee within easy reach. But no. Not these guys. Competitive to a fault, Walker and Thompson exchanged a glance, ran to the edge of the dock, dove off, and swam at full speed through the salty water with Park tight on their heels. It was half a mile across the bay to Mission Point Beach, and from there a two-hundred-yard sprint over the peninsula to the ocean side and a fifty-yard dash to the main tower.

Walker was a legendary surfer and a champion swimmer. He'd been rookie of the year in his first season, and this year Thompson was a shoo-in for the same award. Neck and neck, the two of them tore across the sand in the final sprint, touching the tower at arguably the same time. Sopping wet and heaving for air, they high-fived each other, then peered through the window and spotted Park. The former Navy SEAL was dry and dressed, cradling a steaming mug in his hands. He greeted them with a wave, feigning surprise as though it had taken them so long to arrive that he'd forgotten they were even coming.

2

BIG DON

Lieutenant Donal "Big Don" Roberts of Oceanside PD clasped his hands behind his back as he gazed out at the choppy sea from the observation deck at Oceanside Port Authority Headquarters. Next to him stood his protégé, Sergeant Taylor.

"Looks like it's gonna be a big one, sir," Taylor observed.

Lieutenant Roberts made no reply and kept his eyes on the harbor. It wasn't fair to the former Special Forces soldier at his side, of whom he was exceedingly proud, but he simply wasn't in a talking mood. After thirty years of fighting crime, his attitude had turned sour and he knew it. What Big Don really needed to do was retire and spend his golden years with his wife, kids, and grandkids.

He'd become eligible for it six months earlier, but he was staying on to close an especially troublesome case, and it was that case for which he and Sergeant Taylor were monitoring the entrance to the harbor. As he waited for his confidential informant to arrive in a small white yacht, his mind drifted back to better days. Roberts thought of his college football team, the SDSU Aztecs, and of two players in particular, his best friends both then and now: David Goode and Jason Molloy.

David Goode was uncommonly tall and wide and as nimble as a circus acrobat. After going All-American every year of high school, Goode had received many D1 scholarship offers, but he had chosen San Diego State to stay close to his family. The massive Black man could have dominated at any position, from lineman to receiver—quarterback even—but he played tight end, setting scoring records that remain on the board to this day. Jason Molloy, a stocky running back, was just as tough as any man alive, and Big Don knew he'd never have a more loyal friend.

"Sir, weren't you going to tell me about the case?" Sergeant Taylor interrupted, violently derailing Big Don's happy train of thought.

Roberts plastered on a smile and turned to meet the eager gaze of the newest member of the narcotics task force. "We haven't made much progress," he replied. "Have you heard of the North County Kings?"

"Yes sir."

"You know you don't have to call me 'sir,'" Roberts said, though he was secretly pleased at the show of respect.

"I know."

"What do you know about them?"

"Not much. Local biker gang."

"Correct. They're also one of Jack Cage's biggest clients. We know Cage smuggles drugs and guns from Mexico into Southern California, but so far we haven't been able to locate him or the source of his contraband. That's why this is such a big break for us. The digital files Cage's accountant is delivering today should give us a lot to go on."

Sergeant Taylor must have sensed Big Don's irritation, since he nodded, swung his gaze back to the sea, and said no more. This gave Roberts a chance to resume his trip down memory lane, so he delved back in, mentally replaying the best football game of his life: the 1985 National Championship in the small college division.

They were in the huddle. Big Don, the quarterback, was screaming at his fellow Aztecs to push past their pain. "Now's the time!" he yelled. "This is what we've been praying for, busting all our asses for. Keep fighting!" He looked across the circle to lock eyes with an exhausted Jason Molloy, who'd given it everything he had. When their starting running back had dislocated his shoulder in the first two minutes of the game, Molloy had been sent in to replace him. It was a daunting task, since the Air Force Falcons' massive defensive line was all over them, with two of their best on David Goode. Early in the second quarter, Molloy had been tackled so hard he couldn't stand up for several minutes. He had to be helped off the field and down to a bench, where a doctor checked him out, but after a series of cringeworthy plays made by the third-string RB, he'd lied and said he felt okay.

Molloy's return to the field had been met with roaring cheers from the home-field fans. Seizing the opportunity presented by the Falcons' double coverage of Goode, he took the handoff from Big Don and outran one defender after another. Some of his incursions into enemy territory were stopped short and some weren't stopped at all. In total, Molloy ran for over two hundred yards and three touchdowns, taking a brutal beating in the process. Now he could barely walk, but the Falcons didn't know that. In this final play of the game, they'd be on him like government money on a bad idea.

The stadium was packed with chanting fans, filling both teams with heightened aggression akin to bloodlust in a battle. The Aztecs were down thirty to thirty-seven. Five seconds left. The entire season had come down to this one moment. Big Don glanced across the huddle at David Goode, who nodded once. He knew what to do. Big Don would fake the handoff to the injured Molloy as Goode charged forward like a steel-cast locomotive, engaged his defender for a two count, broke free, and looked for the pass.

"Set hut!" Big Don barked at the start of the play. He faked to Molloy and looked downfield. Goode was open. Firing the ball like a rocket straight down the middle, he threw a perfect pass, not to where Goode was, but to where he was going to be. Goode trapped it easily and plowed through two monster defenders. Then he outran the rest of the Falcons, bringing the score up to 36-37. Handing the ball to the referee, he jogged back to the huddle with zero celebration. If they didn't make the two-point conversion, they'd still lose the game.

Big Don then called a variation on the same play. "Set hut!" he yelled, feigning the handoff to Molloy again, but he faked the pass to Goode and ran the ball in himself, diving into the end zone with his head down and his arms tucked in. The defense nearly crushed him under their collective weight, but when the dogpile was picked apart, Big Don still had the pigskin, protecting it in a fetal position. As one, the Aztec fans leapt to their feet in a raucous celebration that lasted for the rest of the day and well into the night.

The following year, David Goode left college early to join the Los Angeles Raiders. He performed moderately well in the NFL, since at that level everyone had been a college standout, but in his second season he suffered a severe knee injury. The only football he played after that was catch in the park with his son, David Goode, Jr., who would grow up to be a close friend of Jeff Walker's.

After graduation, Big Don was hired as a police officer up in Oceanside. He became a respected member of Molloy's and Goode's church, Hillside Baptist, where no one cared that he was white.

Jason Molloy, the only Black member of every team he'd ever swum for, found work as a beach lifeguard, and was eventually promoted to lieutenant. In the ensuing thirty years, he participated in many high-profile rescues, whether at sea with the Coast Guard, at the shore between jagged rocks and towering waves, or rappelling down rocky cliffs to save a patient.

Molloy, Roberts, and Goode often brought their families together for Sunday barbecues, where they'd sit in the shade and relive the glory days while watching their kids grow into adults.

Big Don Roberts drew a deep breath and let it slowly out, his spirits restored by the memory. As he returned his focus to the waves and the gathering storm, his phone buzzed in his pocket. The caller was Jason Molloy.

"Big Don! How you doin', doc?" came Molloy's booming voice over the line. "Listen, we jus' pulled out a gunshot victim. White male, 'bout fifty, no ID. He was headin' north in a white cabin cruiser named *Poseidon*."

"That's my witness. Is he deceased?"

"Yes."

"I appreciate you, brother. We're on our way," Roberts said as the first heavy raindrop fell on his head.

***

Despite the tireless back and forth of the rescue truck's windshield wipers, Tony Park's visibility was dangerously poor. Blustery wind shook the red pickup as he drove it over the bridge to lifeguard headquarters. With his eyes forward and both hands gripping the wheel, he said, "Ever seen a gunshot wound before, Thompson?"

"Yeah, but not as bad as this," the rookie replied from the rear jump seat. "Do you think the patient had any chance at all?"

"No way," Park said. "Not even if we'd arrived in a waterborne ambulance."

"I agree," Walker added from the passenger seat, but he still felt guilty.

Park hung a right, then plowed the truck through a flooded parking lot and pulled to a stop in a pond. The trio jumped out, splish-splashing fifty yards to the front door through pouring rain. As instructed, Thompson waited in the lobby while Park and Walker threaded their way to the back of the building.

They found Lieutenant Molloy supporting his burly arms and shoulders on his desk; there wasn't much desk to be seen. Among the many plaques and photos on the walls, a large framed picture took pride of place, showing seventy young, mostly Black faces from the past, looking mean in their football uniforms.

Four chairs faced Molloy in a semicircle, two of which were taken. Walker knew Big Don from Hillside Baptist, but he didn't recognize the other guy. Everyone stood to shake hands.

"Y'all have had a *long* mornin'," Molloy began, motioning for them to take a seat. "So let's not make it any longer than it needs to be. The man you pulled out of the water was on his way to meet with these gentlemen."

"Morning guys," Lieutenant Roberts said with a brief tight-lipped smile as the rain thrashed the windows and thunder rattled the walls. Big Don was as large as Park, with a full head of graying hair. "Your patient was the accountant for a smuggling operation we're investigating. It's urgent that we recover that bag you saw thrown overboard."

Sergeant Taylor turned to face the lifeguards, his face hard and stern, his white polo shirt strained at the neck, chest, and biceps. He looked about thirty-five, just a few years older than Park and Walker. "The bag contains a laptop with crucial evidence on it," he told them. "But here's the catch: certain members of the Oceanside Port Authority can't be trusted, and we have our doubts about the San Diego Harbor Police. This is highly confidential, by the way."

Big Don nodded. "What we're proposing is a joint recovery operation with your dive rescue team. We think five or six members should be enough, and it would have to be tonight. Assuming the lightning dies down and you agree. Taylor and I would be patrolling the surface."

As the leader of the dive rescue team, Park gave the first reply. "It's an easy dive," he said. "Only thirty feet. But I'll have to call everyone before I can commit. What do *you* say, Jeff?"

Walker shot his friend a dubious frown. "It's an easy dive if we don't run into anyone else down there," he said, then looked to Big Don. "Why not take the whole team?"

"Good question, Brother Jeff," said Lieutenant Roberts. "It's a balancing act between confidentiality on one hand and defensive strength on the other. I want to minimize the chances of a lifeguard leaking secret details while making sure your team is strong enough."

Walker raised his eyebrows. "Strong enough for what?"

"We *know* it's a lot to ask," Molloy interjected from the other side of his desk. "But you're the bes' we got. I'll be there, too, of course."

"Fine," Walker said, with some reluctance. He was reminded of the last time Molloy had called him and Park into his office and given them a special assignment. Back in April, he'd sent them to Hawaii for a week on an exchange program. It had literally been a hell of a spring break.

The meeting broke up shortly after that. Lieutenant Roberts and Sergeant Taylor left for the Medical Examiner's Office and Molloy debriefed all three lifeguards with regard to the morning's incident. Then Park drove Walker and Thompson back to the main tower.

Opting for hot tea instead of a third cup of coffee, Walker waited out the storm in a chatty circle of lifesavers, though he had difficulty matching his colleagues' excitement. As the only witness to the murder on the yacht, he knew first-hand just how serious these smugglers were. And if the data on the laptop was as crucial as Taylor had said, the crooks would definitely be coming back for it.

3

TACOS AL PASTOR

Piloting the ski boat through heaving whitecaps, which the gaudy blue craft's 7.4-liter V8 managed with ease, was the most visually intimidating of Jack Cage's three guard captains. Through wet sunglasses, former U.S. Army Sergeant Peter Miller gazed straight ahead, making minute corrections to the vessel's trajectory, unperturbed by the inclement weather. As he raced up the coast in high wind and heavy rain, bouncing from crest to crest, his enormous hands steadied the wheel and his lantern jaw flexed with resolve.

Forty yards back, the second of Cage's men, a former Marine named Carlos Maldonado, stood on the upper deck in command of the *Poseidon*. Irritated by Miller's ignorance—willful or otherwise—of the difference in maximum speed between the two vessels, he put his thoughts briefly to work on what kind of violence he might like to do to his comrade, but soon cleared his mind of it for a variety of reasons. Maldonado was tall and lean, his cruel features oddly elongated as though they'd been vertically stretched, his cheeks and eyes sunken like those of a man already dead.

Also aboard the small white yacht was the last of the guard captains, always last, ex-U.S. Army sniper Rick Daniels, who sat indifferently below decks with his eyes glued to a video game despite having been told by Maldonado to search for the laptop.

Even at a solid six-one, two-twenty, Daniels was the smallest of them. All were under forty, all still in top shape, their hair still buzzed short in accordance with military specifications.

The boats were presently racing toward Cage's Carlsbad facility, a secluded waterfront residence retrofitted such that it resembled a small fortress more than the luxury home it had formerly been. Their orders were to carefully search the *Poseidon* for the laptop, which was one of Daniels' two reasons for disregarding Maldonado's instructions; the task would be accomplished much more quickly with tools and the three of them working in concert. The second part of Daniels' rationale was that one of his fellow men, equal in rank, had issued those instructions. Both Maldonado and Miller were always telling him what to do, and he was sick of it.

One after the other, the two boats veered to starboard, cruising through the two jetties at the mouth of Agua Hedionda Lagoon. They navigated across the outer body of that aquatic reserve, then passed under the freeway into the inner lagoon, where the conditions were decidedly calmer. Thunder rumbled and driving rain still fell in sheets as they made their way to the other side, where a tiny inlet hove into view. They slipped into the narrow channel and motored slowly toward one of the many costly residences built on the banks of the waterway. The giant Miller pressed a pair of buttons on his dashboard, causing two of three boathouse doors to slide up and open, and once the boats had coasted into the cavernous space, the retractable panels glided back down behind them.

Daniels' heavy boots hit the deck as he clambered out to tie the lines, and then they all set to work on the task ahead. Searching everywhere on the small white yacht for the damning evidence, they sliced open the upholstery and used power tools to remove every one of the interior panels. Finding nothing, they took off their sopping-wet boots and trudged in single file up a short flight of stairs, settling uncomfortably into a comfortable sitting room.

It was Maldonado's job to place the call. "D2 for D1," he said when Cage answered wordlessly.

"Go ahead."

"We made it to the facility without incident, but the item is not aboard."

"What about the rat?"

"He had an unpleasant morning."

"That's funny, D2, but the item is still unaccounted for."

"Yes sir. We know the traitor ditched it 'cause he was carrying a bag at the docks and it wasn't in the boat when we took command. But there was only one part of the trip where we didn't have eyes on him."

"Good. Then that's where we'll find it. Leave the new boat where it is and get your asses up here. Out."

Maldonado, Miller, and Daniels dutifully trooped back into the boathouse and stepped aboard the ski boat with D2 at the helm. They made the five miles up to Oceanside Harbor in no time, and they were recognized on arrival by several Port Authority agents who had a duty to report the sighting, yet the crooked lawmen went about their business as though they hadn't seen anything at all.

***

At Windansea beach, the thick gray cloud cover continued to hide the sun, but the surf had settled down and the once-abundant precipitation had dwindled to a mist. Dropped off by Johanssen, Walker descended the long set of white stairs to the beach, stored the closed sign in the shed, and sat anxiously in his chair on the flat boulder until he no longer could. Then he hopped off his perch to clear the shore of driftwood, seaweed, and a great amount of other debris, thus disposing of what would otherwise have been a nerve-wracking afternoon. As he worked, his mind reeled with the memory of the murder he'd witnessed earlier that day, at that very spot, and his fears about what might happen later on the recovery dive. At dusk, he marched back up the stairs to the parking area and swung a leg over his ride.

The black Kawasaki was over ten years old, but Walker, with diligent and regular application of his mechanical skills, had kept it impeccable. At thirteen years of age, he'd landed his first job at a motorcycle shop in Mexico, where he was tasked with menial duties, the most interesting of which had been sweeping the floor and fetching things. Yet his boss had allowed him to peer over his shoulder as he worked, explaining what he was doing, and gradually assigned Walker greater responsibility.

He slipped on his helmet and started the ignition, pausing to appreciate the rumbling purr of a well-tuned motorcycle engine, his favorite sound on the planet. Then he lifted his legs and motored away, riding cautiously through the slippery neighborhood, increasing his pace once he merged onto I-5. The cars all around him kicked up spray that collected on his visor, hindering visibility, so to solve this problem, he flipped it up, but the irritating mist now began to gather on his sunglasses. Resisting the urge to toss his Ray-Bans into traffic as he zipped along, he drew a calming breath and slipped them into his pocket.

Now the spray was stinging his eyes.

"Fuuuck!" he roared into the wind, twisting the throttle toward himself in anger.

After a dangerous ride he knew he shouldn't repeat, Walker skidded to a halt in a parking lot and stomped up the stairs to his apartment. It was a one-bedroom unit, with few decorations but for a pair of beach-themed posters and a framed photo of his parents on their wedding day. A comfy sofa and a large flat screen beckoned him to take a load off in the living room, where three surfboards leaned against the wall with an attitude and a heavy-duty weight bench dared him to attempt fifty reps. Walker enjoyed weightlifting; it helped him blow off steam, but his groaning stomach kept him moving toward the kitchen. Peering into the fridge, he saw he'd have to go back out to eat, and with a sniff of his armpit, he found out what his first order of business needed to be.

He wasn't a big drinker, but his favorite place to eat was a bar. El Papagayo served authentic Mexican tacos to a predominantly brown-skinned clientele. As he pulled open the glass door and stepped in to the aggressive sound of Chicano rap, he spotted a group of unsmiling Latinos at a corner table drinking. They glowered at first, but when they saw who he was, their scowls disappeared and they held up their arms in salutation. Walker ambled over to chat with them for a bit, then grabbed a seat at a table of his own.

He was still bobbing his head to the beat when Alejandra sashayed up to take his order. The curvy waitress treated him to a delightful smile, and he rose to give her a faux-kiss greeting.

"Hey you," she said in Spanish as he resumed his seat. "Long time no see. How've you been?"

"Hey yourself," he replied in the same language. "Doing good. Happy to see you," which he said with more longing than he should have. He and Alex had dated for months, but that was years ago and now she was married.

Her features fell into a businesslike configuration. "Ready for your regular double order of tacos? With an ice-cold Sierra Nevada?"

"Yes, ma'am, but with club soda, please."

She nodded and left him alone. By himself as usual, Walker set his elbow on the table and rested his chin on his fist. He closed his eyes and wished he were sitting across from his soul mate, the sexy, intelligent, kind, and loyal girlfriend who he was certain was out there somewhere. Who at that very moment, he thought, might possibly be wishing she were sitting there with him. Then a dark whirlwind of emotional memories swirled in his mind at the thought of a different kind of soul mate. Sadly, this one was gone for good.

Walker's favorite day of the week had always been Sunday, his mother's one day off. Ever since he could remember, she'd packed a picnic lunch and driven him from their house in Tijuana, Mexico, to Rosarito Beach. It was a half-an-hour trip. The Chicano rap faded away, replaced by the rhythmic squawking of seagulls and the salty smell of the coast as he saw his six-year-old self walking hand in hand with her, gentle waves lapping at their heels while the sun toasted their backs.

When Alejandra returned with his food, he wiped his cheeks and forced a smile. A friendly one, nothing else. Each of his ten *tacos al pastor* was made from two small corn tortillas quickly fried, then topped with grilled marinated pork, chopped onions, and cilantro, also known as coriander. He spooned on a healthy glob of fresh red salsa and ate as slowly as he could, which wasn't slow at all. Then he finished his club soda, went to wash his hands, and took his place at a pool table.

With a piercing smack that split the acoustic space like a close-range gunshot, he broke the rack of balls, scattering them across the long expanse of green felt. When they rolled to a stop, he played against himself as if he were two different people, which wasn't half as fun as playing with Tony Park and David Goode.

He won, of course. While re-racking the balls, he saw his phone light up on the table and strode over to take the call. "Hey dude."

"What's up, man," Park replied with a casual air. "You ready?"

Despite his caller's pretense, Walker knew Park wasn't feeling casual or relaxed. Not at all. The guy's final mission as a Navy SEAL team leader had gone terribly wrong, so now, before any kind of incident response or risky operation, he always suffered from severe anxiety. Park was on the mend, however; the long days he spent in the sun on the lifeguard tower gazing out at the sparkling waves were helping him to heal from that traumatic disorder.

"You bet I'm ready," Walker replied. "Who volunteered?"

"Almost everybody, but I chose Crawford, Hall, Fowler, and Johanssen. Listen. Visibility's only five feet. And the water's cold and rough."

"We'll be fine," Walker said reassuringly, while in reality he harbored at least as many reservations as his team leader. "Burgers and beers at Sammy's this weekend?"

"Now you're making me hungry," Park said with a chuckle.

"See you soon, man."

"Ride safe, brother."

Walker grabbed his helmet, waved—a friendly—goodbye to Alejandra, nodded to his buddies in the corner, and made for the double glass doors. In the parking lot, as he straddled his bike, a sudden sense of terror twisted his guts and froze the blood in his veins. He wished he'd voted no back in Lieutenant Molloy's office, but now it was too late to do anything about it.

4

THE MASTER SMUGGLER

J ack Cage settled into an executive chair behind his solid mahogany desk, his slacks and collared shirt stiffly pressed, his aging features also stiff—but still chiseled, he hadn't failed to note that morning in the mirror. As he waited for his computer to boot up, his gaze drifted from the monitor to a framed oil painting that hung on the wall facing him. The artist had painstakingly captured a woody scene with snow-capped mountains in the background, their frozen peaks sloping down to a bright-blue pond in the middle of a pine tree forest. Flanking that relaxing landscape were two others created by the same talented—and well paid—painter. Behind Cage, on the opposite wall, a bookcase stood crammed with thick volumes on topics including aeronautics, seamanship, and international law.

He leaned forward to press a button on his desk phone. "Maria, get your cousin on the line."

"Yes sir."

A minute later, a younger man's voice came through the speaker. "What's up?"

Cage might have slapped the kid if he'd been standing there in his office. "Good afternoon sir," he barked. "What can I do for you?"

"Good afternoon sir," the young man repeated. "What can I—"

"You can tell me about this morning's incident."

By means of and despite the lifeguard's interminable babbling, Cage learned that the late accountant had, in fact, thrown a bag overboard at Big Rock and that, as expected, the dive rescue team was preparing for a recovery operation scheduled to begin at eight p.m. that same day. In addition to the lifeguards' dive boat, two Boston Whalers manned by armed police officers would be patrolling the shore. And the dive team leader's name was—

"That's enough," Cage said, checking his watch. "Listen. We will also be arriving at about twenty hundred hours. Your objective is to disable or delay your team."

"I understand. Thank you si—"

Cage ended the call, rose from his chair, and strode over to a long window where he twisted a plastic rod to open the blinds. Down on the ground floor, his warehouse was crawling with illegals counting money under guard, weighing and handling narcotics, hefting crates of weapons into trucks at the loading bay. The master smuggler scanned his domain for any sign of trouble. Satisfied that he'd seen nothing unusual, he closed the blinds again and headed back to his desk, but not with his usual swagger. For one thing, he was afraid that his employer, a Mexican criminal organization known as the Cartel del Norte, would find out about the missing laptop. For thirty years Cage had been working for that vicious gang under the explicit threat of death and now he wanted out, regardless of the outcome of that day's recovery dive. Unfortunately, he couldn't just give two weeks' notice and submit his résumé elsewhere; he'd have to pull a vanishing act, and it was the careful planning and preparation for that disappearance as well as Oceanside PD's investigation into his activities, and now the additional loss of the laptop, that was causing a dangerous and prolonged spike in his blood pressure.

There came a knock at the door. "It's Maria," his executive assistant called out from the other side.

Cage drew a calming breath as he stood, and let it out on his way across the room, disengaging a high-security lock to pull open the door.

"Your guard captains are here," Maria said as she handed him a file folder, sweeping her long black bangs out of her eyes with her other hand.

Cage ran his gaze over her glossy hair and flawless skin, then paused to appreciate the way her pant suit clung to her curvy figure. After that, it was back to business. "Thank you," he said with a thin smile. "Tell them to come in."

With the barest hint of a flirty grin, she spun on her heels and click-clacked down the hall to her post in the reception room.

When Maldonado, Miller, and Daniels marched in, Cage was standing between the warehouse window and his desk, deep in thought. The muscular trio stopped before him in a row with their hands clasped behind their backs, wearing tactical trousers, combat boots, and black T-shirts.

"We're going to have to fight for the laptop, gentlemen," Cage said, looking each of his men in the eye. "We'll take the dive boat with a crew of two and drop anchor at Point La Jolla. From there, we'll swim under water to Big Rock, which should take twenty minutes with the DPVs. So make sure those are ready. And I want three more guards in the ski boat with an RPG and a full load of rockets."

His guard captains stood straighter than before, nodding vigorously, ready to storm down the stairs and muster their men.

"All right, let's do it. We'll move out in thirty."

Once his men had filed out the door, Cage resumed his pacing and raised both fists, punching himself in the mouth, jaw, and cheeks, drawing blood. Now breathing fast and hard, he fell into push-up position and snapped out an easy forty. *Just a couple more missions and it'll all be over. Soon I'll be sipping drinks in paradise.*

***

Tony Park's racing pulse pounded in his ears. He closed his eyes and filled his lungs, then let the air escape on its own, soothed by the sound of the waves lapping against the dock. Feeling better after several cycles of this, he opened his eyes to check his watch. It was 8:00 p.m. exactly. "Listen up!" he boomed. Four young men and one young woman gathered around him, all clad in black neoprene wetsuits. He scrutinized their faces. They looked nervous, all except Walker, who wore an angry scowl as usual. Lieutenant Molloy and Big Don Roberts waited attentively in a rescue boat docked close by, and Sergeant Taylor and Detective Van Brussel stood in an identical craft, ready to cast off.

"Okay guys and gal," Park began, "it's only thirty feet deep out there, so we won't need to worry about decompression stops. And unless we make unfriendly contact, which I don't expect to happen, our main challenge is going to be visibility. Which is bad enough as it is, so don't stir up the silt even more. Remember, head down, feet up. Avoid touching the bottom. Finally, as you can see, the water's still rough. You are not to surface anywhere near the rocks for any reason. Once we've recovered the bag, we'll swim away from the reef and ascend together. Any questions?"

No one had any.

Jeff Walker, Marcus Crawford, Jenn Fowler, and Paul Johanssen piled in to the silver dive boat and took a seat in the aft deck area on two long benches that faced each other. The hull of the thirty-four-foot Munson, the largest expenditure Lieutenant Molloy had ever had to justify, was built with quarter-inch welded aluminum. Driven by two V6 inboard/outboard engines that made 330 hp each, the vessel was just as fast as the surf rescue boats escorting it.

Park also stepped aboard but went the other way, heading forward to the wheelhouse. There he joined Ethan Hall, who would remain on the boat as divemaster while the recovery operation was under way.

Molloy and Big Don Roberts pushed out of their berth and motored off, leading the convoy through the channel. At the wheel, Molloy leaned his lower back against a curved backrest. Directly behind him, Lieutenant Roberts hung on to a pair of handles welded to that backrest. Like Molloy, he wore a ballistic vest and a tactical helmet, but slung across his back was an M4 carbine with a night vision scope.

The silver dive boat was next in line, followed by the second Boston Whaler, with Detective Van Brussel at the wheel and Sergeant Taylor holding on to the back support. Both men were equipped with vests, helmets, and rifles, just like Big Don, their boss.

As the dive boat emerged from the brightly lit harbor into the chilly darkness of the open sea, Park left Ethan Hall in the wheelhouse to issue last-minute instructions to his team, who sat facing each other on the aft benches. "We'll swim side by side, five feet apart!" he told them, shouting over the engine noise as the vessel's bouncing hull blasted everyone with salty spray. "Make sure you can see the two divers beside you at all times."

"Tony, what can you tell us about the bag we're searching for?" Marcus Crawford asked. "Like who does it belong to or what's in it?"

Park frowned and shook his head. Crawford knew that was confidential; he was probably just nervous.

"Why don't you think we'll run into anyone else down there?" asked Jenn Fowler as she tied her long blond hair into a ponytail, tucked it into her wetsuit, and pulled her hood into place.

"Good question, Jenn," Park replied. "If we see any other boats, we'll turn back. And it would have to be a hell of a crew that would dare to mess with five pro divers guarded by a team of well-armed policemen." Despite his words, Park's heart thundered in his chest. If there was one thing in the world he was afraid of, it was that someone on his team might suffer an injury. He wished he'd listened to Walker back in Lieutenant Molloy's office instead of agreeing so quickly to his supervisor's plan.

"Yeah, Fowler, you've probably got more to worry about with Crawford down there than with enemy divers," Johanssen said, in reference to Crawford's reputation as a ladies' man. All the divers erupted into anxious laughter as Hall dropped anchor far outside the break line.

"Be right back," Park told them, heading forward to the wheelhouse again. Once inside, he pulled open a storage compartment and brought out his Navy Sig. Eyeing Hall sternly, he said, "I'm trusting you, man. If anyone catches you with this, just say you found it in the glove box. It's registered to me and I'll take responsibility."

Hall nodded and took the offered pistol. He knew how to use it. Park and Walker had taken him and Crawford to the shooting range many times.

"Okay then. Good luck, bro." With a final pointed look, Park offered his younger colleague a knuckle smack and made his way back to the benches. All five divers watched him in silence as the boat rocked from side to side. He felt proud to be working with them on this mission, and their faces told him they felt the same way. "This is it," he said. "The faster we get in and out, the better, so let's swim as quickly as we can while staying aware of our surroundings."

The divers helped each other don their heavy tanks, giving their buddies' gear a final check. Then, one by one, they held their masks to their faces and leapt into the ocean as the red rescue boats sped off to circle the area.

The water was cold, but their wetsuits would warm them up in a minute or two. They surfaced and formed a circle. Park gave and received the OK hand signal from everyone, deflated his buoyancy compensator, or BC, and submerged, kicking himself downward with long and sturdy fins, descending headfirst into the murky world below. The beam of his dive light didn't fall on a single sea creature, as if even the fish knew better than to stick around for a bloody fight.

5

FIRST CONTACT

The night was cold and cloudy and the sea as dark as motor oil. Cage stood on the rear swim platform of his fifty-foot dive boat, rolling in the chop as he and Maldonado adjusted their full-face masks. They exchanged a nod and leapt in together, their fins slapping at the surface. When they popped up, they turned back around to receive the diver propulsion vehicles handed down by Miller and Daniels, who then joined their fellow divers in the water and took their own DPVs from the pair of guards who would remain aboard.

Cage initiated the comm check as the foursome deflated and descended. "This is D1, how do you read? Over."

"D2 loud and clear, over," came Maldonado's voice crackling through their headphone assemblies.

"D3 loud and clear, over."

Daniels, who hated being D4, echoed Miller, his former sergeant in the Army. "D4 loud and clear."

At twenty feet, Cage glanced at the illuminated face of his wrist-mounted diving compass, checking his team's direction of travel. He led them south at that depth in near-total darkness, spotting the lifeguards' roaming dive lights after one mile.

"Shut 'em down, guys," he said.

Without switching on their own lights, the smugglers stashed their DPVs and hovered with neutral buoyancy a few feet off the sandy bottom. They unsheathed their knives and prepared to strike.

***

Minutes earlier, the dive rescue team had stopped their initial descent just before reaching the sea floor. Park made a circle with his light and five identical signals came back immediately, meaning everyone was okay. He led them to the base of Big Rock, where they lined up in a row, with Walker and himself at either end. Then they propelled themselves out to sea for a hundred yards, combing the bottom with their roving dive lights, finding nothing. After that, the lifeguards headed back to the underwater shoreline, scouring the next parallel section of the search area to no avail, so again they oriented themselves toward the open ocean to search a third parallel section, and so forth until they'd covered half the designated area with no sign of the laptop bag.

Park scanned the sediment below him as he swam along, maintaining as much peripheral awareness as he could. That's when he detected movement straight ahead and his heart leapt out of his chest! By waving his dive light back and forth, he told his team to stop swimming and gather around.

The tryout process that Park had endured on the road to becoming a Navy SEAL had been brutal. Every day, starting at zero four thirty, he and the rest of the candidates were made to perform calisthenics for four hours, with negligible rest between sets, and the real work began after breakfast. That year, the washout rate had been eighty percent. Once he and the rest of the passing twenty percent were officially Navy property, their superiors had subjected them to harsh drownproofing and deep-water simulation exercises that tested their response to fear even more than to oxygen deprivation. The idea had been to expose the seamen to extreme conditions with safety parameters in place before facing real danger in combat zones. Over the following eight years, Park was involved in over thirty underwater missions, so while his need to please Molloy had put him and his fellow divers in a mortally dangerous situation, he was uniquely qualified to see them through it.

His suspicions were confirmed as the enemy divers approached. Again he waved his light back and forth, quickly this time to indicate an emergency. He pointed his finger in the direction of the danger, then looked into his teammates' eyes as he switched off his light. They followed suit.

As there was little moonlight to glance off the rival divers' gear, their silhouettes were virtually indistinguishable in the gloom, but soon their dark shapes, then their cold, determined faces, and finally the knives in their hands came sharply into view. Having covered this contingency back at the docks, the rescue divers fanned out into an inverted V formation with Park at the apex. Everyone unsheathed their own blades. Eye contact was held. Underwater combat was inevitable.

Park found himself confronted by a tall man whose elongated face, hollow cheeks, and deep-set eyes lent him a skeletal appearance. With his black neoprene hood, he looked a little like the Grim Reaper. With one look at his attacker's gear, Park knew what to do: he kicked himself brusquely past and whipped back around to cut the guy's air supply hoses. The man fought back immediately, turning to slice Park's skin through his wetsuit in several places, but soon he was out of air and forced to ascend.

Park made a conscious decision not to stab the man as he swam away, hoping the patrol boats would pick him up, and also hoping he wouldn't later regret that act of mercy. His regulator hissed and clicked as he breathed. The canned air was dry and sterile. He swiveled his gaze in all directions and didn't like what he saw: Walker, the only visible member of the dive rescue team, was being attacked by two other divers! One of them was tall and trim; the other even taller and twice as wide, about Park's own size, so Park kicked himself closer, colliding with the larger of the two. Each quickly immobilized the other's knife hand, their joints and muscles straining in a deadly contest of wills. Both men dropped their knives and lights in the struggle, and if it continued like this, Park knew, they'd both likely drown, so even as he fought, he took seven or eight deep breaths in rapid succession and unclipped his backpack-like buoyancy control device. He wriggled out of it, escaping from his adversary's clutches, although he'd just surrendered his air supply. Park then darted down to the seabed, snatched up his knife, and whirled around just in time to see his rival coming in for the kill! He plunged his blade into the man's outstretched arm, spooking him. As the man swam away, he left a blooming trail of blood behind him.

Park's chest was on fire. Resisting the instinct to breathe, he kicked himself upward with medium intensity to conserve what little oxygen he had left. As he ascended through the final ten feet, his brain screamed in his face like an irate BUD/S instructor ordering him to inhale. Yet he suppressed that urge, swam on, and finally broke the surface, where he gasped for air and thanked his lucky stars.

The clouds had dissipated enough to let the moon shine through, casting its pale light on a waterborne battle unfolding fifty yards away. Cracking gunfire echoed through the night as the lifeguards' two rescue vessels and a blue ski boat raced by each other and circled back around for another pass. From the ski boat, an RPG operator fired a blazing rocket, but it didn't connect with either of the rescue boats. That's when Park spotted something even more distressing: over at Big Rock, the shorebound current was dragging a helpless diver toward the shore, the towering waves threatening to smash him or her against the jagged rocks, and it was Park's team's emblem on the diver's hood! He put his face down and raced to give assistance, his brawny arms and legs propelling him through the churning sea like the twin 330-hp engines of the silver dive boat.

***

At first contact between the two opposing forces, Marcus Crawford had followed Park's lead and kicked himself closer to danger. He'd gripped his dive knife in one hand and his light in the other, illuminating an enemy whose hard eyes glared at him from behind a full-face mask, mesmerizing him for a terrifying split second. That's all his attacker needed; the man shot out a hand and bent Crawford's arm behind his back, forcing him to drop his knife.

Through the pain of the armlock, Crawford kept his eyes open and snapped a mental picture, then ditched his dive light. This freed his left hand to reach up and unhook the clasp on the other diver's mask, which, unlike Crawford's own traditional visor, contained his breathing apparatus. Before the other diver regained his bearings and swam away, Crawford made a flat hand and struck him repeatedly in the eyes and throat.

As he collected himself, gratefully inhaling the dry air delivered by the cylinder on his back, another diver popped out of the gloom and smashed his metal scuba tank into Crawford's face. Had it been someone from his own team? It had happened too fast to know for sure.

Now Crawford's mask was cracked and leaking, and his regulator wasn't supplying air as it was designed to do. He felt faint. All he could do was kick himself weakly to the surface, where he dropped his broken mask and treaded water for a moment, sweeping his gaze in all directions, looking for his team's dive boat. Through the noisy chaos of the waterborne battle being waged all around him, he spotted the glinting silver hull. Only fifty yards away, but since stray bullets were snapping over his head with alarming regularity, he ditched his weight belt and BC/tank assembly, took a massive breath, and swam under water all the way there.

As he climbed aboard by the port-side ladder, Crawford saw no sign of Ethan Hall or anyone else, just the two aft benches to the right and the empty wheelhouse to the left. Shivering from nerves as much as from cold, he kept his head down and thought carefully about his next move. Hall might well be lying on the bottom of the ocean, with an enemy shooter hiding behind the wheelhouse, waiting to kill the lifeguards as they came aboard, so Crawford snuck around the front of the wheelhouse in a crouch, keeping his head below the windows and approaching from what he hoped was an unexpected direction. As he came around the front of the wheelhouse to the starboard side, he saw nothing, but he thought he heard footsteps.

"Who's there?" he shouted involuntarily.

"Stand up slow and turn around," someone called out from behind him.

Too late, Crawford realized that whoever it was had hurried around the other side of the wheelhouse to catch him from behind, playing the same trick on him that he had tried to use. As he gradually rose and spun around, his eyes went wide and his mouth fell open. There stood Ethan Hall, just out of reach in a perfect two-handed shooting stance, exactly like Park and Walker had taught them. Hall's eyes glinted with deadly intent as his finger curled around the trigger and his features twisted into a terrible scowl.

6

FEAR

When the two recovery teams first collided, Walker's light fell on a pair of crooks who looked more like astronauts than scuba divers, their features obscured by high-tech gear. He noted, in the split second before the underwater scene burst into violence, that one of them was older, tall with gray eyes and a closely cropped gray beard, while the other looked like a white-skinned Incredible Hulk whose wetsuit threatened to split at the seams. Pressing their advantage, the smugglers swam toward Walker with black knives in their hands, clearly intending to slice him into bloody chunks of fish food.

Walker kicked himself backwards, stalling for time, and it was at that instant that Park came crashing into the Hulk, evening the odds.

Graybeard feigned a swipe. When Walker took the bait, reaching out with his left hand to immobilize Graybeard's right, the latter executed his actual plan, cranking Walker's other arm toward the outside of his body. Lightning bolts struck at all three joints, forcing Walker to drop his knife, and that's when the other shoved his own blade into the lifeguard's thigh.

A brilliant shower of sparks and colors exploded in Walker's brain. Over the years, he'd had motorcycle crashes, horrific surfing wipeouts, and injuries sustained in street fights that had put him in the hospital on both sides of the border, but none of it had produced such a sinking feeling as the one that now gripped his guts at the bottom of the ocean. An overwhelming rush of dizziness dragged him toward unconsciousness as blood gushed out of his thigh like a jacuzzi jet. In the manner of a wounded animal fleeing from a hunter, he wildly kicked and pulled himself upward with his three good limbs, but he knew he'd never make it to the surface. With twenty feet still to go, Walker pressed the button on his BC to inflate it before—

***

Back at initial contact, Jenn Fowler had drawn on her regulator, expecting a full dose of air, but she only received a fraction of a breath. Her heart rate shot to double as her eyes darted to the air pressure gauge. Her tank was all but empty. Knowing the only way she could have run out of air was if she had a leak, she initiated an emergency ascent, but stopped short when her dive light fell on a dark, oddly rectangular shape down on the sea floor. With a last partial breath, she swam to the bag and took hold of it, then pushed off the bottom with her fins, kicking immediately, spitting out her useless regulator and resisting the urge to breathe. Spots danced before her eyes on the way up, but she broke the surface soon enough and replenished her lungs with cool night air.

Yet relief gave way to fear when she felt herself moving. Fowler heard the threat before she saw it. Whirling around, she froze for a moment as a real-life nightmare unfolded before her eyes: not only was the raging surf dragging her toward Big Rock, but it was also exploding on the jagged boulders that ran along the shore. She'd be lifted up like a rag doll and dashed against them!

Jenn hastened to ditch her heavy gear, all except for the laptop bag, which she slung over her head by the shoulder strap. She immediately pivoted, kicking with strong legs, pulling with desperate arms in a futile effort to survive. As the terrifying booming behind her grew louder and louder, she squeezed her eyes shut to imagine her parents and brother standing in the open doorway of their family home, beaming joyful smiles and reaching out their arms in welcome.

***

Jenn Fowler was seconds from being swept up and hurtled into the jagged boulders, but Park was almost upon her. *Gotcha!* he thought, roughly spinning his colleague back toward the shore, both of them looking directly at a life-changing injury at the very least. As a killer wave sucked them up and over the falls, they exchanged a worried glance, but Park had a plan. To the left of the rock face they were flying toward sat a tiny cove where the sea was calmer, so he led her as in a dance, rotating backwards to plant his dive boots on the craggy rock wall and pushing off into the inlet, both lifeguards performing a sideways dive just as the wave slammed into Big Rock with a force like that of a moving motor vehicle.

"You okay?" Park asked on the way to safety.

"Yeah, I am, thanks to you, man," she replied, clinging to a boulder, the swell rocking her back and forth.

Park shook his head at himself. His entire team could have been killed. Again.

***

When Maldonado clambered aboard Cage's dive boat, his subordinates took care of his gear, which allowed him to head directly below decks, leaving a trail of puddles on each varnished wooden step as he emerged onto the lower level. There he saw Daniels sitting on a bench, rubbing his windpipe and blinking red eyes, but otherwise D4 looked okay. Miller was a different story altogether: clutching his arm, the big man stood dazed in a puddle of seawater and blood, so Maldonado stepped forward to inspect the damage. He unsheathed his knife to cut off Miller's wetsuit sleeve, uncovering his forearm. The muscle had been pierced clean through, yet no major blood vessels appeared to have been severed. Since professional medical treatment was preferable to a clumsy field suture, Maldonado simply irrigated Miller's wound with an alcohol solution and wrapped a tight bandage around it. "What happened?" he asked, surprised that anyone could have gotten the best of his hulking comrade.

Miller shrugged. "I don't like the water. Almost drowned when I was a kid."

Unless their boss came back with the laptop, the guard captains knew, they'd failed in their mission, so it was with gloomy anticipation that they peered through the hull-side windows and waited for Cage to return. They watched as the lifeguards' rescue boats darted into the ski boat's range, the lawmen firing short bursts with their rifles. Then the twin Boston Whalers carved hard turns in opposite directions to avoid the return fire laid down by the ski boat.

Maldonado's lips curled into a grin when one of his guards set a rocket-propelled grenade launcher on his shoulder and pulled the trigger, the warhead blasting off to connect with one of the rescue boats, and a wave of delight washed over him as a massive orange fireball mushroomed into the night sky.

***

When Jeff Walker found himself up against a pair of smugglers resembling spacemen due to their military-grade diving gear, he hadn't been alone. Not at first. Swimming beside him, Paul Johanssen had recognized both "enemies." Graybeard was Mr. Cage, a man who'd been exceedingly generous to him and to his cousin Maria, and the Hulk was Peter Miller, the most frightening mass of ill-directed muscle Johanssen had ever had the displeasure of knowing. Encouraged by the hefty sum he'd be paid for his disloyalty, he left Walker to the two killers' mercies, swimming toward the third teammate he intended to betray.

The first had been Jenn Fowler. At the buddy check, after she had carefully and good-naturedly inspected his gear, he had jabbed an embroidery needle into her regulator hose several times.

Always jealous of Marcus Crawford's easy way with women, Johanssen felt a twisted sense of satisfaction when he saw his fellow lifeguard trapped in Daniels' armlock. He waited in the shadows, cursing as Crawford escaped from the man's attack by pulling his mask off and nailing him with finger strikes, but when the time was right, he charged his distracted teammate at full speed, whirling around to smash his scuba tank into Crawford's face.

Having scored three big points and with no further opportunities in sight, Johanssen ascended. He felt sure that none of his teammates had seen him assisting the smugglers, but in any event he'd already decided to accept Cage's standing offer of employment, so when he surfaced, he headed for Cage's dive boat instead of his own. Swimming toward it, he spotted Maldonado standing on the rear platform. The wiry killer was aiming a rifle directly at him, but Johanssen wasn't worried. As soon as

Maldonado recognized him as Maria's cousin, he'd surely reach out a hand to help him aboard.

***

Just as intelligent as Cage if not more so, Maldonado was aware that the best course of action would be to put a bullet in Johanssen's shoulder and send him back to his team a hero, thus preserving Cage's source of information in the lifeguard service. But he wasn't thinking about long-term outcomes. Maldonado was an addict and he knew it and he didn't care. Peering through the illuminated reticle of his night vision scope, he sighted the kid's head and fired twice, savoring the sensation of all-consuming power that flooded his body.

***

"Sorry, man," said Ethan Hall, lowering Park's Navy Sig and engaging the safety.

Crawford's heart continued to slam into his ribcage like a jackhammer as he trudged back to one of the aft benches and took a load off. "It's okay," he said, reaching back to unzip his wetsuit.

"I'm serious," Hall insisted, handing Crawford a towel. "I apologize. I thought you were one of the bad guys."

"No worries, bro. I would have done the same thing," Crawford replied as he rubbed his long hair dry, then swept his eyes over the moonlit ocean, his gaze falling on the smoldering remains of one of the rescue boats.

Hall followed his buddy's line of sight, frowned, and nodded grimly. He waited for a silent moment before speaking again. "At least Lieutenant Molloy and Big Don Roberts made it. They're over at Big Rock picking up Park and Fowler. And a big dive boat just came for the smugglers and sped off with the ski boat, so we're out of danger."

"Yeah, I saw 'em leave."

"Crawford!" a voice boomed from down in the water. It was Sergeant Taylor swimming up to the dive door with Walker in tow. Detective Van Brussel was right behind him, applying pressure to Walker's thigh with both hands.

Crawford's heart sank when he saw his good friend and mentor floating lifelessly in the sea, astonishingly pale.

"We need to get a tourniquet on him immediately," Taylor said as he climbed aboard. "He's got a deep knife wound, probably a severed femoral artery."

The lawmen pulled Walker up to the deck while Hall fetched the medical kit and twisted on a tourniquet above the wound. At the same time, Crawford hustled up to the bow and raised the anchor, then scrambled into the wheelhouse to shove the throttle forward.

"I thought you guys were dead," Hall said to Taylor as they raced back to Mission Bay. Kneeling over Walker between the two aft benches, they were steadying what looked like a corpse so Van Brussel could bandage the wound.

"The RPG operator took too long to fire," Taylor replied. "Van Brussel saw him and yelled at me to jump ship. Thanks, partner."

Van Brussel glanced up, nodded once, then turned back to his patient.

In the wheelhouse, Crawford reached for the microphone and held down the PTT button. "Marcus Crawford to Lieutenant Molloy, over," he said, steering the craft with one hand, alternating his gaze between the navigation screen and the rough water he was charging through.

"Go ahead, Crawford."

"Walker's badly injured. He needs a blood transfusion and emergency surgery. We're on our way back to Mission Bay and I've already called for an ambulance."

"Roger. Is everyone accounted for?"

"No sir. There's no sign of Johanssen."

"Okay. We'll stay here and search for him."

As Crawford continued to push the twin engines to their limits, Sergeant Taylor set his ear on Walker's chest, looking toward his patient's feet, listening for a heartbeat and watching for the rise and fall of respiration.

But Walker wasn't breathing.

7

A GOODE FRIEND

David Goode, Jr. signaled the end of the song with a leap and his band cut off just as his feet hit the stage. Then he dropped into a kneeling position and hung his head with dramatic flair, causing the crowd to burst into roaring cheers that followed him and the rest of the group all the way back to the green room, where fruit bowls and sandwich platters were set out on a table and plush chairs and sofas, makeup mirrors, bathroom facilities, and an oversized cooler packed with a predetermined selection of drinks on ice had been provided for the sweaty entertainers' refreshment.

With only twenty minutes of downtime before he'd have to change into his second outfit, Goode grabbed a seat and gulped fresh orange juice from a glass beer stein, which, in accordance with his contract, had been kept at room temperature so as not to shock his vocal cords. The first set had gone an hour twenty, and the second would run even longer. He released a sigh and sat still for a moment, breathing slow. Finding his center. That evening and the next, he was performing at Humphrey's Concerts by the Bay, a prestigious venue that paid good money plus comped tickets and a suite package for every member of the band.

Goode set his half-empty mug down on a coffee table and took out his phone, scrolling absently through social media until he came to a post created by Dr. Bernice King, Martin Luther King

Jr.'s youngest daughter. Just as he was liking and reposting it, the device buzzed in his hands. The caller was Tony Park.

"Jeff just got out of emergency surgery. His femoral artery was punctured but not severed and his prognosis is favorable," Park concluded, having first provided his close friend with some non-secret background information about the recovery dive.

"What can I do to help?" Goode asked.

"Nothing right now. Just thought you'd like to know."

"Definitely. 'Preciate you, brotha. Are there visitin' hours yet?"

"From eight to nine. That's a.m. though."

"Very funny. See you then."

"Yeah, I'll be there."

Emotional after hearing the news, David Goode lifted his stirring baritone to every heart in the crowd, offering his fans a second set that was even more uplifting than the first. When his bandmates launched into improvised solos, he'd slip out of the spotlight, swaying to the beat, focusing on what they had to say. At high points he'd shout out to lift them higher still, and when he felt that some encouragement was in order, he'd coax them into giving more. That was his mission in life, as a matter of fact, not just to direct his band and inspire his fans, but to lead everyone he could, starting with himself, so that the circle he inhabited might be better and do better.

The packed house danced and sang along unabashedly. Some fans cried, like many folks did at church. At one point, as the band played on, Goode stepped down into the audience and boogied with a woman close to his mother's age, who beamed with delight as he gave her a twirl.

After the encore, the band broke it down, playing softly and sparingly while Goode thanked the crowd for coming. He introduced his fellow musicians, then saluted every corner of the theatre and jogged offstage, riding the ecstatic cheers into the green room like a surfer on a wave.

An hour later, after the VIP meet-and-greet, the weary entertainer was winding his way through the puddles in the parking lot to his brand-new Ford Mustang Shelby GT500 when two melodious female voices rang out behind him:

"Dave! So did you want to take us to that party?"

"Yeah, it's been a long time, babe."

Goode wheeled around slowly, not sure he wanted to lay his eyes on his astonishingly attractive backup singers, both of whom he knew in the biblical sense. For a second he let his gaze roam up and down their curvy bodies, but he tore it away, politely declined, and waved a friendly goodbye as he squeezed himself into the confines of his street-legal race car.

The sparkling GT500 sported a classic look. Painted in Oxford White with Kona Blue over-the-top racing stripes, it was a dream car for sure, yet too small for Goode's massive frame. He weighed the same as Tony Park and stood an inch taller. As he roared over the Mission Bay Bridge into Pacific Beach, the singer frowned and wished he'd given more forethought to the recent purchase.

The following morning, Goode didn't open his eyes to bright midday sunlight for a change. Counting his blessings as he padded out to the kitchen, he felt grateful for his health and strength, and for the many people in his life who loved him. His profession brought him joy and he was well paid for it. Too well, if he was being honest: his home was a penthouse suite on the sand and he'd just bought himself a hundred-thousand-dollar car.

Shaking his head with a frown, he wondered how many of his distant African cousins were trekking through miles of blistering desert with weighty pots on their heads at that very moment, only to stand in line, fill the vessels with contaminated water, and trudge back home. Every day. All while he was standing there feeling blessed, peering through floor-to-ceiling windows at the golden beach scene ten floors below.

The storm had passed, leaving behind unusually large waves that had attracted a great number of surfers. Which brought Jeff Walker to mind. As he sliced a banana into a bowl, Goode thought back to the first time Walker had shown up at Hillside Baptist Church, brought by a girlfriend as a guest. She hadn't lasted long, but Walker had stayed for years. Seven, if memory served.

After breakfast, he took a seat at the keyboard. Placing one foot on the sustain pedal, he set his fingers on the keys and jammed freely for a while, then slowed his groove and moved up a key, transitioning into a new tune he'd been working on: a love song for his girlfriend.

The piano had always been a place of healing for Goode, somewhere he could relax and let his active mind explore every combination and permutation of the harmonic network that he was so intimately familiar with. This was where he was free, connected to something bigger and better than himself. This was where divine inspiration flowed through him like benevolent electricity, but only when he was tuned in closely enough to let it happen.

As Goode played on, he let his rich voice pour forth from the depths of his belly, making sure to keep his nasal passages open, thus allowing the high end of the sound spectrum to come out clean and resonant. He sang his guts out for a half an hour and closed the session with a freestyle rap, a soliloquy on the power of love. His heart finally in the right place again, he covered the instrument and cut the power, then reached for his phone to call Lynn Peters, a second-year law student at USD.

"Hey, sweetheart," she answered.

"Hey, babe. How *you* doin'?" he joked, in an imitation of Joey from *Friends*.

"I've been studying for the past five hours. That's how *I'm* doin'."

"Five hours? It's only seven thirty."

"I know."

"Sounds like *you* could use a night off," he said. "Y'wanna come over later on, maybe have a glass of wine, watch the sunset? I'd *love* to make you dinner."

"Sounds heavenly. Forget the wine, though. I'm going to need some coffee."

***

Jack Cage hadn't slept well after the disastrous operation of the previous night, but he'd kept his habit of rising early to knock out his five-mile run, then driven to the warehouse compound before Maria or any other day-shift worker arrived. He strode past the empty reception area, headed down the hall to his office, and settled into the executive chair at his desk. While waiting for the guard captains to show up, he thought back to his difficult childhood for some reason: a violent and occasionally revolting time in his life. Fortunately, his men marched in to derail his train of thought.

Cage did not rise to greet them, gesturing instead toward a pair of brown leather sofas set in an L shape around a glass coffee table, where Miller took a seat more gingerly than the other two.

"I don't suppose any of you know who shot our lifeguard," Cage began, staring at each of them in turn.

All three shook their heads, but it was an easy guess as to who had done it. Cage locked back on to Maldonado's dark eyes. "That was stupid," he said. "Johanssen could have helped us for years."

Maldonado tilted his head so subtly that the nod was hardly perceptible. It might have been a concession, though it certainly wasn't an apology, and in either case it didn't matter. The lunatic would soon have to fend for himself, and Cage suspected that his was a story that wouldn't end well.

"Now," Cage went on, "since Oceanside PD was running the show, we can bet they're keeping the laptop at their headquarters. Maldonado, tonight you will lead Daniels and three of your guards in a second—and final—recovery operation."

"Yes sir," Maldonado replied, his sunken eyes gleaming.

"Mr. Cage," Daniels broke in, surprising his boss by speaking up for once in his life. "That's not a large enough attacking force. The building will be heavily guarded, with security doors, bulletproof glass, and an alarm system."

"Normally you'd be correct, D4," Cage returned. "But it won't be heavily guarded tonight. As for the security doors and the bulletproof glass, I don't know whose idea it was to put a police station in a shopping mall, but you'll be breaching the wall it shares with the public library."

"And the alarm?"

"You'll just have to get in and out as fast as you can. But I'll discuss all of this in detail later. For now, I want you two to get some rest, and be back here at twenty hundred with your men, geared up and ready to go. Miller, you've got the night off."

Once his men had filed out of the room, Cage rested his elbow on the desk and his chin on his fist as he ordered his thoughts and priorities. With the police tightening the net around him and the cartel watching his every move, he had a number of loose ends to tie up before he could disappear. If ever there was a time in Cage's life when he needed to get everything right, it was now.

8

GUNS AND GIRLFRIENDS

Jeff Walker let out a self-pitying groan. After a long night in a
hospital bed, sleeping in dreamless, opiate-addled fits along
with several other patients in the same ward, most suffering
worse than he, the postoperative patient checked the clock on
the wall for the millionth time and finally it read eight a.m.,
the start of the only visiting hour in the ICU. No more than
a minute later, a pair of familiar voices echoed in the hallway
outside, lifting his spirits considerably. He peered over the
safety rail as a cheery nurse swept in, followed by Tony Park and
Lieutenant Molloy.

"Morning, Brother Jeff," said Molloy, offering his hand.
Walker's boss's grip couldn't have been described as crushing,
but still Walker winced from his injuries. "You doing all right?"
Molloy asked. "How are the nurses treating you?"

The nurse giggled. She took Walker's vital signs and bustled
back out, closing the door behind her.

As Park approached his buddy's bed to clasp his palm in a
soft Hawaiian handshake that didn't hurt, Lieutenant Molloy's
features tightened with concern. "I have bad news," said the
former running back. "We found Johanssen's body. He was
shot twice in the head."

Walker groaned again.

"That's not all. We recovered Jenn Fowler's gear and found a neat set of holes in her regulator hose. Most likely made by a large needle."

A pensive silence followed, after which Walker was the first to speak. "It wasn't Crawford and it wasn't Hall," he said. "Those guys are our brothers."

Molloy nodded. "I know."

"We think it was Johanssen. Jenn's dive buddy," said Park, with a frown and a discouraged shake of his head. "When he was checking her gear."

"As for who shot 'im," Molloy resumed, "Roberts and Taylor are good friends of mine, and no one else on our team was armed." He leveled on Park a pair of dubious, knowing eyes. "Right?"

Park avoided the eyes as well as the question, hastening to ask, "But if Johanssen was working for the smugglers, why would they shoot him?"

"That's what I can't figure out," Molloy replied, dropping his heavy frame into an orange plastic chair. He blew out a sigh as Park headed for a sturdier bench seat by the window.

Molloy looked uncomfortable. He cleared his throat before speaking again. "Roberts and Taylor wanted to be here this mornin', but they couldn't come. So I'm speaking for them as well. The smugglers we fought las' night are dangerous criminals led by a man known as Jack Cage, and I owe both of y'all an apology for askin' you to get involved."

"It's okay, boss," Walker said. "I doubt Roberts and Taylor told you the whole story when they came to you for help."

"No, they didn't, but it was still a bad call."

"I'm sorry, too, Jeff," Park said. "I should have said no back at headquarters."

"Bro, you saved my life last night. Twice. Jenn's too. I'd say we're even."

Park left it there, but he didn't look any less ashamed.

"And we don't think Cage has a reason to come after y'all," Molloy went on, "but Don Roberts is gonna put a twenty-four-hour watch on your residences anyway. What's your rehab timetable, Walker?"

"Two weeks of bed rest before physical therapy. A month before I can walk with no restrictions. Two till I can run."

"All right, then. So that's two months' leave from beach duty. Come in to headquarters after the first thirty days and we'll find somethin' for you to do. Then it's back to the beach, assumin' you don't rip open your wound before it has a chance to heal."

"I won't."

"You'd *betta* not," Molloy said, standing to wring out Walker's injured hand once again. "I'll stop by your place with some groceries, since I *know* there's nothin' in the fridge." With a nod, the senior lifeguard strode out to begin his day, crossing paths with David Goode in the hallway just outside the door. "See you tomorrow at the barbecue, Brother David?" he boomed.

"Yes sir," Goode boomed back, then entered the room. With a sympathetic frown, he came beside Walker's bed. "Hey dude. Leas' you get a vacation," he said.

"Yeah," Walker replied dryly. "I'm looking forward to some carefree time off. It'll be like playing cops and robbers."

"But with your legs tied together and no gun," Park called out from the other side of the room. "Let me bring you one."

Walker shook his head. "I don't have a license."

"You don't need one," Park countered. "According to California Penal Code Section 12026, and I quote, with minor changes for the sake of brevity, any citizen or legal resident of the United States over the age of eighteen who is not a convicted criminal or a mental health patient who carries, either openly or concealed, anywhere within his or her place of residence, place of business, or on private property owned or lawfully possessed by the citizen or legal resident, any pistol, revolver, or other firearm capable of being concealed upon the person, is not guilty of carrying a concealed firearm."

"So he can keep it in his apartment," Goode summed up, showing no amazement at his friend's recitation. Both he and Walker had long known that Park was blessed with a photographic memory.

"But it would be Tony's gun, not mine," Walker countered, then looked to Park. "Wouldn't I have to buy it from you?"

Park wagged a finger in the air. "Good question, but no. Lawful possession of a firearm means the person who has custody of the weapon either legally owns it or has the permission of the lawful owner or a person who—"

"I understand," Walker cut in, cracking his first smile of the day. "It's legal for you to loan me a gun."

"Can he carry it when he goes out?" Goode asked.

"Another good question," Park answered as he crossed the room to join his buddies. "Yes, he can keep it in his car or on his person, but only if he believes himself to be in grave danger." Eyeing Walker, he said, "You'd have to notify your local police department in advance if possible. Let me know, man. I know you're not a gun lover, but it might just save your life."

"I will, bro. Thanks. And I appreciate you coming to check on me."

After Park left for lifeguard headquarters, Walker told Goode about the previous night's dive in general terms, providing strictly necessary, non-sensitive details about Oceanside PD's investigation.

"I agree with Tony," said Goode, now with a better understanding of the situation. "You're gonna want a gun, at least until your leg heals. It would be easy for the smugglers to find out who's on the dive rescue team and come lookin' for ya. They probably won't, but you'll sleep better knowin' you have it."

"Fine. I'll tell him."

"Promise."

"Come on, bro."

Goode laughed. "All right, all right. Hey, you wanna come to the barbecue on Sunday? Everyone'd love to see ya."

"Thanks for the invitation, but I can't. No walking for Walker for two weeks. Say hi for me, please."

"Will *do*." Goode offered Walker a fist bump. "Ya know ya always welcome, brotha. See ya later."

Walker hadn't been back to Hillside in years. The congregation would always be his family, but more like distant relatives now that he'd drifted away. He sometimes thought about returning for a Sunday service. Or not. Only if he felt like it. But one thing was for sure: he missed the self-confidence he'd had when he'd been in the habit of following his conscience all the time. And now, lying there in the hospital, as the desire to be guided by goodness came into his heart, regardless of whether he ever went back to church, a wave of benevolent electricity rushed through his body, making all his hair stand on end.

***

Carla Reyes took a dangerously hot cup of coffee out of the microwave and hurried to the small table in her breakfast nook to set it down. She lowered herself into a solid-wood chair and peered through the window to admire her little garden, rain-soaked and glistening in the early morning sun. Since Park was at the hospital visiting Walker, she ate alone, nibbling thoughtfully at a slice of unbuttered toast.

They were in love—she was sure of that—but Tony was so focused on his career and his buddies that she often felt like a piece of property rather than a life partner, and now was one of those times. *Why is he so distant?* she wondered, leaving her coffee to head back to their room. *Is it me?* She hiked up her nightshirt to look in the mirror at her butt and thighs. *Definitely not,* she decided, letting the fabric fall and turning her critical eye on her brand-new boobs. She shook her shoulders from side to side and watched them jiggle. A smile tugged at the corners of her lips. She loved them, and she knew Tony did, too.

Carla was the manager at Bella, a hair salon and spa located ten blocks from her cozy duplex unit, so she'd walk to work after getting ready. Her first appointment was a special one: David Goode's new girlfriend was coming in for a cut and style. As Carla pulled on a pair of skinny-fit jeans, she hoped Lynn Peters would turn out to be a good person. Dave deserved that much. Ever since she'd known him, he'd always had a girlfriend, often more than one, but to her they'd always seemed like gold diggers. He'd invariably pour his big heart into the relationship while they rode him for all they could. *Literally.*

She ambled back through the kitchen to the breakfast nook, dejectedly wishing Tony would pour *his* big heart into their relationship. At least once in a while. Then she picked up her plate and dropped her unbuttered toast in the trash.

***

Lynn Peters' alarm woke her up at five. She made a cup of tea and read two chapters on intellectual property law before stepping out for a run: four miles in thirty minutes through a smelly neighborhood she was dying to move out of. Back home, she read for another twenty minutes in the kitchen over a bowl of cottage cheese and peaches.

Lynn's mother had often said that looking one's best is a crucial survival skill, especially when one is not *feeling* one's best, so since she was scheduled to speak at an important luncheon that day and nervous about it, she'd made an early appointment at a beauty salon her new boyfriend had recommended. Hopefully they'd know what they were doing. *For seventy bucks, they'd better,* she grumbled to herself. The speech was a condition of her scholarship; when she'd applied to USD Law, she'd been selected out of three thousand female applicants for a single full ride, which had come with the annual obligation to address the current year's finalists. Today she'd be using the analogy of salmon swimming upstream to lay their eggs as a means to inspire the young women to continue their struggle against a system rigged to keep them down.

At the end of every semester, Lynn's academic performance was reviewed to make sure she finished in the top ten percent of her class (*try top one percent,* she scoffed). Yet it came at a cost: on those rare occasions when she'd lay her books aside to go out on a date, she'd inevitably find herself mentally reviewing what she'd been reading at home, wishing she had a pen and paper in front of her instead of a handsome young man who hadn't gotten tired of her yet.

As she buttoned up a sky-blue blouse and brushed her long blond hair, she studied her reflection in the mirror, seeing an intelligent, confident, and beautiful young woman who was nonetheless living an unbalanced lifestyle. *Nothing I can do about that right now*, she thought as she grabbed her keys, then marched outside and drove to Bella with the stereo off, reciting her speech four times without making a single mistake.

***

Tina Garcia swung her locker door shut with a metallic clunk after a long night at the EMS base station. As she trudged through the sterile corridors of Scripps Mercy Hospital, her mind replayed the recording of a gory car crash to which she'd responded only a few hours earlier. A red sports car had blown its tires drifting on a curve, causing it to skid out of control, slam into a tree, and burst into flames, killing both occupants. Whether the victims had been conscious at the time, Tina couldn't know for certain, but the way she imagined it, even if the impact had knocked them out, the agony of being burned alive had probably shocked them awake. When she'd arrived on scene, a citizen responder had been attempting to put out the raging flames with a fire extinguisher, but the white blasts had served only to blow them aside for a moment, exposing a pair of charred, skeletal corpses in the two front seats.

The sun wouldn't be up for another half an hour. As Tina wound her way through the puddles in the parking lot to her Kawasaki Ninja 650R, she looked forward to some home-cooked food, a hot bath, and twelve hours of sleep, in that order and preferably with no nightmares. She walked around her ride in a three-hundred-sixty-degree inspection, devoting particular attention to the condition of her tires. Satisfied, she tucked her long black hair into her leather jacket, popped on her helmet, and swung a leg over the machine. When she hit the ignition, the even grumble of a well-tuned motorcycle engine brought a smile to her lips. It was her favorite sound in the world. Then she gave the throttle a twist and blasted off.

It was a short ride from Downtown to Chula Vista, where her family home was the nicest building on the block. The two-story yellow house was painted every year whether it needed it or not. Every screw was tight, every hinge oiled, every corner swept. Her father had built it from the ground up, performing or supervising every bit of work from the pouring of the foundation to the installation of the bathroom accessories. Lovingly decorated with portraits, plants, and comfortable furniture, the Garcia residence was where every family gathering was held. Tina rolled up onto the short driveway and braked to a stop, leaning the black-and-white sport bike on its kickstand before heading inside. When her eyes fell on her mother waiting for her in the kitchen with her arms outstretched, both women broke into beaming smiles.

Mamá was the best cook Tina knew. From traditional to fancy Mexican food and international favorites such as chicken cordon bleu and spaghetti carbonara, the kindly matriarch could do it all. That morning, breakfast was chilaquiles, a peasant meal that can feed a family for a month for the price of a tank of gas. Tina knew the recipe well: first, yesterday's tortillas are cut into chips and toasted in oil. Then yesterday's salsa is poured on top and the mixture is stirred and briefly fried. Chilaquiles can be topped with diced onions, cheese, a fried egg, and/or shredded chicken, possibly with refried—meaning yesterday's—beans on the side. As she savored a forkful of the spicy comfort food, her mother told her of a tricky situation unfolding among her uncles and aunts.

Following a much-anticipated hot bubble bath, Tina assumed her accustomed sleeping position, pulled the blankets over her shoulders, and closed her eyes, but she was unable to shut off her thoughts, her stubborn mind refusing to drop the subject of her ex-boyfriend. In the end, the cons—specifically his selfish ways and sleeping around—had far outweighed the pros; still, there had been positive aspects, the absence of which made the breakup feel like a loss. Before drifting off, Tina resolved to see the recent separation as a win, as a chance to focus on her family and on herself for a change. Which brought to mind something her mother had said as they'd been washing the dishes, that only when she was content with being single, with her own life, would she be ready to find the right person to share it with. Tina wondered what her future soul mate was doing at that very moment. Maybe thinking of her!

9

TAYLOR'S PROMISE

When Cage had purchased the twin Jeep Cherokee SRTs for his guard captains to use, which in his mind represented their share of a bonus he'd received from the cartel, Maldonado had fallen in love with the blacked-out vehicles. They weren't the publicly available four-by-fours that came standard with a sport-tuned suspension, upgraded brakes, aggressive bodywork, and a 6.4-liter Hemi V8 engine producing 475 hp; these custom models were further equipped with armor plating, undercarriage IED protection, ballistic glass, electrified door handles, and one other secret feature. Maldonado's fascination had dwindled to disillusionment, however, when he'd tried to outrun a Highway Patrol helicopter and was nearly caught due to the additional weight of the aftermarket armor.

With Daniels riding shotgun and three guards in the back, D2 was driving one of these Jeeps to Mission Plaza Real Shopping Center, cursing his boss's refusal to invest in a pair of Trackhawks, which are essentially the same Jeep Cherokee but with a 707-hp supercharged Hellcat engine. He cranked an angry turn onto Mission Avenue, accelerating through the curve as he mentally rehearsed the tactical plan: first, they would break in to the Mission Branch Library and blow a hole in the west-facing wall. After gaining entry to the police station, they were to eliminate all survivors, find the evidence room, and recover the laptop once and for all. At the briefing, Cage had said that several police officers would be dispatched at the last minute to respond to an emergency, so only a skeleton crew was likely to remain: one patrolman, one sergeant, and, by coincidence, night shift commander Lieutenant Donal "Big Don" Roberts.

In Maldonado's opinion, the only area in which Daniels showed any special skill or talent was lock picking. It took Daniels ten seconds to open the front door to the library, which activated an ear-piercing siren. Dressed in dark tactical gear and balaclava masks, the five intruders hustled to the community room, affixed an explosive device to the west-facing wall, and took cover as the blast hurled concrete chunks into the bookshelves and thick smoke billowed up from both sides of the breach. Maldonado thought he heard a momentary scream just as the bomb went off.

***

Two minutes earlier, Lieutenant Don Roberts had been sitting in his office, gazing at the family photographs on his desk. His eyes were first drawn to his wife's precious smile, which lit up every picture she appeared in. Then to his children. Having raised them with so many family outings and hugs and kisses over the years, and now to be able to sit back and watch them steer their own ships was an extraordinary privilege. Even if it were all over today, Big Don told himself, he'd been blessed. He next turned his attention to a larger picture on the wall to his left, the group photo of his college football team, in which his younger self stood proudly beside his then-and-current best friends David Goode, Sr. and Jason Molloy. He was looking forward to seeing them at church the following morning, with a backyard barbecue in the afternoon.

A shrieking alarm split the silence. It was a common occurrence easily triggered by teenagers fooling around, stray dogs, strong winds, or library employees who couldn't remember the code. Muttering under his breath, Lieutenant Roberts headed for the front of the station, walking along the east-facing wall as his thoughts drifted to the waterborne battle of the night before. It was all about the laptop. *And it still is*, he realized with a chilling jolt of panic. "Get down!" he screamed at his fellow officers as the explosion snapped his bones, boiled his blood, and tore him apart.

***

Maldonado's red laser sight cut through the smoke as he and his men picked their way through the rubble, stepping over the dismembered remains of the night shift commander, with two separate alarms assaulting their ears. He gestured for his men to fan out, which they did in a fluid, coordinated motion as they cleared the labyrinthine space. It was Maldonado who found the two other policemen sprawled out on the floor with broken limbs and head trauma, so he swiftly targeted their hearts, one after another—Crack! Crack!—then directed his team to the evidence room, where Daniels' only talent proved useful once again.

As he ran back to the SRT with his brothers-in-arms beside him, Maldonado reveled in the crisp night air, his sharpened senses noting all of the stars in the sky, the smell of every flower, and each clomp of their steel-toe boots.

Life didn't get any better than this.

***

A hush fell over the sanctuary as Pastor Williams stepped up to the pulpit. His commanding voice soared to every corner of Hillside Baptist Church as he praised Big Don's commitment to his community, and it fell to a reverent whisper when he spoke of the man's devotion to his family. Mrs. Roberts, her children, and their children sat in the front pews, nodding tearfully as the pastor urged them to be strong in their time of grief, to remain courageous and trust that better days would come. Among the many regular church members who'd gathered to pay their respects were Lieutenant Molloy, David Goode, Sr., and David Goode, Jr. Even more numerous were the non-members, including Sergeant Taylor, every employee of Oceanside PD, a large contingent of men and women from the rest of the San Diego law enforcement community, and a great number of friends and relatives.

Pastor Williams cried openly as he and David Goode, Jr. offered a moving rendition of "Amazing Grace," with the elder Goode providing accompaniment on the organ. One by one, every mourner rose, many waving open hands in the air with tears pouring down their cheeks as they sang along.

As the hymn came to an end and the crowd settled down, Pastor Williams called for anyone who wished to say a few words to come up and do so. Sergeant Taylor strode straight up the chancel steps, sensing the collective weight of a thousand eyes bearing down on his back. He took his place at the pulpit and looked out at a sea of expectant faces.

"Good morning, everyone," he began with confidence, though his throat caught when Big Don's widow lifted her brokenhearted gaze to his. She was family. "I know it's not much consolation, ma'am," he said, with tears in his eyes, "but I want you to know I'm going to be looking out for y'all for the rest of my life." His words almost faltered, but he powered through it, his voice rising from a cracking whisper to a growl, and his promise echoed through the pews as many other funeral-goers vowed the same support.

Mrs. Roberts nodded bravely and tried to smile, but her hands shot up to her face and she hung her head, heaving and shuddering as she wept.

Taylor then locked eyes with every member of the narcotics task force, his best friends, and thundered, "I swear to y'all that I won't rest until we find whoever was behind this and lock them up for good!"

All those gathered burst into applause, many of them leaping to their feet and shouting out in solidarity, some calling for much harsher forms of punishment than a prison sentence as the new leader of the narcotics unit stomped down the steps and dropped into his seat.

The last part of the service saw five hundred people form a tight circle around the Roberts family. Everyone within reach laid a hand on their shoulders as Pastor Williams implored the Holy Spirit to protect and provide for the grieving clan and Deacon Goode played inspiring chords behind him.

"Oh, Don!" Mrs. Roberts wailed as her people lifted her up in prayer. "What am I going to do without you?"

10

ENTER VERONICA

Walker's two weeks of bed rest had finally passed. He'd read a couple of thriller novels, listened to some tunes, but spent most of his time wishing he were out surfing or riding his motorcycle. Guys like him don't deal well with forced inactivity; after all, Walker had lived for sports and stunts since before he could tie his shoes. So it was, on this fifteenth day of the postoperative period, that he'd risen before dawn and waited anxiously for the sun to climb high enough, then grabbed his bag and eased down the stairs to the parking lot. As he hobbled to his Corolla, he nodded to a pair of plainclothes policemen standing near their unmarked unit.

The sand felt cool under his feet as he limped along. He chose a suitable spot, spread out his towel, and sat gingerly down, stretching his legs toward the ocean. With the still-gentle morning sun growing warm on his shoulders, he swept his gaze over what he'd been missing all this time: long rows of glassy waves cruising in to shore, crumbling, crashing, sliding up the sand in rhythmic fashion. One after another. Time and again. The melodious calling of the gulls and the salty, earthy smell of fresh coastal air coaxed him down onto the towel, yet when he closed his eyes he couldn't halt his rushing thoughts. Nor was he able to catch a full breath, as he'd been excessively nervous since the recovery dive. *No, it had started before that,* he corrected himself, *with the shooting off of Big*

Rock. This was the sort of thing, Walker knew, that Tony Park had been forced to endure in the Middle East, many times, and it gave him some measure of insight into the cause of his buddy's panic attacks.

As he flipped onto his stomach, the now-blazing sun on his back recalled a hot and dusty tactical course he'd taken with Park, Goode, and eighteen other people serious about self-defense. Having paid a thousand dollars each to sleep on the desert floor for a week, they were awoken each day before dawn by a special operations instructor who led them on ten-mile runs before breakfast. Then in hand-to-hand drills with a surprising amount of contact. When the heat was at its worst, they'd marched into a massive tent for classroom instruction on topics including firearms and small unit tactics. Then it was back outside for gun and knife drills, skirmish games, and a final sunset run that made you want to puke. The food was bad. The ground was hard. It had taken Walker a week to recover from the ordeal and the same amount of time to forgive Park for convincing him to sign up for it, but the experience had proved useful many times. And Goode was right: he *was* sleeping better with a P226 in his nightstand drawer. At the moment, the pistol was right beside him in his bag, loaded, chambered, and de-cocked.

Walker sat up to study the waves again, his mind whirling with memories of his mother, as it always did whenever he went to the beach. He blew out a long sigh and pictured her younger, healthy smile, deliberately not fast-forwarding to the disturbing one that had been burned into his memory as if by branding iron. This was where she'd given him his first surfboard. Thirty-five miles south of where he now sat, in Mexico but on the same stretch of sand.

Eight-year-old Walker had long been relegated to dry sand, forced to watch the bigger boys paddle out every Sunday. As his interest in the sport grew into an overwhelming desire to join them, his mom had watched him leap in the air and spin around in imitation of their aerial stunts, waiting until she felt he was old enough. Then she'd asked around, chosen a board that was just right for his undeveloped body, and surprised him with it on Easter Sunday. Her heartfelt smile as she handed it over was proof of the joy she took in giving.

A cheery voice behind him dragged him kicking and screaming back through the years to the present time. "Hi!"

Shielding his eyes from the sun, Walker turned to see a dark-haired beachgoer about his age, barely clad in a black bikini that covered virtually none of her perfect bronze-hued slopes and valleys. She was Latina, his favorite flavor, and her full lips bloomed into an inviting grin. "Sorry to bother you," she said, holding up a bottle of sunscreen, "but I'm all by myself and I don't want to get burned. Would you mind?"

"Hi yourself," Walker replied coolly. "Of course not."

He started to crawl to his feet, but she took one look at the bandage on his thigh and plopped herself down in front of him, facing the waves. "My name's Veronica, by the way," she said over her shoulder.

"Jeff," he replied, squeezing out a glob on his hand, setting straight to work on her slender neck and shoulders. "But most people call me Walker. Do you live around here?"

"No, up in Orange County. But I'd always heard about Mission Beach, so today I finally came down to see what the fuss was all about."

When he patted her shoulder to let her know he'd finished, she swiveled around to blast him again with that heart-stopping smile.

"So what's the verdict?" he managed. "Does it live up to all the hype?"

"It's perfect," she replied cheerily, looking around at all the natural beauty and smelling the air as though savoring the aroma of a mouth-watering meal. Then her gaze dropped to his leg. "Hey, what happened?"

"Bar fight. You should've seen the other guy."

She giggled, then pushed out her lips in a theatrical pout. "Bet that hurt. Let me guess, you're a bouncer and some punk was making trouble at the door."

"Nope."

"So what do you do?"

"We're actually sitting in my office," he said, gesturing grandly toward the chain of towers that trailed off in the distance. "I'm a beach lifeguard."

"So if I needed mouth-to-mouth, would you give it to me?" she joked, setting her hand on his shoulder as they shared a laugh and caught each other's eyes.

Walker was in a good mood for the first time in far too long. It was just what he needed: to soak up some vitamin D, rest his gaze on the ocean, and flirt with a scantily clad creature such as she.

All of a sudden, Veronica spotted someone in the distance and waved excitedly. She stood, then stooped to brush the sand off her legs. Walker also rose, his attention fully engaged.

"I'd love to see you again," she said. "Do you want to call me sometime?"

Of course Walker wanted to call her sometime. He thumbed her number into his phone before she turned to go, her perfect rear end switching back and forth as she skipped away.

Two days later, they were flirting again, this time at an outside table at Sammy's Bar and Grill, which was right on the Pacific Beach boardwalk, just a few hundred yards from where they'd met. A cheerful waitress bustled up to the table with a glass of red wine for her and a frosty mug of pale ale for him.

Veronica wore stretchy black leggings and a bright-red off-the-shoulder blouse. Her long glossy black hair, curled only slightly, tumbled down to her cleavage, and her generous lips awoke in Walker a primal yearning to crawl over the table and fall on top of her.

They clinked glasses and beamed at each other, sipping their drinks as the sun bade the beach community a glittering farewell, its golden rays glancing off the sea as it drifted toward the horizon line.

It came up in conversation that her bloodline was Mexican, so he excitedly rattled off a witty phrase in perfect Spanish, but her confused expression dashed any hope of a good match in that regard.

"So you were born and raised in Mexico?" she asked.

"Yeah, my mom left the U.S. when she was pregnant with me."

She set down her wine with a sly, knowing look. "I couldn't help noticing that you don't have any cuts or bruises on your hands from that bar fight."

Walker hadn't forgotten Lieutenant Molloy's warning about the confidentiality of Oceanside PD's investigation, but his strong emotions were clouding his judgment, as they tended to do. "Okay," he admitted. "I was attacked while scuba diving the other night."

She gasped. "Oh my god! I'm glad you're okay."

"Thanks. Sorry I didn't tell you before."

Her exotic eyes drew him in as she leaned closer from across the little table. Her perfume was intoxicating. "That's okay, Jeff," she cooed. "I appreciate you being honest with me, more than you know. I really like you."

"Me too," he said, moving in for a kiss, but he stopped short when he noticed two large men towering over the table. It was Park and Goode, who had come to meet him for dinner since Veronica needed to leave early. "Hey guys," he said sheepishly, clambering awkwardly to his feet to make the proper introductions.

"So what do you think of Sammy's?" Park asked Veronica once they'd all sat down.

"I'll be back," she replied, sticking her nose in the air with a comically pompous expression. "It's an upscale venue, but not pretentiously so," she declared like a food critic delivering a review, deflecting the ensuing laughter by putting the spotlight on Park and Goode. "So are you guys scuba divers like Jeff? My brother and I are going diving at the cove on Sunday."

Park hesitated. "Uh, I know La Jolla has some great spots, but no, I'm not a diver," he lied.

"Me neither," said Goode.

A notification sounded on her phone, so she checked the device and looked back up with an apologetic smile. "My ride's here."

"I'll walk you out," said Walker.

They laughed and held hands as they stepped out the front door, strolling toward a gray Jeep Wrangler parked at the valet station. Walker peered through the passenger-side window and locked eyes with the driver, a large square-jawed man with a military-style buzz cut.

"That's my brother, Tim," Veronica said.

Tim's features warmed slightly, and he offered Walker a pleasant nod, which the latter returned before refocusing his attention on his date.

She stepped close. "Do you want to hang out tomorrow? Maybe Sunday? I'm in town all weekend."

"I'd love to," Walker replied as he came in for the kill. He slipped his arms around her waist and softly said, "May I call you tomorrow?"

"Of course you may," she whispered as they brought their lips together in a deliciously long first kiss.

Grinning like an idiot, he held the door for her as she settled into the passenger seat, and as Tim merged into the passing flow of cars, she waved goodbye and hit him with a dazzling, delighted smile.

Back at the table, the guys' conversation was subdued compared to their usual rowdy banter. Park sat with his back to a corner, scanning the room for trouble. Walker's head was still in the clouds, and Goode also seemed lost in thought, unusually sad for some reason.

That's when Walker remembered Park's lie. "Why'd you tell her you weren't a diver?" he asked.

Park shrugged. "Just got a funny feeling. It's probably nothing."

"There's no way she's involved, bro," Walker said, taking the last swig of his pale ale and setting it down. "We bumped into each other at the beach. It was totally random."

After devouring three plates piled high with steaming French fries and juicy cheeseburgers washed down with another round of drinks, they were waiting for the check when Goode asked, "Have y'all ever been to The East End?"

Park and Walker said that they hadn't.

"It's a huge, newly renovated concert hall downtown and I'm performin' there in three weeks. Y'all wanna go? I can get ya two tickets each and a fistful of drink vouchers."

It was an easy decision to make. Goode's shows were always fun. Then the trio argued over who would get the check and the charismatic singer prevailed. At the curb they went their separate ways: Park strolled five blocks through an upscale beach community to Carla's cozy duplex unit, Goode only two to his oceanfront high-rise, and Walker slid behind the wheel of an old economy car and drove twenty miles south to his one-bedroom flat.

11

A REVEALING SECOND DATE

A chilly morning wind blew through Walker's hair as he limped along the packed wet sand of La Jolla Shores Beach, restricted by doctor's orders to merely a mile a day of careful walking. To his right, a pair of surfers bobbed in beginner waves, both outfitted in full wetsuits. Straight ahead, at the south end of the beach, a contingent of kayakers was just putting in. Walker had to laugh at himself when it occurred to him that he was scanning the beach for trouble even when he wasn't on duty.

It was nine o'clock on Sunday morning. At ten, he'd be meeting Veronica at a nearby café for breakfast, and he was glad it was nearby, since at this snail's pace he'd need forty-five minutes just to get back to the car. As he inched along, he felt like a gorilla in a cage; his inner child begged him to sprint to the south end, take a flying leap, sail through the air, slice into the surf, and power around the point. But he'd most likely feel something tear along the way. In the best of cases, he'd be set back a month or more; in the worst, he'd drown or bleed to death, so Walker dutifully hobbled to the end of the beach and back, focusing on his idyllic surroundings.

She was already waiting for him at an inside table, decked out in tight-fitting blue jeans and a black T-shirt knotted at the midriff, exposing a flat stomach and a sparkling belly button ring. "Hey!"

she called out, rising from her chair. Walker strutted up for a kiss and a very curvy hug.

"How was the dive?" he asked a minute later, now sitting across from her.

"Cold," she answered, then sipped her coffee and set it down. "Plus my brother used to be in the Army, so it felt more like a training exercise than a family outing. He's pretty hard core."

"I hear you," Walker said, cradling his own steaming mug with a cold pair of hands. "Park's like that, too."

"Speaking of the military, did you ever serve? You're so serious. Formal, like a soldier."

"No, but my dad did. I never got to meet him, though."

"Really?" She was such a good listener.

"Yeah. He was killed when my mom was pregnant with me."

"No way! I bet you've tried to find the guy who did it. You look like a man of action."

"I am. And yes I have. I even know his name. When I first moved up here, I tried for years to find him, but I'm not a relative, so I couldn't access his service record, and there wasn't enough evidence for the police to reopen the case. All I know is, he and my dad flew in different squadrons out of NAS North Island. The public record shows his discharge, but that's it. After that, there's no trace of him."

Veronica nodded encouragingly, her lovely, almond-shaped eyes focused only on him. It was almost too good to be true.

"Hey, do you want to go to a concert with me?" he asked. "It's downtown, at a place called The East End. My friend Dave Goode's the lead singer. You remember him and Park from Sammy's, right?"

"Sounds great," she answered noncommittally, and smiled, but with little warmth. This seemed odd to Walker; he'd thought she would say yes right away.

"We could go to dinner with Park and Carla before the show," he persisted, hoping that if all went well she might be amenable to a post-concert sleepover.

"When is it?" she asked clinically, her smile gone.

"In three weeks," he replied as his gaze fell to her bulging black T-shirt. *So she's in a bad mood. Everyone's entitled to an off day every once in a while.*

Veronica was about to eat a grape off her fork, but she stopped the utensil on its way to her mouth and shot him a wink. "Maybe we can have a pajama party afterwards. With or without pajamas." Her alluring grin was back. Then she popped the fruit into her mouth, chewed it, swallowed it, and said offhandedly, "Hey, about that guy who killed your dad. I forgot to tell you I have a friend who's great with computers. Maybe he could help. What's the killer's name?"

"Trent Bolton, final rank lieutenant junior grade."

"Do you have any idea what he looks like or where he might be?"

"Yeah, I do. At least what he *used* to look like. I've still got my dad's NAS North Island yearbook," Walker said, though it would be the last piece of information he shared with her; alarm bells were finally going off in his head.

Her next invasive query had to do with the incident at Big Rock. She wondered whether anyone had died in the attack, but Walker sidestepped the question and raised his hand for the check, cursing himself for not being suspicious when they'd "randomly bumped into each other" at the beach. As usual, he'd let his emotions control his behavior while semi-deliberately switching off his brain. And now that he'd semi-deliberately switched it back on, he thought back to their date at Sammy's, when she'd abruptly changed the subject to ask whether he'd *really* been in a bar fight: another dead giveaway. And of course she hadn't actually gone diving that morning, not so early and not under the current weather conditions.

He tossed his fork onto his plate with a clatter and looked her dead in the eye.

She held his gaze, her cold features full of contempt, giving Walker a glimpse of who she really was. "I'll be back in a minute," she said.

As she strode back to the restroom, Walker whipped out his phone and placed a call to David Goode.

"Whas *up* brotha?"

"Morning, bro," Walker said quietly. "I don't have much time to talk. I need a huge favor."

"Name it."

Once she'd slinked back to the table, they sat in silence while waiting for the tab. He didn't accuse her of dishonesty, since he knew she'd lie about it, and he kept his expression as hopeless as possible, as though she'd hurt his feelings, which she had, and as though he didn't have a plan, which he did. Soon, as before, a message was sent to her phone, informing her that "Tim" was waiting at the curb, so he saw her out, but obviously not with any kind of romantic pretension; he wanted to get a good look at the car, the driver, and the license plate.

Instead of the gray Jeep Wrangler, it was an all-black Jeep Cherokee that pulled to a stop outside. Its tailgate badge identified it as an SRT, which Walker knew stood for Street and Racing Technology. The custom Jeep Cherokee had no license plates, just a sheet of paper taped to the inside of its tinted rear window.

Walker didn't hold the door for her as she climbed into the passenger seat. Once again he locked eyes with the guy she'd said was her brother, but this time the staring contest didn't end with any warm expressions or pleasant nods.

He tore his gaze away from the driver's eyes and stared into those of the two-faced floozy in the passenger seat. Her sneering lips and unapologetic eyes made her look much uglier than before.

When the SRT sped away, a white GT500 with blue over-the-top racing stripes grumbled to life two blocks up the street. Goode and Walker acknowledged each other with upward nods as the Mustang took off after it.

Minutes after limping back inside the café to retrieve his credit card, Walker found himself stuck behind two slow-moving luxury cars. He slammed his hand on the steering wheel, honking and screaming at the wealthy locals with nothing to do. Grabbing his phone off the passenger seat, he checked Goode's current location: I-5 north, just past UCSD. Still not far away. When one of the sleepy drivers blocking him finally changed lanes, he stood on the gas pedal and weaved in and out of traffic until he hit I-5. It took the Corolla some time to reach its top speed of 118 mph, but as long as "Tim" didn't spot the Mustang, Walker knew he'd catch up soon enough. Near Del Mar, he glanced left at the Pacific Coast racing by. The water sparkled in the sun like a bed of diamonds, much like "Veronica's" belly button ring, or whatever her real name was. He reckoned she must have been sent to ask about the attack at Windansea or Trent Bolton. Or both.

At Cardiff, he finally caught sight of Goode, trailing the target vehicle at a moderate distance of around two hundred yards. As Walker came alongside the GT500, the rich tones of the Mustang's supercharged V8 reminded him of Goode's own voice: deep and powerful in the low register, clear and precise in the upper range. He eased up on the gas and dropped into formation.

They followed the black SRT to Oceanside Boulevard, skidding through the wide left turn in a drift, then accelerating hard onto the straightaway, heading east, away from the coast. For the first fifteen miles there was plenty of traffic to hide behind, but much less as they neared the foothills. Tim never seemed to notice them, possibly distracted, Walker thought, by his passenger's prominent and prominently displayed physical attributes. The black Jeep veered off the boulevard and wound its way through a maze of side streets, ultimately arriving at an industrial park. Goode chose not to follow it in, pulling to the side of the road instead, which Walker did as well. The massive entertainer squeezed himself out of his sports car and hustled back to the Corolla. "Whatchu wanna *do*, brotha?" he asked through the open driver-side window.

On the one hand, Walker had no desire to put his close friend in any more danger than he already had. On the other, Whatever Her Real Name Was had been far too interested in Trent Bolton for there to be anything but a solid connection between her and the man who'd murdered his father. Even more important than finding his soul mate, Walker's deepest desire was to come face to face with Trent Bolton. For over a decade he'd yearned for a fight to the death with the man who'd sunk his mom into such a state of grief that her body had eaten itself alive. That's how he saw it, anyway; he believed his mother's cancer had resulted from the combination of her broken heart and the stress of raising him as a single mom in a foreign country.

"Let's take one car," Walker said.

It took them an hour to search the massive development, which was laid out like a tiny city. They rolled past countless manufacturing plants, office buildings, convenience stores, and grassy recreation areas. Goode's knees pressed up against the dashboard as he steered his race car, while Walker looked everywhere for the SRT. It wasn't until they'd reached the most distant corner of the sprawling complex that he spotted something suspicious. Up ahead on the right was a massive property with a guard house, a solid-steel gate, and high walls topped with concertina wire. The facility looked out of place, more like a military installation than any of the factory buildings and offices they'd driven by.

Goode drove slowly toward the gate as Walker peered past the security station into an internal parking lot, and there it was! There *they were*, to be more precise: two identical black SRTs parked on either side of an enormous crimson pickup, with a gray Wrangler at the end of the row. The blacked-out Jeeps and the blood-red 4x4 were imposing. Sinister even. But it wasn't a motor vehicle that made Walker's jaw fall open.

12

HATE VERSUS HATE

J ack Cage eyed each of the framed landscapes on the wall, but even his favorite paintings couldn't calm his nerves. He leapt up from the desk to pace his office and consider the issues at hand: it was only a question of time before Oceanside PD raided the warehouse facility in which he presently stood, so he set a conservative deadline to abandon it, calculated how many truckloads he'd still send out before then, and compiled a mental list of all the evidence he'd have to destroy or remove. Once all of that was done, he and his guard captains would relocate to Mazatlan, where the cartel would most likely put them up at the oceanfront complex they always stayed in. Cage would continue to take advantage of the Cartel del Norte's hospitality until he'd collected a couple of outstanding payments and his new identities were ready, at which time he'd leave his men in Mazatlan and travel to Cairns, Australia, where the construction of his new house was already under way.

As he trod to and fro on the shiny tiles of his private domain, Cage heard the soft thud of the main door closing, then footsteps clacking in the hallway. He put his thoughts on hold and wheeled around to see his executive assistant waiting at the open door to be nodded in. It was Sunday, so she wasn't wearing one of her sleek pant suits; she sported tight-fitting jeans and a black T-shirt knotted at the midriff.

A week ago, he'd given Maria the names of the rescue team divers and told her to find out what was known as to his identity, his properties, the guard captains, Oceanside PD's investigation, Paul Johanssen's murder, the laptop, and anything else that might come back to bite him in the ass. Tony Park had been first on her list, but the former SEAL was always taking long, indirect routes whether by foot or by truck, looking over his shoulder and packing a pistol, so Maria had moved on to Jeff Walker. She'd approached his fellow lifeguards on the sand, claiming to be a grateful swimmer he'd saved from drowning, and they said he trained in the mornings at Mission Beach. So she'd gone there every day for a week and finally run into him. At their "chance encounter," after giving him her number, she hadn't actually spotted any friends in the distance; she'd hurried off to catch a ride back to the warehouse and report what she'd learned, chiefly that Walker had been the diver Cage had tried to kill. This had prompted the master smuggler to perform an internet search, and when he saw Walker's picture, he realized with a surge of dread that the reason the lifeguard's emerald-green eyes had looked so familiar to him was that they were just like those of his father, Lieutenant Thomas Walker, whom Cage had shot dead thirty years before. Thus, before Maria's next two dates, he'd told her to find out what Walker knew about his father's death and killer.

"So," Cage said, resuming his seat at the desk as Maria gracefully sorted herself out on one of the brown leather couches. "What did you learn?"

She recounted the details of the conversation sustained at the breakfast café, leading Cage to decide he had no other choice but to erase Jeff Walker. On her way out, she passed Miller in the hallway, who lumbered up to Cage's desk in a state of concern. "Sir, I think there's a vacuum leak in my SRT, but I can't find it," he said.

That's when Cage hit his boiling point. Ever since he'd dragged himself out of bed at 0500 for his goddammed daily run, he'd been increasingly irritated by one inconvenience after another, his anger meter creeping ever closer to the red zone. In a rage even before his arrival at the warehouse facility, he'd then been hit by Maria's disturbing news about Jeff Walker, and now this!

Cage leveled a withering gaze on Miller, as if the mechanical failure had somehow been his henchman's fault, and stormed down the stairs to the parking area. He popped the black Jeep's hood and stuck his head in to take a look, but before he was able to identify the problem, he sliced his hand on the radiator. Cage froze. That did it! Far past anger, now in the calm before a dark and violent storm, he ever so slowly placed his palms on the open hood, then slammed it down with all his power. He closed his eyes to take a shuddering breath and saw himself in his imagination dousing all four of his vehicles with gasoline and tossing a lit match—*whoomp*—then torching the entire complex while he was at it. Just then, from the road on the far side of the guard house, there came a squealing of tires and the deep rumble of an engine large enough to propel a city bus. Cage peered past the security station to see a white Mustang driving slowly past, and his features twisted into a hateful scowl when he recognized the green-eyed, blond-haired lifeguard staring back at him from the passenger seat.

***

As the security gate slid open, Walker fished his phone out of his pocket and snapped a few pictures of the man he'd all but identified as Jack Cage a.k.a. Trent Bolton, and of "Tim," the square-jawed brother. When the pair of crooks jumped into one of the SRTs and bounced out onto the road, Goode put his foot down. The supercharged GT500 quickly pulled ahead even as a storm of bullets slammed into its trunk and punched two holes in the rear window, barely missing Goode's and Walker's heads.

"Did ya bring Tony's pistol?" the massive singer asked, keeping his eyes on the road as he hit a hundred and thirty.

"If I did, I'd already have it out," Walker answered as he reached for the overhead grab handle.

As they raced through the industrial park, Walker thought they'd lost their pursuers, but all of a sudden, straight ahead, the black SRT skidded around a corner and came charging toward them. Goode cranked the steering wheel left and skidded onto a side street, avoiding a head-on collision just as Tim fired from the open sunroof—CRACK! CRACK! CRACK!—but none of his rounds found their mark.

Goode's tires squealed in protest as he whipped through the maze of streets, shaking off his tail once again. And this time he found the way out, leaving Walker's Corolla behind. Back on I-5, with the sparkling coast on the right, the GT500 hit its electronically limited top speed of 180 mph. Safe for the time being, the guys exchanged a glance.

"Nice driving," Walker said. "Sorry I got you into this."

"Happy to help, brotha," Goode replied. He nodded once and turned his attention back to the road.

Walker's first priority was to get his hands on Park's .40-cal. Then he'd break the news to Lieutenant Molloy and Sergeant Taylor.

***

Minutes earlier, Cage had spotted Walker, jumped into the SRT, stomped on the gas, and bounced past the security gate onto the road. The cobra emblem on the white Mustang's trunk meant it was a Shelby, as was his own Ford F-150. "Fuck!" Cage yelled, wishing he'd opted for a pair of supercharged Trackhawks instead of the slower SRTs. The black Jeep wouldn't do well against the rapidly disappearing Mustang, but still he had to try.

Miller hit the sunroof button and planted his boots on the leather passenger seat. He used his seat belt to strap his legs to the backrest, then worked the charging handle of his Kalashnikov to chamber the first round with a metallic click-clack.

Despite Cage's familiarity with the layout of the industrial park, his target had eluded him. *Think, man!* he ordered himself as he sped along, still raging from his hell of a day. *Where could they be?* In a flash of inspiration, he cut right, racing up to the next block, then turning in the same direction again. And there they were, heading straight toward him. Miller fired, but the Mustang's driver darted onto a side street.

Cage trailed his adversaries to the best of his ability, out the main access gates and onto the public road, but the chase had come to an end. He pulled over, crunching to a halt across the street from an abandoned blue-gray Corolla. "Give me the rifle," he said.

Miller dropped into his seat and did as he'd been told.

Cage got out, slammed the door, and approached the Corolla. He peered through the rear window at a red duffel bag on the bench seat, with "SD LIFEGUARD" printed on the side pocket in white letters. When his eyes fell on the word, a dark anger took control of his body, operating his arms and legs like a puppet master as he strode back across the road and leveled his weapon. He sighted the fuel tank and pulled the trigger—CRACK!—but nothing happened, so he steadied his aim with a breath and fired again. This time, there came a pop, a whoosh, and a plume of fire that rose into the sky. Cage stood transfixed, the flames' reflection dancing in his eyes as the vehicle burned from the inside out, just as his own hate was destroying him from within.

***

Two days later, when Walker limped out of his apartment and down the stairs, nodding to the plainclothes policemen, he made his way to a silver Honda CR-V, a rental provided by the insurance company. He pulled out onto the street, far from impressed by the Honda's initial response, though its suspension felt tight, and once the rental hit forty, it surprised him with a passable amount of juice. He merged onto I-5 and cruised north to Mission Bay, where he ultimately pulled to a stop outside lifeguard headquarters. Thanks to the disability placard provided by the hospital, he only had to walk a short distance to the front steps, and as he did, he took stock of the facts of the case in preparation for the meeting he was hobbling into: before Don Roberts' tragic death, the lawman had been investigating the presumably criminal activities of Jack Cage, the largest supplier of narcotics in North County, one of whose biggest clients was a biker gang known as the North County Kings. Cage had most likely orchestrated the shooting of the accountant on the yacht and the attack on the dive team at Big Rock, along with the theft of the laptop and the murders at the Oceanside Police Station. And now there'd been a new development, the reason for his appointment with Lieutenant Molloy and Sergeant Taylor: in light of the evidence Walker held in his hand, Cage's former name was almost certainly Trent Bolton, the same drug-running naval aviator who'd shot his father in cold blood.

Disinclined to interrupt a serious conversation, Walker waited at the open door to his boss's office until the latter looked his way to invite him in. Molloy sat at his desk, with puffy bags under his eyes and a week's worth of stubble. "Mornin' son," he said, extending a strong hand.

On the other side of the desk, the new leader of the narcotics task force looked fresher than the senior lifeguard. His shirt was pressed and his eyes were bright, but, then again, he was twenty years Molloy's junior. "What have you got for us, buddy?" he asked, offering a second solid handshake.

"A photograph and the whereabouts of the man who killed my dad," Walker replied as he grabbed a seat next to Taylor. "I'm pretty sure it was Jack Cage."

That got their attention.

Walker began with the story of his father's execution in the gas station, including the final telephone call between his parents. After his mom had hung up, he said, she'd driven to a hotel in Ensenada and waited there for a week. Then she'd rented—and later bought—a house in Tijuana, where she'd given birth to Walker and raised him for sixteen years before her untimely death. The second part of his narrative included the major details of his involvement with Whatever Her Real Name Was, how he'd met her, their two dates, and it concluded with the sighting of Bolton at the industrial park. Walker produced the pictures he'd taken with his phone and cracked open his father's Navy yearbook for comparison. Even after thirty years, the former fighter pilot's chiseled features, his intense, intelligent gray eyes, and that haughty scowl were unmistakable.

"It's the same guy," Taylor confirmed. "But that doesn't mean he's the man we know as Cage."

"Yes it does," Molloy disagreed. "The shooting at Windansea, the fight for the laptop, and the bombin' at the police station occurred one after another, so they're related. And why would he chase a car that was just passin' by his warehouse?"

Taylor nodded in agreement. "Because he recognized Walker from the dive. And that's why he sent the girl to spy on him. But it's still not enough for a warrant. I'll have my analyst run these photos through the databases."

"You should also have him track down the owner of the warehouse," Molloy pointed out, then turned back to Walker. "So why did Bolton shoot ya daddy?"

"It's a good story," Walker began.

Thirty years ago, one Saturday at noon, Lieutenant Thomas Walker and a slightly pregnant Mrs. Christine Walker strode arm-in-arm into the officers' club at NAS North Island. A lone high diver stood on the ten-meter platform, towering over an Olympic-size swimming pool that rippled and sparkled under the San Diego sun. The diver made a slow and steady approach to the edge, then threw his arms over his head and took the leap. He held his knees to his chest and flipped forward, once, twice, still rotating as he opened up, keeping his eyes on the water. After a blazing series of four front flips and a double twist, he sliced into the pool headfirst with no splash at the last possible split second.

Mrs. Walker raised her eyebrows and gaped at the feat, but her husband scoffed at the Speedo-clad acrobat as they stepped into the O-club and headed for a large circular bar in the center of the room. Later in the day, it would be surrounded by a thick ring of officers clamoring for adult beverages, which is why they'd come early, to get a dose of vitamin D for her and the unborn baby, and so he could swim in the pool before the crowd showed up.

"Two club sodas, please," Lieutenant Walker said, spotting an acquaintance over the barman's shoulder: Trent Bolton, normally strong and fit but looking oddly haggard that day. If the rumors were true, he thought, his fellow fighter pilot was out of his mind on drugs and drink. Bolton was engaged in an argument with a skinny man dressed in loose-fitting beige coveralls. A maintenance worker, perhaps.

"You've cheated me for the last time, asshole!" the thin man yelled. Spittle flew from his lips as he stood over the seated Bolton. "Meet me outside and I'll teach you a lesson!"

"Lesdoitrighthere," Bolton slopped out, staggering to his feet, tipping his barstool over onto the floor.

"You fuckin' rat," the thin man hissed, then drew back his fist to throw a punch. But on second thought he stopped and raised his voice to reach every nearby observer. "Saying you serve your country while running drugs for Marco Del Real!"

"Shuthafukup!" Bolton screamed, reaching into his pocket for a six-inch blade. He snapped it open and took a clumsy swipe, but the thin man easily stepped out of reach.

Lieutenant Walker hustled around the bar to grab Bolton from behind, wrenching the man's arm behind his back. "Drop it!" he growled, using one hand to force Bolton's arm up toward his head, obliging his fellow aviator to comply before his shoulder broke, and the other hand to grab Bolton's neck and rub his nose on the floor in a hammerlock restraint.

The barman vaulted over the counter and scooped up the knife while Mrs. Walker made a call to the military police and the thin man slipped out the door.

The MPs arrived in minutes. Based on the bartender's and the Walkers' statements, they handcuffed Bolton, arrested him, tested his blood, searched his house, and found a surprising amount of cocaine. This led to the court-martial trial at which the Walkers were later called to testify.

As Jeff Walker reached the conclusion of what he thought had been a fascinating and well-told anecdote, he saw his boss's gaze flit from a tall stack of paperwork to his watch.

"So Bolton shot ya daddy to keep 'im from testifyin' at a trial," Molloy said dryly with a frown.

Walker felt his face go red. That's all he should have said.

But Taylor's expression brightened. "That's it!" he exclaimed. "Marco Del Real is the head of the Cartel del Norte, a Mexican gang split off from the Sinaloa Cartel. So they must be the source of Cage's contraband!"

Walker managed to contain his temper for the rest of the conversation. But as he stormed through the hall and exploded out the front door, forgetting about his doctor's orders, his features contorted into a hateful scowl. As if his limbs were being operated by a wicked puppet master, his right hand balled into a fist and hammered the palm of his left, several times before he even knew what he was doing. More than ever before, he longed to heap pain and suffering on a fellow soul. He'd snatch up a bat and shatter Cage's bones, starting with his hands and his feet, then move on to his ankles, knees, elbows, arms, and legs. Walker would delight in the man's screams of terror as he came in for the kill, raising the wooden club one last time to bash out the brains of the man who'd destroyed his family.

13

FIGHT NIGHT

Jack Cage's blood-red muscle truck grumbled to a halt in the parking lot outside the boxing gym where he trained. The driver-side door swung open and his black dress shoe stepped onto the running board. Then the smuggler himself hit the asphalt and strode confidently toward the front entrance. His senses were sharpened by the adrenaline that invariably coursed through his veins on fight night, though he wasn't in the best of moods. As he walked, he scowled when he thought of the long list of complications surrounding his plans to leave the country, but he reminded himself to keep his focus on the goal: the new clifftop residence in Cairns, Australia, where he'd spend the rest of his life in luxury, and how content he'd finally be when he stepped onto the balcony on the night of his arrival. He'd revel in the sweeping view of the Coral Sea, then ease himself into the steaming jacuzzi with a naked female companion. Or two. Or three!

Cage realized he'd forgotten to lock his truck, so he swiveled back to press a button on his key fob, pausing for a moment to admire his custom Shelby F-150. The menacing front end featured Tuscany's ram-air hood, honeycomb grille inserts, and fender vents, all designed for maximum cooling of the five-liter V8, which, like that of Goode's Shelby GT500, was supercharged to over 755 hp. In a second similarity to the singer's Mustang, Cage's one-hundred-and-twenty-thousand-dollar truck boasted front-to-back double rally stripes, though they were black, not blue. And it was fully armored, like his twin Jeep Cherokee SRTs. Sadly, he'd soon be selling this massive pickup at a fraction of its cost.

When he threw open the gym's front door and marched past the punching bags, he thrilled at the sights, sounds, and smells of hard work and aggression, nodding to several men on his way back to the locker room.

Cage's warm-up routine included stretching and calisthenics; then he hit the speed bag, the double-end bag, and the hanging bags. Dancing around the heaviest of those, he shouted out in anger as he darted in to surprise his imaginary opponent with deadly combinations.

Sweaty, he grabbed his towel and plonked himself down on the bench next to his fellows, sitting ringside to watch a fight already in progress. In a rowdy chorus, every man shouted heckles and cheers; they all loved fight night.

Before long, Coach Lenahan called out, "You're up, Jack!"

Cage was slated to fight a new guy named Derrick, who would probably give him a good workout, he figured, as most of the men who trained at Jerry's were seasoned pugilists. Now and then you'd get a few white-collar guys, but Coach knew better than to match Cage up with them. As soon as he heard his name, Cage leapt up from the bench and bounded up the steps, lifting the ropes to enter the ring. He swung his arms back and forth and looked to the other side of the canvas, sizing up his opponent: Derrick was twenty years younger, forty pounds heavier, and two inches taller. When the beefy kid caught Cage's gaze, he shot the smuggler an overconfident smirk, his first mistake.

The fifty-year-old former collegiate champion popped in his mouthguard, breathing slowly through his nose as he waited like a racehorse at the starting gate. At the bell, he advanced quickly, smacking Derrick with a consecutive pair of jabs, then dancing out of his reach.

The kid's footwork was solid and he kept a tight guard, but his second mistake was to start swinging for the knockout while Cage was still fresh. The elder combatant pretended not to notice a clearly telegraphed overhand right until the last possible moment, when he stepped off-line to the left and continued to rotate into a devastating left hook. Derrick stumbled but stayed up as Cage kept the pressure on, exploiting the opening with a practiced succession of rights and lefts. He had to admit that the younger fighter held his ground, but the kid's eyes started to roll back into his head, and he swayed and staggered with diminishing awareness as Cage let loose another well-drilled combination, pounding Derrick's nose and eyes, then his gut, then back up to his mouth and his newly broken nose. The final uppercut toppled him like a chain-sawed pine.

As Derrick lay immobile on the blood-spattered mat, Cage's fellow boxers cheered. Initially, anyway. But when the younger fighter climbed unsteadily to his feet and Coach Lenahan shouted "No!" from down on the floor, the only other sound in the building was Cage's shoes slapping the canvas as he sprinted forward, winding up for a crushing haymaker, his target a wide-open chin. He just couldn't resist the temptation.

BOOM! Derrick's legs buckled and his brain rattled around in his skull, the heavy silence split by the echoing thud of his body hitting the mat. His arms and legs twitched and spasmed for some time before going fully rigid.

Cage eyed his fallen opponent with little concern while ignoring the outraged shouts of his fellow boxers. It was no big deal. He'd been knocked out plenty of times: as a kid by his youth care counselor, in countless confrontations on the street, and also in formal competition. He snatched up his bag and strutted back to the locker room, where he showered and changed, then made his way back through the building and out into the cool night air. No one dared to stand in his way on this, the last of his visits to Jerry's Gym.

On his way home, Cage bullied every car out of his path, screaming at the other drivers and even lowering his window at one point to challenge one of them to a fight. He was out of control and he knew it and he didn't care. His truck's massive tires squealed at the corners as he wound his way up the hill, zooming recklessly through the exclusive development in which he lived. Each stately home was fronted by a carefully manicured lawn and an imposing wrought-iron gate, one of which slid open to let him in.

His black dress shoes padded across the hardwood floor as he stormed to the kitchen and poured three fingers of Macallan Estate Reserve, then added one more in case the first three didn't do the trick. He raised his tumbler, swirled the amber liquid around, brought the glass to his lips, and slowly sucked on liquid fire, savoring the sensation as it all snaked its way down to his belly. Ahhing in satisfaction, he next set the empty tumbler on the counter and pulled open a cabinet to remove a second glass, taking everything with him into a sitting room where he parked his backside on a white leather settee.

Mercifully, his mind had gone clear at fight night, but now it was time to get back to work. One of his assets had informed him that the new commander of the Oceanside PD narcotics task force was a former Special Forces guy named Dominick Taylor. Taylor had reportedly sworn to hunt Cage down, as he'd been a close friend of Lieutenant Don Roberts. This meant Cage had to assume the worst, which was that Taylor had recovered all the data from the laptop. With such an overwhelming amount of evidence, the lawman could easily obtain a warrant, so the master smuggler resolved to speed up his timetable. He gave himself two days to abandon the warehouse facility, then poured himself a second drink, took a fiery sip, set it down, and moved on to the second reason for his current state of anxiety. In the end, he concluded that Jeff Walker could not be allowed to remain alive. The kid was a major risk to the perfect future he'd been planning for over half a year. So he grabbed his phone and made a call to Maldonado, who showed up at his door soon thereafter.

"We might as well hit Park, too," Cage said to his second-in-command while standing over the coffee table to hand him a drink. "But Goode might be overkill. Literally."

Maldonado shook his head as he rose to take the offered glass, then resumed his seat on a facing leather sofa. "I disagree, boss. It's always better to err on the side of caution. Goode's concert is the best place to strike and the singer's going to be there anyway."

"Fine," Cage said. "I'll be running the op from here, so you, Miller, and Daniels will have one target each."

Cage and his cadaverous number two proceeded to nail down the details of the multiple homicide they intended to commit, toasting each other for another hour. Once Cage was alone again, he ambled down the hall to bed, breathing much easier than before. Cairns was so close he could reach out and touch those naked tits in the jacuzzi.

***

"Hey. I'm not calling too late, am I?" Carla asked, using her shoulder to pin the phone to her ear as she stirred a batch of brownie mix.

"No," Tina replied from miles away. "*¿Qué pasó, carnala?*"

"You know how Tony's friends with David Goode, the singer?"

"Yeah."

"Well, we have an extra ticket to his concert this weekend at a *reeeaally* nice place. Want to come?"

"Sure!"

"Cool. But before the show, Tony and I are going out to dinner with a lifeguard buddy of his named Jeff Walker. Are you ready for a double date?"

"I don't think so. He sounds white and preppy and that's not my thing. Not anymore, if you know what I mean."

"I hear you, but I think you'll like him," Carla replied. "Yes, Jeff's white, but he's not preppy. He was born and raised in Mexico, so he speaks better Spanish than you do. Plus, he's got a great body."

"Well, since you put it like that ..."

***

On the day of the concert, Park's hand trembled as he put the mayonnaise away. He'd intended to prepare two sandwiches but ended up making only one, since he couldn't eat after suffering another panic attack.

On return from his last tour of duty in the Middle East, cut short due to a tragic final mission, he'd been diagnosed with PTSD and given a medical discharge. Once home in San Diego, he'd been plagued by recurring flashbacks, suicidal thoughts, and vivid nightmares. Worse yet, sharp noises such as popped balloons or shattered glass often resulted in crippling anxiety attacks or dangerously violent outbursts. The docs had prescribed him all sorts of meds, but they'd been more hindrance than help. What *had* produced a positive effect was Park sitting on the lifeguard towers for half a decade, soothed by the beauty of nature and his stable relationship with the sweet, sweet Carla Reyes. Now, his disorder lay mostly dormant with little effect on his day-to-day, but it didn't take much to trigger the occasional episode, and that's what had happened to make him lose his appetite.

Earlier that morning, while he and Carla were jogging along the shore at Pacific Beach, they had passed a pair of tourists sitting on beach chairs. One of them whistled loudly and called out, "Nice tits!"

Park brought the jog to an immediate halt and lumbered up the beach in their direction.

Carla grabbed his hand to stop him. "No, honey. Tony. Look at me. You do not want to go to jail," she said, pleading with her big brown eyes. "We've got a concert to go to."

Park could not let the matter go. At the very least, he was going to make Dumb and Dumber apologize. Dropping her hand, he marched straight up to them. "What was that?" he asked, staring hard.

"Come on, man," Dumb replied. "It was a compliment."

"Yeah, get over it," Dumber added, popping a cold soda with a sharp crack.

And that was all it took. Hurled back through time to the staccato sounds of bloody combat, Park suddenly couldn't catch a breath, and his heart beat so fast it hurt. His face flushed, his ears buzzed, and the beach scene spun in circles. Clutching his chest, he dropped to his knees on the sand, afraid he was about to die from a heart attack.

"It'll pass," Carla said, leading him up the beach to a bench on the boardwalk. She took a seat beside him and stroked his back as he placed his head between his knees. When the pain and panic eventually subsided, she held his hand and walked him slowly home, just a few blocks through the neighborhood back to her cozy duplex unit.

Park frowned as he left the kitchen, shaking his head at himself. He set Carla's sandwich in front of her on the table in the breakfast nook, gave her a grateful kiss, and trudged back to their bedroom to lie down, though he had a hard time sitting still. After tossing and turning for twenty minutes, he grabbed his phone off the nightstand and punched the button for Walker's cell.

"Hey bro."

"What're you up to, champ?" Park asked.

"About to finish up with the junior lifeguards. Then I'll hobble back to headquarters to work in dispatch."

"Still can't run?"

"I *feel* ready, but the doctor said one more week. You sound nervous. You okay?"

"I just had another panic attack."

"I'm sorry to hear that."

"But I'm fine now," Park assured himself. "So we'll see you and Tina at Sammy's at eighteen hundred?"

"Eighteen hundred at Sammy's," Walker echoed. "That's affirmative."

Park cracked a smile. "All right, soldier. Stay frosty," he said, clicking off just as Carla came into the room. In a delightful start to an anxiety-suppressing afternoon of Netflix and chill, Park's curly-haired Latina treasure wiggled out of her bikini. His grin widened; those new breasts had been worth every penny.

***

"How *you* doin'?" David Goode joked, holding his cell phone to his ear.

"Not so good," came Lynn Peters' discouraged voice on the other end of the line.

Goode let out a long sigh of resignation. He'd been expecting this call, hoping it wouldn't happen but knowing it probably would.

"I'm running late," she explained, meaning *I still have several hours of studying to do*. "I'm sorry, but I won't be ready in time for you to pick me up. I'll just meet Carla and Tina at the box office."

"No problem, love," Goode replied, leaving out that he'd really been looking forward to introducing her to the band backstage and hanging out at intermission. After they said goodbye and ended the call, he hopped in the shower to get ready for the performance.

In the ramp-up to the show, he'd been interviewed on several TV and radio programs, and many music industry VIPs would be in attendance that night, both celebrities and executives. Sure, Goode was nervous, but like a SWAT team leader, he was used to the stress, and he'd even learned to enjoy pre-deployment fear. So he strode coolly over to his walk-in closet and eyed his collection of tailored suits, counting ten—far too many for a man to have, in his opinion. The thing was, with so much disposable income, he often had trouble finding ways to dispose of it. For a time, he'd considered getting a motorcycle like Walker's, but then he figured if he was going to risk his life in a speed machine, he'd prefer the protection of a steel frame and a safety belt. Which is why he'd opted for the Shelby GT500, a smart decision, he'd thought, yet foolishly he'd failed to take it for a test drive before slapping down a small fortune for it. If he had taken that precaution, he'd have noticed the car wasn't designed for bodies as large as his.

As he buttoned up a silk vest over a shirt and tie, Goode had a thought that offered him some consolation: at least he wasn't generous just to himself. Before he'd bought the Mustang, he'd already purchased a new house for his parents, two more for their parents, and his weekly donation to Hillside was always triple the expected tithe of ten percent. Pushing a silver cufflink through the four folded buttonholes of his dress shirt, Goode paused on his way out to gaze down at the coastal vista below, where an endless succession of perfect glittering waves was rolling in to shore. He closed his eyes and drew in a breath, thanking God for all the joy in his life, asking that he'd always see his blessings as tools to help those who needed it most. Then he slung his garment bag over his shoulder and pressed a button on the wall to call up his private elevator.

A minute later, he squeezed himself into the white Mustang and pressed another button: the ignition! Relishing the roar and grumble of the high-performance engine as he cruised up Grand Ave. to the freeway, Goode felt sure he was about to hit it out of the park. He was right, but it would be to a vastly different and greater extent than he or anyone else could have imagined.

14

SITTING DUCKS

When Jeff Walker pulled up to his blind date's house and knocked on the door, he was greeted by a burly Mesoamerican man. Shorter than Walker, but roughly the same weight and width, Tina's father looked about fifty, and Walker made certain to address him as *Señor*.

"She's running late," said the broad-shouldered patriarch in Spanish. "Come in. Would you like some lemonade?" He gestured toward a pair of sofas in the living room, where, after handing over a friendly glass of refreshment, he and Walker sustained a deadly-serious conversation on non-serious topics for ten minutes that seemed to stretch into eternity.

When Tina finally made her appearance at the top of the stairs, she flashed a heart-stopping smile before gliding down to the sitting room. Draped in a modest black dress that couldn't hide her curvy figure, she'd pulled her glossy black hair into a ponytail except for a pair of curlicue dangles that fell to her cheeks.

"This is my daughter, Tina," Sr. Garcia said in Spanish as he rose, and Walker also stood to shake the young woman's hand. Her exotic almond-shaped eyes, full lips, and flawless bronze-hued skin were further beautified by a masterful application of cosmetic products, and her warm and honest grin continued to light up the room.

Walker stuck with Spanish out of respect for her father. "I'm Jeff," he said. "Thanks for agreeing to meet me."

"My friend Carla speaks well of you," she returned in the same language.

As she pulled a gray shawl over her slender shoulders and kissed her father goodbye, Walker was struck by her remarkable resemblance to "Veronica."

As he pulled away from the curb, Walker said, in English now and for the rest of the night, "That's a nice bike on your driveway. Do you have a brother?"

She clicked on her seat belt and shook her head. "It's mine."

"Cool! I ride, too," Walker replied as he steered through his own stomping grounds; by coincidence, he and Tina lived less than a mile apart. "Mine's a five hundred though. Do you take it out a lot?"

"Every day, but just to work. I used to be in a riding club, but I didn't like it."

"No?"

"Nah, just a bunch of married men telling misogynist jokes and trying to hit on me. What about you? You got to meet my dad. Do *your* parents live in town?"

"No," said Walker with an icy edge. She seemed nice, but so had the other girl.

In the tense silence that followed, now on I-5 heading north, Walker glanced left at the Coronado Bridge, its two-mile silhouette winding to the island over the moonlit ripples of the bay, while Tina peered through her window in the opposite direction, her attention drawn by the multicolored lights of the crowded downtown skyline.

He held the front door open for her as they stepped into Sammy's, and a beaming hostess took them to a table where their dinner companions were already seated. Carla, clad in a stretchy brown dress that complemented her curly brown hair and eyes, rose to greet them with big hugs and bright smiles. Park, who wore a double-XL suit and tie, also stood to give Walker a Hawaiian handshake and Tina an appropriately Mexican cheek-to-cheek greeting.

After a bit of small talk and a round of drinks, Park turned to Tina with an impish grin. "Do you want to hear how Jeff got burned while trying to impress a girl on the beach?" he asked.

"Sure," she replied.

Walker didn't like this story, but that was the point. His buddy was just playing around, trying to lighten the mood as usual.

"Everything was going fine at first," Park began. "Our hero's jogging on the sand, showing off his pecs, and he catches the eye of this bikini-clad sunbather lying on her towel. She's cute, so he stops to chat her up and ask for her number. She wrote it on your arm if I'm not mistaken."

"Good memory," said Walker dryly, already searching his own recollections for a story about Park that would prove even more embarrassing.

"So Jeff says he'll call, flashes her a winning grin, and struts away. But as he goes, he has a flash of inspiration!"

Carla suppressed a giggle. She knew the punch line. And when Walker saw Tina listening with rapt attention, he had to admit Park was a great storyteller.

"Wanting to impress the girl even more, Jeff jogs down to the water, leaps high, and dives into the surf with perfect form, fixin' to swim off into the sunset. But then he feels his belly scrape against something as the tide goes out, leaving him stranded on a rock formation like a beached whale!" Park mimed a futile swimming motion while Carla cackled and snorted and Tina hid a smile with her hand.

"I see how it is," Walker said, offering Park a sporting grin and a fist bump, having already selected a perfectly devastating anecdote of his own. Halfway through the meal, he set down his fork on his plate with a dramatic clatter. "All right," he said, twisting his lips into a devilish grin as he dabbed his mouth with a white cloth napkin. "Here's one even *you* might not know, Carla." Walker looked around the table and caught Tina's dark, liquid eyes. God, she was beautiful. "One day, after many hours of training in the hot desert sun with the Navy SEALs—"

"This one's not appropriate for the dinner table," Park cut in, which of course caused Carla and Tina to lean in with greater interest.

"After hours of training in the sun," Walker repeated, over the vehement protests of his good friend, "Tony's standing at the urinal when he feels his face flush, his head spin, and a growing roar in his ears. He knows he's about to pass out, so he rushes toward the door at full speed, hoping to make it to the bench outside. But he doesn't. Halfway there, he blacks out and veers off-course, his momentum carrying him all the way into a concrete-block wall. A minute later, when he opens his eyes, he's got a fat lump on his head, his pants around his ankles, and a big group of tough guys standing over him, offering sharp commentary about the big red hearts on his underwear!"

Walker roared with laughter, but since no one else was amused, his chuckles quickly trailed off into silence.

"Awwww," Tina cooed. "I hope you weren't hurt."

"Thanks, Tina," Park replied with exaggerated sadness. "The boxers were a gift."

As Carla wrapped her arms around her man and planted smooching kisses on his face, Park caught Walker's eye and shot him a taunting grin.

Later, as their plates were being cleared away, Carla turned to Tina and asked, "What about you? You're a paramedic. I'll bet you've got lots of stories."

"Sure," Tina replied. "I've brought three patients back from a flat line and done a fair amount of field surgery. And I still get letters and presents from all the people I've saved."

While Tina went on to provide greater detail, Walker decided his blind date was even cooler than he'd hoped for. Despite his awkward refusal to discuss his parents in the car and his failed attempt at payback, Tina was fitting in with an established family.

An hour after that, as the foursome strolled down Market Street toward The East End, the venue came into view and the topic of conversation turned to its massive glass-walled lobby, which was packed with well-dressed concertgoers sipping on pre-show drinks.

Lynn Peters was waiting for them outside the box office. Smiling brightly, she shot her arm into the air and waved to gain their attention, her long blond hair spilling over the shoulders of her faux-fur coat. Once she'd handed everyone their tickets, Park held the glass door open, providing rear security as they all filed into the grand foyer.

Now on the far side of a pat-down screening station and a metal detector, Walker was feeling more relaxed. Even more after a drink at the bar. Then the lobby lights began to flicker on and off, meaning it was time for them to find their table. The group followed the signs that pointed the way to platform B, where David Goode's beaming family and friends welcomed them to a long, elegantly appointed table with hugs for everyone. Excited conversation ensued as they took their seats, and soon the house lights dimmed and a hush fell over the crowd.

***

Two hours earlier, at exactly nineteen hundred hours, after bathing, shaving, and shrugging on suits, Rick Daniels and his comrades marched out of the surveillance center and into the warehouse, heading upstairs to the offices. As they settled themselves on the leather sofas that faced their boss, who sat at his desk, Cage said, "Who are you slick motherfuckers and what have you done with my grubby guard captains?" The joke earned him a hearty laugh. Then his features fell serious and he jutted his chin toward the glossy photos he'd already laid out on the coffee table in front of them. "Make sure you know those faces."

The guard captains reached for the images of Walker, Park, and Goode and studied them for the umpteenth time as Cage went on. "Miller, what are the main and alternate exit points?"

"Main is the foyer and the alternate is the south entrance," the giant man replied immediately.

"Good," Cage said, slowly turning his head to level a doubtful frown on Daniels. "What will you do once you exit the building, D4?"

That was an easy one. "Run three blocks east to the extraction point sir!" Daniels barked in reply.

"But what are the cross streets?"

Daniels was mortified. He'd known the answer just a minute before, but now he was drawing a blank.

His comrades were staring at him.

Cage was scowling with impatience.

"4th and C," Maldonado finally answered for Daniels after a nerve-wracking silence.

Cage shook his head in disappointment. "I knew it," he said to Daniels. "That's why I put you and Maldonado together. Just follow him and you'll be fine. Okay, that's it, guys. Call me on the hour." He stood by the door and clapped them on the back as they marched out.

An hour later, at The East End, while Maldonado and Miller were up in a top-level luxury suite snapping on nitrile gloves and screwing suppressors onto their pistols, Daniels was down in the foyer watching the door, waiting for Walker and company to arrive. When they did, he eyed them from a distance as they ordered drinks, then followed them to their table to see where it was. Daniels next took the elevator to join his comrades up in the skybox, which offered an aerial view of the auditorium.

Maldonado stood by the wall-sized window, looking down at the gathering crowd. "It's like a shooting gallery at an amusement park," he said. "Two sitting ducks and a singing one."

"Put these on," Miller instructed, apparently not in the mood for jokes as he handed Daniels a pair of gloves and, once his directions had been followed, a suppressed Sig Sauer along with a fixed-blade combat knife, all of which been stashed in the suite since the day before.

After the opening act and a lengthy intermission, when David Goode finally strode onstage and launched into his first song, the kill team pulled on full-face balaclava masks and stole through the hallways at a cautious run, nodding to each other as Daniels and Maldonado peeled off toward platform B and Miller took the elevator to the ground floor.

Daniels drew his gun and looked to his partner. Maldonado didn't seem nervous at all; the man was bounding into violence with all the delight of a boy rushing to open his presents on Christmas morning.

15

SHOWTIME

P rior to the construction of the San Diego Music Center, The East End had been the largest performing arts venue south of Los Angeles, though it was called by another name. Designed by a visionary architect and built by the city in 1964, it was home to Broadway in San Diego, the San Diego Opera, and the California Ballet. A few years before David Goode's concert, however, its new owners had poured millions of dollars into its renovation, tearing out the tiered seating to erect ten ascending platforms such that when the stage performers looked out at the gathered public, they might see a giant set of stairs, each step being large enough for twenty long dinner tables. In place of the orchestra pit, they installed a dance floor, but it turned out that most concertgoers preferred to boogie near their seats.

A table at The East End didn't come cheap, yet the heaviest price tag by far was that of the luxury skyboxes, which offered a commanding view of the auditorium, a catered dinner package, and a fully stocked bar. Cage's three guard captains left this refreshment untouched, having rented the space for the sole purpose of stashing their weapons there in advance.

The house lights flashed once again, signaling the end of intermission. A few minutes later, when the theatre was plunged into darkness, an expectant silence descended upon the auditorium. Suddenly, the centerstage spotlight illuminated the microphone stand as well as the instruments set up behind it. There was another quiet pause. Then, when Goode strode onstage in his tailored suit, the crowd showered him with applause, female shrieks, and masculine chants that reminded the hometown hero of a pack of barking dogs. His boys! Goode plucked the mic off the stand, smiling and waving to all his fans while the rest of the band took their places inconspicuously.

"Thank y'all for comin' out," he said as the audience settled down. "I'd like to start with a new song I wrote for my girlfriend, who's here with us tonight. I love you, Lynn." He blew a kiss up to where he thought she might be, since with the light in his eyes and the great distance between them it was impossible to know for sure.

The drummer kicked off the show with a medium-slow R&B groove. After sixteen beats, the bassist joined in, his solid low notes grounding the harmony. Then the guitarist and the woman at the keyboard completed the mix both rhythmically and melodically with syncopated contributions that helped Goode know what notes to sing. The joyful interplay among them was contagious.

Dancing freely to the beat, Goode beamed at his band in appreciation, his powerful muscles stretching out his double extra-large suit as he turned back to his fans. Then, when he lifted his voice, his soulful lyrics mesmerized the crowd from the verses to the chorus, to the bridge, and ultimately the reiteration of his message: a declaration of love. At the cutoff, the house erupted in a roar. Without waiting for the noise to die down, the band transitioned into a recent hit, bringing everyone to their feet.

***

Lynn clapped, hopped, and cried tears of joy. Tina and Carla screamed Goode's name while Park and Walker traded semi-jealous frowns.

Lately, Park had noticed that Walker was making a habit of situational awareness, which, he thought, might have been motivated by his own example. At the moment, for instance, the blond lifeguard was scanning his surroundings, and this reminded Park to do the same. He saw each of the two hundred concertgoers on platform B dancing by their tables, blissfully lost in the music. None of them—including himself, unfortunately—were armed. If things went pear-shaped, he and Walker would have to coordinate a response with the other men in the group: David Goode Sr., who was even bigger than his son but had a bad knee, Brother Christensen, similarly large and mean but also past his prime, and John, Goode's sister's boyfriend. John was white and quiet, a slim academic type, but behind his eyes there was a surprising amount of steel. Maybe something from the Goode family had rubbed off on him, or better put, Park joked to himself, one person in particular.

That's when he saw them. At the far side of the platform, two masked men in dark suits came charging toward his table, flowing through the sea of dancers, leveling their pistols in his direction.

"Get down!" Park screamed. Glasses and wine bottles exploded on the tabletop as everyone slipped under just in time, eyeing each other with uncertainty.

"Stay *low* and follow me to the side doors!" barked David Goode, Sr.

Sure that he and Walker were the killers' targets, Park turned to his buddy and saw what he'd expected to see: a hardened game face matching Park's own tactical plan. With a single mutual nod, the two friends agreed to stand their ground so that everyone else could crawl away. Problem was, with each spit of the silenced pistols, Park was growing more and more apprehensive. For the second time that day, his heart was hammering out of control and he couldn't catch a breath. He felt as though he were deep under water with no air supply.

Park couldn't believe it. Never, ever, not *once* in his life had he been too scared to fight. It was a point of pride passed down by a long line of warriors. Yet as the gunmen strode closer, he grew increasingly unable to react, even as Walker shook him by the shoulders and screamed his name.

***

"Tony!" Walker yelled, but it was to no effect. Park was clutching his chest and staring straight ahead, apparently unaware that he was about to be murdered.

Walker reached up to the top of the table, feeling around for anything he might use as a weapon. His hand found an empty champagne bottle, which he brought down and held by the neck like a club. Then he crawled on the floor to the left end of the table and peered through a gap in the tablecloth: one of the killers was aiming his gun at the Goode family! The masked man was tall and wiry with intelligent eyes. The other one, who looked to be about Walker's size, stood farther back, panning his pistol in every direction, either searching for a specific target or covering his partner.

Walker pushed the tablecloth aside and flew at the lanky shooter, cocking the heavy bottle as he charged. The shooter whirled on Walker and fired, shattering the champagne bottle. Walker's heart leapt out of his chest, but still he held fast to the jagged remainder and swiped the broken bottle at the shooter's face, making sure to keep his adversary between himself and the other gunman. As the would-be shooter reeled from his injury, Walker dropped his improvised weapon to take hold of the man's silenced pistol and the wrist that gripped it, and endeavored to separate the two. With all the blood pouring down his adversary's face and the mask now sliced to shreds, Walker had little difficulty taking control of the firearm, stepping out of reach, and lining up the second hitman in his sights.

"Drop it!" Walker ordered the second one, who glared at him as he tossed his pistol onto the carpet. "Take off your masks, both of you." By then, the music had stopped, and the sea of panicked spectators was stampeding toward the exits located on either side of every platform.

The first hitman, the wounded shooter, peeled off his shredded mask to expose a strangely long face with hollow cheeks. Multiple parallel gashes ran diagonally from his forehead to his lips, and a sheet of scarlet flowed down onto his shirt and coat. He gave a red-toothed grin as he wiped his eyes clear and prepared to pounce. For an instant Walker wondered why, but it didn't matter; he had the advantage. He lined up his sights and pulled the trigger. Click! All in an instant, the bleeding hitman closed the distance, wound up for an overhand right, and knocked Walker senseless. Then he reached under his shirt for a knife and fell on Walker to finish the job.

***

Goode hadn't heard the first of the silenced gunfire over the music, but as the crowd began to part like the waters of the Red Sea and his band dropped their instruments and rushed offstage, a sinking feeling gripped his guts. Knowing that his friends and family were the most likely targets of any kind of attack, he let go of the mic, took the six-foot drop to the dance floor, and sprinted for the side stairs, stopping short when he saw someone blocking his path. Thirty yards ahead, a masked man about his own size was training a pistol on him from a kneeling two-handed stance. Only the man's hard eyes and the top of his nose showed through his black balaclava's face opening.

Goode flew into motion, juking right and left like his father had done on the football field, dodging the big hitman's coughing rounds as he flew forward and tackled his adversary to the floor. The gun skittered away in the struggle, but the big hitman recovered quickly, sliding his arm around Goode's neck in a rear naked choke and rolling onto his back for better purchase.

Goode was three seconds from oblivion. He instantly threw his arms and shoulders up and brought his chin down, breaking his assailant's hold just as he'd been taught in the desert, then slipped out, stood up, and backed away.

The masked man also rose, and he pulled up a pant leg to unsheathe a long fighting knife. With bloodthirsty eyes, he adopted a bladed stance, shifting his weight from leg to leg, holding his weapon back in a reverse grip and his front arm up in guard.

Goode stayed low like a wrestler, his muscles tensing for fight, flight, or freeze. But he knew it wasn't going to be flight and it wasn't going to be freeze. He figured his best bet was to control the distance with his legs. Maybe break the guy's knee with a side kick. Just then, a set of double doors swung open and two yellow-jacketed security guards snuck up on the hitman from behind, so Goode threw a high round kick to give them time to maneuver, which the hitman dodged as he came forward and lashed out with his blade.

Goode was cut, but the fight was over. The guards grabbed the hitman from behind, each of them controlling one arm. Since it wasn't clear they could handle the guy, Goode ran forward to deliver a straight knee to the hitman's chin, dropping him like a bag of bricks.

With a nod to the security team, Goode raced up the side stairs two at a time, desperately worried about his family and increasingly frustrated by the never-ending ascent. Growling, he redoubled his efforts and finally emerged onto platform B, which he found deserted except for a bloody-faced hitman looming over Walker with a long knife in his hand and another one with brown hair cut short like a soldier's. As the bleeding hitman drew back his blade, Goode didn't break his long stride; he dashed through the sea of tables just in time to kick Walker's attacker in the head like a punter in the Super Bowl.

As Goode kicked the bleeding hitman's consciousness into the farthest reaches of outer space, the other man scooped up a pistol from the floor and trained it on him, but he didn't pull the trigger. Before this last guy could make up his mind, there was a raging giant towering over him.

With one hand, Goode forced the indecisive hitman's shooting arm straight out, and with the other, he smashed the guy's elbow joint upward from below with all his strength, dislocating it with an extended grinding crunch. The man screamed in agony, dropping to his knees as Goode relieved him of his gun and helped Walker up. It took them several minutes to calm Park down to a point at which he could be led downstairs.

***

No sooner had Goode started up the side stairs than Miller opened his eyes, but only slightly. He saw one of the yellow-jacketed security guards standing nearby, leaning on the stage, happily playing with his confiscated P220 Legion Full-Size .45 auto with a high-grade titanium sound suppressor as if the firearm were a toy.

The second security guard came striding toward Miller with a taser in one hand and a pair of handcuffs in the other, so Miller feigned unconsciousness until the approaching guard came within striking range, then leapt up and smashed the tip of the guard's chin with a plate-sized palm strike. Next, he took a single step toward the other guard, who immediately handed over his silenced pistol. With a grunt, the giant hitman accepted the peace offering, hustled up the stairs, found his comrades, and helped them back down to the alternate exit. As he ran to the pick-up point, he dreaded the debriefing session that would be conducted in less than one hour.

***

Jack Cage paced back and forth across the deep-pile carpet of his mansion's sitting room, practically wearing a path into it as he waited for his men to call. The constant movement wasn't helping to settle his nerves, so he dropped onto one of his white leather settees and assumed a laid-back position, but he felt ridiculous; his mood was anything but laid back, and posture wasn't going to make any difference. Bing-bong! It was the doorbell. *Finally.* He downed his drink, strode to the front door, threw it open, and crossed the driveway to the front gate, where his gaze came to rest on a high-end hooker. His lips curled into a predatory grin. So did hers.

Soon Cage was back in his sitting room, alone again, down a thousand bucks, and even more unsatisfied than before. He poured himself another drink but left it on the coffee table, staring at it for a full minute before he hurled it into the wall. The new owners could deal with the damage. For the price they were getting, he felt, they should be happy to clean up the mess.

Troubled by the delay in communication, he headed back down the hall to his room and lay face up on his bed, studying the off-white ornamental plasterwork on the ceiling as he thought back thirty years. Lieutenant Walker's murder hadn't been a crime of passion—more like an unfortunate accident. The two fighter pilots had simply crossed paths on Walker's way up and on Cage's (then Bolton's) way down.

Shortly before the elder Walker's last day on Earth, the Cartel del Norte had ordered Bolton to silence both man and wife. Thus, after following the first half of that order at the gas station, Cage and his men had driven back to the Walkers' house and kicked in the door, only to discover that Christine Walker had left in a hurry. No one went looking for her. Both he and the cartel had had more urgent matters to deal with.

The buzzing of his telephone in his pocket snapped him back to the present. Cage took the call and held the phone to his ear, saying nothing.

"D2 for D1."

"Go, D2."

"Mission failed. Zero tangoes down and D4 is a casualty. We're on our way back now."

"God *dammit!* Meet me in the surveillance center."

"Copy that."

Cage stormed to the kitchen, grabbed a clean tumbler, gulped down the second drink he'd denied himself earlier, and fumed all the way to his truck. As the three-and-a-half-ton pickup barged down the hill to the industrial park, he realized he was slipping further and further away from where he needed to be mentally.

His truck was in better shape than he was.

16

NONCOMMITTAL NODS

As soon as he hung up with Walker, who'd called to let him know about the attack at the concert, Lieutenant Molloy met Park, Walker, and Goode at San Diego Police Headquarters, and they all piled in to his Ford Explorer. The senior lifeguard then drove the group to the newly rebuilt Oceanside PD police station.

"Appreciate you coming in so late, sir. Or is it early?" Sergeant Taylor asked, clasping each man's hand as they stepped into his office, Big Don's former domain. "Please," he said, gesturing to the four chairs facing his desk.

Molloy was the only visitor who didn't sit right away. He kept his back to the group as he paused to study a large framed photo on the wall, the same picture that adorned his own office.

"I couldn't bring myself to take it down," Taylor explained.

Nodding grimly, Molloy finally took his place in the only empty chair. "To answer your question," he grumbled, "it's late. For all of us, includin' you. 'Preciate you drivin' down from LA in the middle of the night."

"Of course," replied the new commander of the narcotics task force. Since his military days, Taylor had let his coarse black hair grow longer, but only by an inch or two, and his height and weight fell somewhere between those of Park and Walker, so when he leaned forward to rest his elbows on his desk, there wasn't a great deal of available workspace.

The conversation initially centered around the incident at the concert hall, with Park, Walker, and Goode reporting from their points of view. Most of the credit naturally went to Goode, but Taylor also commended Walker's and Park's decision to stay at the table and fight. "And don't worry, Tony," he said. "I came back from Afghanistan with PTSD, too. Just keep watching the waves from the lifeguard tower and don't skip your counseling sessions. You'll get better."

Park did not lift his head from its lowered position, but he did nod to show he'd understood. A puddle of tears had formed on the floor below him.

A clerk bustled in and out to deliver a steaming round of coffee, and little of importance was said while everyone took first sips of the hot refreshment. Then a young man in his early twenties with long, disheveled hair and droopy eyes showed up at the open door. Taylor nodded him in and stood to shake hands, moving behind his seated visitors to allow the young man free rein of his desk. "Guys, this is Sean Choi," he said, "our best freelance technology analyst."

"Good morning," the young man mumbled, offering the barest hint of eye contact before turning the computer monitor so everyone could see it.

"Good morning, Sean!" Taylor thundered pointedly. "What've you got for us?"

"Quite a few interesting findings, sir," Choi replied more clearly and in a stronger voice. After inserting a flash drive in Taylor's computer, he made an effort to look his listeners in the eye. "I can confirm that Jack Cage was formerly known as Trent Bolton. His name change petition was filed up in Sonoma County, which made it hard to find." With deft keystrokes, he called up an image of the court order that had authorized the administrative procedure.

"Good," said Sergeant Taylor. "What about his discharge?"

Choi seemed to come alive as he delved further into his presentation, though he did steal a wistful glance at the steaming mugs on the desk. "For those of you who don't know," he said, "Oceanside PD subpoenaed Bolton's service record, but most of it was classified, redacted, or missing. So here's the full version." He scrolled through several pages on the display.

"Excuse me. How did you find that?" Walker asked. "I've been looking for it for years."

Choi's eyes, sharper now, darted to those of his boss.

Taylor chuckled. "Let's just say Sean's an expert programmer specialized in the circumvention of cybersecurity."

Walker reckoned that meant "hacker," which would explain why the young man was employed on a freelance basis.

"I've summarized the most important points," Choi went on, reading from a report he'd called to the screen. "At a general court-martial, former Lieutenant Bolton pled not guilty to one specification of wrongful possession of a controlled substance with the intent to distribute, one of wrongful use of a controlled substance, and another of aggravated assault with a dangerous weapon. The case was dropped on appeal for technical reasons, but the dishonorable discharge was maintained due to a long history of conduct unbecoming an officer and a gentleman. Interestingly, Bolton's discharge was upgraded to fully honorable two years later, with no reason given."

Taylor harrumphed. "The reason not given is that the Cartel del Norte paid someone high up in the food chain to illegally process his status change."

"And redact his service record," Molloy added. "But why the name change?"

"Good question, sir," Choi said, calling up another official document. "Besides Bolton's military record, his civilian criminal history lists two arrests for possession with intent to distribute, with plenty of evidence against him, but again the charges were dropped, in both cases. He filed for the name change shortly after the second arrest."

"To hide his criminal record," Goode concluded.

"Right. No one can hide behind a name change, but that must have been his intent," Choi explained, double-clicking the mouse to produce the first of several satellite images, an overhead shot of the industrial park from which Walker and Goode had escaped in the Mustang. "Now with regard to the laptop. You'll recall that Cage stole it back when he stormed this police station, but not before I had cloned the hard disk. Among the encrypted data I managed to recover were various records of deliveries made to a pharmaceutical company based in Vista. Some of them bear his name and signature."

"That's enough for a warrant," said Molloy, with a tight-lipped smile.

Taylor nodded thoughtfully. "Yes, it is."

Choi's fingers flew over the keyboard and the image zoomed in on Cage's warehouse complex, showing both black SRTs parked next to a massive blood-red truck. "As you can see," he proceeded, "the facility consists of two main structures, with an internal road between them and a fenced-in field behind the larger building. That grassy area appears to be surrounded by thick walls."

"That's where we'll gain entry," Taylor remarked.

"By explosive breaching?" Park asked hopefully.

"Yes, but I can't let you get involved."

Park frowned and turned back to the monitor.

Once more the hacker focused a pitiful pair of eyes on the steaming brews that were being savored by everyone but him. Walker figured the poor guy had been up all night just like the rest of them. "One more thing," said Choi, now eyeing Walker. "I got the facial recognition results from the pictures you took. One of the men in the photos was Jack Cage, and the other was Peter Miller. Ex-U.S. Army, final rank sergeant. And with the security footage from The East End, I was able to identify the two hitmen who took off their masks: Rick Daniels, who served overseas under Miller, and Carlos Maldonado, a former Marine who was dishonorably discharged just like Bolton a.k.a. Cage." As he spoke of the three mercenaries and their leader, the technology analyst showed their photos, one by one. "I've printed everything out, sir," Choi concluded, handing Taylor a thick manila envelope from across the desk.

Taylor couldn't contain his grin. "Brilliant work, Sean. Thanks for handling this on such short notice. And you know you don't have to call me sir."

"Yes sir, I know."

Once Choi had taken his leave, Taylor resumed his seat. "Lieutenant Molloy. Guys," he said, meeting each of their gazes with a sympathetic expression. "I *am* aware that this case is personal for you. But even if it weren't a risky mission, I couldn't allow you to assist in the service of the warrant." Then, with a hard look in his eyes and a sharper tone of voice, he said, "You are not to go anywhere near that warehouse at any time. Is that clear?"

Walker, Park, and Goode exchanged a three-way look before they turned back to Taylor and gave no reply. So sleight were their nods that agreement was neither expressed nor understood.

17

THE PRICE OF VIOLENCE

Christine Walker is one of three female friends lying on lounge chairs under wide, colorful umbrellas at Rosarito Beach. She still looks good in her one-piece, though fourteen years of double shifts and a nicotine addiction have aged the corners of her eyes and mouth. She manages an English academy Monday through Saturday, in addition to all the time she devotes to her home and her son: picking up after him, driving him wherever he needs to go, folding his clothes, and all the rest of the work she does so that he might focus only on school. Which, of course, he does not.

A warm late-morning breeze brushes over her body and she shivers, which strikes her as odd. Her girlfriends aren't cold. And her son, as he tells her the story of the wave he just caught, is dripping wet, and he seems comfortable. Mrs. Walker is unable to focus on the details of his narrative, as she's been plagued by persistent stomach pain for over a month. Rest, fluids, and analgesics have made no difference. In the past, she's suffered from gastrointestinal problems, of course, the usual kind, but this illness feels alien and corrosive. She's scared to death.

Young Jeff Walker leaps to his feet to demonstrate his ride to glory. His muscles are growing more and more defined. He's going to be big. *Like his father*, she thinks. *Maybe it's time to tell him the truth about what happened.* Wiping a lonely tear from her cheek, she nods encouragingly and tries to smile, but the pain curls her mouth into a grimace.

***

Young Walker smiles broadly as he comes to the exciting conclusion of his tale. He's in his element at the beach, and it's all because of his mom. Even when she's had to be stern or strict with him, she's always encouraged his growth as a student, as a surfer, and in every other aspect of his existence. She's his heroine and the first love of his life. But today, something about her looks off. She's trying to listen, yet her smile is weak. Now she's wincing in pain. Walker kneels to ask her what's the matter but all of a sudden he's hurting, too. He places his palm on his aching jaw. *That's odd*, he thinks. *I know I didn't hurt myself in a wipeout.* Then it comes back to him in a flash. It was Maldonado's overhand right at The East End. *I'm dreaming.*

Walker's eyes flew open and he sat up in bed, his heart racing from the nightmare he'd been about to have, the second part of that story. The clock read eleven a.m. in dark-red digits; one hour before his lunch date! As he bathed, his mind refused to let go of the dream, dragging him back to the worst period of his life: his mother's rapid decline over the eighteen months between that morning on the beach when she told him the truth about his father's murder and her untimely death. The only silver lining in that darkest of clouds was that nothing could ever hurt him worse than seeing his broken-hearted heroine draw her last breath in a hospital bed. He still hadn't gotten over it, and he didn't think he ever would.

A destructive hate surged up within him. It was all Cage's fault! Walker took an impulsive step toward his bat, but stopped himself from smashing up the kitchen, the TV, all the windows, and every other fixture in sight. It was then that he realized his buddy Tony wasn't the only one with PTSD.

After a quick mile in the car, Walker jerked to a halt outside Tina's parents' house. He leapt out, slammed the door, and remembered to scan the street for threats as he strode up the walk to ring the bell.

"¿Quién?" her father barked from behind the door, understandably wary after the ill-fated concert of the previous night.

"Jeff Walker."

Señor Garcia swung open the door and holstered a pistol as he gestured for Walker to come inside.

Walker stuck out his hand with a smile and wished the man a good afternoon, but Sr. Garcia did not return the smile nor echo any kind of good wishes. His grip was gentle, yet the look in his eyes and his tone of voice were far from pleasant when he uttered this simple reply: "Take care of her."

Tina appeared beside her father, clad in tight-fitting blue jeans and a black short-sleeved blouse. She kissed her dad on the cheek and told him not to worry.

***

"You look nice," said Walker as they set off for their destination. Still upset by his dream, he found himself driving more aggressively than usual.

"It's because I took a shower for a change," Tina joked, her long black hair fluttering in the wind.

"Ha!" he replied, pressing a button to raise her window. "You know, we could have taken the bikes."

She looked at him and nodded. "A longer ride would be more fun, though. Do you like apple pie? I know a place up in Julian."

Then she hit him with a spectacular smile, her hair and makeup as perfect as if she'd just stepped out of a beauty salon. Walker had to make an effort to keep his eyes on the road.

When they came to the restaurant and he opened the front door, the door jangler tinkled to announce their arrival. The place was packed. "The food must be good here," he remarked as they stepped into the comforting aroma of a Mexican kitchen at mealtime.

"It's not good, it's great," she corrected him on their way to the hostess stand. "And the prices are fair. My parents used to take us here all the time. They're close friends with the owners."

As they followed a cheerful young Latina to a corner booth, Tina took Walker's hand. Hers was clammy, and when a nearby patron dropped a fork on his plate, she jumped at the noise.

"Sorry," she said, sliding in to her side of the booth and taking an offered menu. "I'm still a little shaken up."

"Me too. Don't worry though," he said, scooting in opposite her and wondering whether he should say anything about the P226 he had concealed under his shirt.

When the waitress brought their beers, they clinked cold bottles and breathed a little easier.

"So what's your favorite thing on the menu?" he asked, studying the laminated list of food options, peering over it to watch the door from time to time.

"Pozole," she answered quickly.

Walker liked pozole, so much that his mom had learned how to make it for him. Loaded with pork and chicken, the spicy red soup also contains nixtamalized corn, which is like popcorn but much heavier and a little chewy. The dish is normally garnished with chopped lettuce, sliced radishes, lime juice, oregano, salt, and/or hot chili powder.

No further mention was made of the previous night's attack. Instead, Tina and Walker traded rescue stories, ultimately concluding that her job as a paramedic was more valuable to the community, though highly traumatic, while his work was easier and better for mental health.

This time it was Walker who startled, when the front door was thrown open and a large young man stormed inside. The beefy newcomer scanned the sea of diners until his eyes locked on to Tina, and his brows drew together in a scowl when he spotted Walker. Immediately striding in their direction, he loomed over the table and opened his mouth to speak, but Tina beat him to it.

"What are you doing here?" she asked.

"Doing well, thanks," he retorted. "I was just passing by and saw you through the window, so I thought I'd come in and say hi." The guy had short dark hair, and he wore slacks and a sweater with untucked shirt tails. Last night's party outfit, Walker guessed, and he also suspected that this was the ex-boyfriend who had cheated on Tina several times.

"Fine. Hi, Ryan. Bye, Ryan," she said, rolling her eyes.

Ryan was undeterred. "I see you have a new boyfriend. What's up, man?" he said with a smirk, catching Walker's gaze.

Walker was not in the mood for restraint. Tina set a calming hand on his shoulder and said under her breath, "Just ignore him."

Walker looked Ryan dead in the eye, saying nothing. He'd had plenty of street fights growing up as a white guy in Mexico, then a few more in San Diego, so he saw through the fragile confidence in the preppie's eyes and knew he wasn't in danger.

Ryan's smirk broadened and he turned back to Tina. "Looks like you're moving down in the world," he scoffed. "I *never* would have taken you to this trashy place."

Tina rose. "You need to leave. Right now," she snapped. "And don't *ever* follow me again!"

That's when Ryan made his first mistake. "Come on," he pleaded, grabbing her forearm. "I was just looking out for you."

Tina's face pinched with suspicion. "Are you drunk?" she asked, pushing him gently away.

Ryan didn't let go. His other hand locked on to her other arm and he pulled himself even closer.

Walker scooted out of the booth and stood up, staring hard.

Still in Ryan's clutches, Tina turned to Walker, her eyes wide with fright, which Walker couldn't understand. *Didn't she see she was safe?*

"No!" she shouted. "Sit down, Jeff. Please."

Ryan let go and whirled on Walker. Second mistake.

"She told you to leave," Walker said, blading his body to protect his groin. "This is your last warning."

Silence descended on the room. All eyes were on them.

"Fuck you," Ryan spat out, squaring off with his hands up.

Walker dodged a clumsy punch and spun the drunken idiot around, hauling him out into the street by his shirt collar. Eager for violence since he'd woken up from his dream, he took his time teaching Ryan a lesson. It was a perfect outcome: the preppie would never bother Tina again, and now that Walker had blown off some steam, his apartment would remain intact.

The door jangler jingled again as he strutted back inside, his heart still pounding and his knuckles bloody. He'd half-expected a round of applause or maybe drinks on the house, but he couldn't have been more off base: many worried patrons were on their feet, some running past him out the door. Walker wondered what had happened until an older man in a kitchen apron spotted him and hurried over with a pale face and a panicked expression. "I'm Javier Velazquez, the owner," he said, out of breath and speaking quickly. "Tina's gone! Two men in boots and masks crashed through the emergency exit, dragged her outside, and forced her into a black Jeep Cherokee."

18

COMBAT 101

"You're going to be raided today."

"What time?"

"Six-thirty p.m., by a fourteen-man tactical team from Oceanside PD and SDPD narcotics."

"Led by Dom Taylor?"

"Yes."

"Understood," Cage growled. Then he hung up on his asset and punched a button on the base of the phone.

"Yes?" answered Maria.

"Get Toño Del Real on the line." An enforcer for the Cartel del Norte, Del Real was Cage's primary point of contact in that organization.

"One moment."

As Cage waited, his gaze drifted to the paintings on the wall. He'd be leaving them behind.

"*¿Qué pasó? ¿Algún problema?*" came Del Real's jeering voice over the speakerphone.

Cage snatched up the handset, his anger meter registering a spike. "Yes, there is a problem, boy," he seethed. "The police are coming to raid us today, so I'm calling to request authorization to evacuate."

"Please hold for my father."

Minutes later, the warehouse facility was a flurry of activity: Maria was pushing the paper shredder to its limit; Cage was on the phone with Marco Del Real, the head of the cartel; Miller and three of his guards were loading equipment into the SRTs, and Maldonado was patrolling the perimeter with four of his men. The only person on site who wasn't rushing around was Daniels, who lay dejectedly on his bed in his quarters above the surveillance center.

***

Earlier that day, Tina Garcia had been ordered to remain seated on a sofa in the surveillance center, where a television and a foosball table stood by, awaiting a dull moment in the security guards' lives. She surveyed her surroundings as she breathed through her nose, since her mouth was covered with duct tape. Some fifty yards to her left, a long C-shaped desk occupied an entire wall and part of both adjoining walls. Two armed guards wearing tactical gear sat at the C-shaped workstation studying monitors, speaking into their headsets, and glancing her way every now and then. These were the goons who had kidnapped her at the restaurant: one was lanky with stitches on his gaunt and sunken face, the other just as tall but twice as wide. Directly ahead of her stood a row of metal lockers and storage compartments bolted to the wall.

To her left, a stocky man with a brown buzz cut eased his way down the stairs. Dressed in a pair of black slacks and a bloody dress shirt, he supported one of his arms with the other, wincing with each step as he made his way to the ground floor. From what Tina could see, and based on what Walker had told her the night before, this man was suffering from a hyperextension injury of the elbow complicated by an anterior dislocation. The joint should have been immediately reset by a medical professional in a hospital setting under local anesthesia, with previous radiographic imaging, but instead it had been left untreated. According to her calculations, fifteen hours had passed since David Goode had run up to platform B to save Jeff and Tony at the concert.

A trim man in his fifties with silver hair cut in military fashion stormed imperiously through the main doors, and when the larger of Tina's two kidnappers set out a chair for the injured man coming down the stairs, she knew what was going to happen next. It made her sick.

"Hold him down," the leader commanded. The long-faced goon placed both hands on the injured man's shoulders to hold him down in the chair, and the giant one knelt to immobilize his legs. The leader took hold of the sitting man's damaged arm, supporting his wrist with one hand, then placed the palm of his other hand over the crook of the man's elbow, the one that had been forced upwards into an inverted letter V. "Dammit, Daniels," the leader muttered, then shoved the bones back into place with a prolonged crunching sound. Daniels screamed.

"Miller, get a sling from the infirmary. Maldonado, you put it on," the leader commanded. He pulled a flask from his pocket and handed it to his moaning subordinate, then strode over to where Tina sat. "Come with me," he ordered her, striding toward the lockers and pulling open a door that led to a descending staircase. "You first," he said, and followed her down.

At the bottom of the stairs, there were three doors to Tina's left. The man opened one of them, stood clear of it, and waited for her to trudge inside. It was a small room with bare concrete-block walls. The only furniture was a pair of metal folding chairs and a table, on which her purse had already been placed. "Sit down," he ordered her, then tore off the duct tape that sealed her lips. "You may call me Mr. Cage. What's your name?" he asked, his steely eyes boring into hers.

"*Me llamo chinga tu puta madre*," she snapped, shaking her head to clear the bangs from her eyes since her wrists were taped together in her lap. "*No hablo inglés.*"

"The only word I understood was *madre*," Cage retorted. "And however true the rest of them might have been, you'd still better watch your mouth." He fished around in her purse to find her wallet. "Cristina Garcia," he said, reading from her driver's license. "Twenty-five years of age, with a Chula Vista address. Of course you speak English. What's your relation to Jeff Walker?"

No response.

"Have you heard anything about a police raid?" he demanded.

She glared at him in silence.

Cage paused thoughtfully, then said, "Speaking of mothers, I bet you still live with your parents. Shall I send one of my men to Chula Vista to see if that's true?"

"I'm Jeff's girlfriend," she replied. "And I don't know anything about the police."

He glanced at his watch and frowned. "You're lucky I don't have time for this. Follow me." He left the room to open the adjacent holding cell, locked her inside, and hustled back up the stairs.

***

"Taylor told everyone he was going to hit at dusk, but he moved the actual time forward in case Cage has an asset on the force," Park told his buddies, sliding his cell phone back into his pocket.

"That was smart," Walker said, shrugging on a ballistic vest.

"I'm surprised he was willin' to tell ya that," Goode remarked, turning away from a wall full of firearms to look at Park, who strode across the room to join him.

"Lieutenant Molloy's a good man," Park told Goode. "He stonewalled me at first, but when I told him about Tina, he gave in.

And he said he wanted to come with us, but I told him I'd report him if he did."

"*Good*. He's too old for it. You should have seen him when he was younger, though. *Toe* fools up on the football field. Well?" Goode prompted, jutting his chin toward all the weapons mounted on the wall.

Park took a moment to survey his ample collection, then lifted a black and gray Sig Sauer P320 off its hanger and handed it over. He pointed at a magazine box, from which Goode took out two full mags, stuffing them into a pouch on his tactical vest, and then a third which he seated in the big pistol's grip. Park next passed his buddy a helmet and a pair of shooting glasses and, once Goode had put them on, a California-compliant semi-auto rifle. "You're Goode to go," he said.

"I've heard that one a million times. It brought me no amusement, Park."

"Ha!"

The three guys took up most of the space in Park's little studio, which looked more like an arms depot than an apartment. There wasn't even a bed, just a cot in the corner, on which Walker sat lacing up his boots. They were too big for him, but much better in a fight than his basketball shoes.

"Ready bro?" Park asked.

"Are you?" Walker snapped.

"I'll be fine," Park shot back evenly. "I'm doing this for you and Tina, so I doubt I'll get shaken up."

Now Walker felt stupid. "Sorry, man. I'm just mad at myself for leaving her alone in the restaurant."

"No worries. I'll be okay, and so will you. Just follow me. Do what I tell you, when I tell you, and we'll be back here sipping whiskey before you know it."

Goode was waiting for them at the door. He flicked his chin toward Walker. "Hey, how did it go with Tina's dad?" he asked with a teasing grin. "Bet that was a *fun* talk."

***

Taylor's tactical team poured out of two unmarked vans and double-timed it to the rear wall of the warehouse property. After breaching the wall, they'd have a long, wide-open approach, so it would be easy to pick them off in the tall grass, particularly since Cage had ordered his guards, many hours in advance, to set up a pair of M2 HB belt-fed machine guns outside the rear doors of the warehouse. Which was why Miller wasn't alarmed when the monitors showed the police pulling up five hours early; all he had to do was send out a crew to the heavy guns. While keeping an eye on the screen to watch one member of Taylor's tactical unit place an explosive charge on the rear wall, he lumbered over to the weapons closet, hearing and feeling the blast as he grabbed a Kalashnikov and seated a curved thirty-round magazine, then chambered the first round with a metallic click-clack. Just like the police, the giant guard captain and his men were equipped with body armor, ballistic eyewear, comm headsets, and tactical helmets.

Maldonado joined him at the monitors, also geared up and ready to go. The lanky killer grinned as he watched the raiding force file through the hole in the wall, running in a crouch through knee-high grass with rifles panning, each man covering a unique sector of fire. Maldonado cackled away but Miller set his jaw when Taylor's team was torn apart by a supersonic hailstorm of projectiles large enough to shoot down a fighter plane.

***

Park was the first to charge through the breach in the wall. Walker followed, and David Goode covered the rear. Cradling Ares SCR semi-automatic rifles and their sidearms in drop-leg holsters, the trio hustled past ten mangled policemen, some with half a head, others missing limbs, all sprawled out in the bloody grass on the way to the rear warehouse doors.

Just inside, they found Sergeant Taylor and his three remaining men holed up behind a stack of crates. When Taylor wasn't surprised to see them, it occurred to Walker that Molloy might have mentioned they were coming. In any event, as bullets snapped over his head, splintering wood and pocking the walls behind him, Walker risked a glance around the corner of a crate. The warehouse was about the size and shape of a football field, with a maze of cubicles, tables, and machinery between the two end zones. Based on the number of guards closing in on them, he concluded they were outnumbered by two to one, at least.

"Go up the right flank!" Taylor ordered two of his men. "Van Brussel and I'll take the left." Then he eyed Park and company. "Y'all stay here and lay down suppressive fire."

With this maneuver, the newly reinforced tactical team sent hot lead tearing through the throats and faces of five approaching guards before Van Brussel fell to the floor at Taylor's feet. Blood sprayed and spurted from the frightened man's throat as he struggled to speak. "Tell Jane and the kids I love 'em." Then his head rolled to one side and a spreading pool of hot blood soaked Taylor's tactical trousers at the knee.

"You bet I will, Mike," Taylor growled as his buddy's sky-blue eyes went vacant. Now alone halfway up the left-side wall, he saw the main doors at the far end of the warehouse crash open to admit a commanding figure. He raised his M4 carbine to take aim, but when a fusillade of automatic fire tore into his surroundings, showering him with wood chips, concrete chunks, and a cloud of plaster dust, he had to hit the deck.

Meanwhile, on the safe side of the crates near the rear doors, the constant noise of heavy gunfire disoriented Walker from all sides. Every beat of his startled pulse brought him more respect for Tony Park.

***

As soon as Cage had locked Tina in her cell, she had started on the tape around her wrists. It took her ten minutes to free herself with her teeth. Not long after that, she heard footsteps click-clacking down the stairs from the surveillance room, so she stooped to peer through the bars in the heavy door. A young woman whose size and facial features were remarkably similar to her own stepped confidently out of the stairwell onto the basement floor. Decked out in three-inch heels, too much makeup, a navy-blue mini-skirt suit, and a low-cut blouse, she looked like a stripper about to peel off a secretary costume.

As their eyes met, Tina was struck by a burst of sudden inspiration. "It's rude to walk into a room and say nothing to whoever's already there," she called out through the bars.

"Not if that person is a little *bitch*," Stripper countered, her heels clacking as she came closer to the door.

"What did you just say?" Tina grabbed the bars and rattled them, showing more anger than she really felt. "I dare you to come in here and say it to my face."

Stripper's eyes widened and she thrust her hand in her pocket, but then she stopped. "No." A victorious smirk crept at the corners of her lips. "Your dumb ass is gonna stay locked up."

"*Pinche cobarde. Puta*," Tina snarled, but her fighting words produced no effect. Apparently, her underdressed visitor spoke no Spanish. *Moving on to plan B.*

"Well, I'm off like a prom dress," Stripper sang out. "Just wanted to see what the fuss was all about and now I know. It was about nothing at all, just another piece-of-shit immigrant."

Tina thrust out her arm from between the bars and flipped the woman the bird. As she did, it crossed her mind that this might be the lying slut who'd tricked Jeff on the beach. So it was with extra cruelty that when Stripper rushed forward to grab her middle finger, Tina caught the woman's wrist, added another hand to the grip, propped one foot up on the metal door, and yanked her visitor's arm into the cell. As Stripper's head smashed into the heavy door with a resounding thud, Tina hung on to her wrist and reeled her in, searched her pockets, and found a set of keys.

She had just let herself out when the first explosion rocked the grounds. In the distance, she heard heavy gunfire, shouted orders, and screaming, dying men. One floor up, metal doors clanged shut and boots stampeded out of the building. "Who's the little bitch now?" Tina muttered as she locked Stripper in the cell, then searched the basement for anything she could use to her advantage. Her purse had been taken out of the interrogation room, and in another larger space crammed with racks of computer equipment, she found nothing useful, so she started up the stairs with the keys in her fist and the longest one sticking out between two of her fingers. At the top, she eased the door open a crack and peeked into the surveillance center. Only one armed guard stood between her and a chance to escape, but he'd just spotted her!

***

Minutes earlier, Cage had been barking orders into a headset mic as he watched the warehouse firefight in the monitors at the C-shaped desk. Beside him sat Daniels, whose right arm, his shooting arm, was tightly bound to his body in a sling. At first, Cage had had no qualms about commanding from a distance; he'd more than earned the right. But when Walker, Park, and Goode showed up to assist and five of his guards went down, he lurched to his feet, hurried to a gun closet to grab a Kalashnikov, and chambered a round with a metallic ker-chick. His own voice echoed in his ears—*You'd better not fuck this up, Jack*—as he hustled out the doors and across the road to lead his men to victory in one last battle.

19

FINALLY READY

Taylor's strategy had proven successful: his tactical team had surrounded and eliminated a significant number of guards, but the opposing force was still stronger and much more familiar with the layout of the warehouse. Park, Walker, and Goode had stayed by the rear doors in a supportive position, but now they were too far from the action; they needed to advance.

"Cover!" Park shouted.

"Coverin'!" Goode answered, popping up to fire at the guards while Park ran forward in a crouch. Then Walker did the same for Goode, the trio thus leapfrogging up the middle and helping to beat the guards back toward the main doors. But when those main doors crashed open to admit a commanding figure, the retreating guards split left and right on that man's order, moving forward again along the flanks.

On the right side, Taylor's two remaining men were poised to shoot, so when their assailants rushed toward them, the result was a short-lived offensive maneuver. Sadly, Taylor's guys hadn't spotted Miller, who'd trailed his comrades and taken cover, then charged out of hiding to exact revenge with two well-targeted bursts of automatic fire.

On the left side, Maldonado and his men were closing in on the isolated Taylor, so Park gave his buddies directions by hand signal before hustling off to his aid. Goode moved right, keeping his head low as he set off to hunt for Miller. This left Walker by himself to cover the center line, on which Jack Cage was striding straight toward him with his rifle leveled.

Walker spun out of danger just as Cage's machine gun rang out like a jackhammer and a burst of bullets chewed up the surrounding obstacles. Timing his counterattack by the ever-louder sound of approaching footfalls, Walker slipped his finger into his rifle's trigger guard, sucked in a breath, and swung around the corner to face his nemesis, firing even before he had a visual. CRACK CRACK CRACK CRACK! For an instant, he wondered why Cage wasn't down on the floor writhing in pain, but a split second later his question was answered by a rifle stock scything through the air and smashing into the side of his head. Walker spun in all directions in an attempt to locate his attacker, but his mind was slow and muddled.

Cage calmly continued his assault with a devastating throat strike that made Walker drop his rifle and forget he had a sidearm. The choking lifeguard fell to his knees, clutching his throat, heaving for breath, the tiny stream of air passing through his windpipe scarcely enough to keep him conscious.

"Can't say it's been a pleasure, kid," Cage said with a rueful frown as he relieved Walker of his Glock, then tossed it aside and took aim with his own rifle.

***

The warehouse fell silent for a moment as both forces hunted each other down. Goode was stalking forward in a crouch, as was Miller from the opposite side of the battleground, and they couldn't see each other from where they were. When the two giants finally collided, they were too close for anything but hand-to-hand. They grabbed and grappled, throwing elbows and driving knees into each other's thighs and groins as they fought in the clinch. The first of those knees to land was Miller's, which he followed up with a front kick that caught Goode just above the knee.

The singer hobbled backward and drew his P320, but he didn't have time to fire since Miller whipped out his knife and threw it into his shooting arm. Goode cried out in pain and dropped his Sig, but still managed to pull the blade out of his bicep and drop into a fighting stance, with the knife in his left hand and his right dangling uselessly.

Miller grinned as he came forward, unarmed since both had dropped their rifles. He stepped easily into Goode's slashing attack, caught his knife hand, wrist-locked it, moved behind him, and twisted the singer's arm up toward his head. Inch by inch, Goode's non-dominant hand lost ground as Miller forced it higher. Since his shoulder was about to be crunched out of its socket, Goode let go of the knife and begged for mercy.

Miller held the armlock but didn't crank it any farther; instead, he glanced across the warehouse at Maldonado, who was fighting Tony Park. Maldonado dodged a heavy punch and caught Miller's gaze. The two guard captains exchanged a nod before turning back to their work.

Anyone who knew David Goode, if asked, would have said no, he was not actually in the habit of crying out for compassion. It had been a ploy. So when Cage's largest man let up for a second to meet his comrade's eye, Goode dropped his chin to cock his head like a hammer, then slammed it back into Miller's nose, breaking it with an audible crunch. Miller let go of Goode's arm just as a pair of gunshots rang out from close range.

Goode whirled around to see Sergeant Taylor firing his M4 and Miller dropping to his knees on the concrete floor. Taylor pulled the trigger again and again as thick, sticky, dark-red fluid spurted out of Miller's neck like water from a spigot. The man's body jerked under the repeated impacts of Taylor's rifle fire, his eyes gradually losing focus and then going blank as he died, face up in a pool of his own blood.

***

Walker struggled to breathe through his constricted throat as he stared down the gaping muzzle of Cage's Kalashnikov. "I know you killed my father," he croaked, rising from a single knee to a standing position with his hands in the air.

"Maybe I did," Cage returned, moving farther out of reach, his finger curling around the trigger as he peered down the barrel of his weapon. "You can ask him yourself in a minute. Even sooner if you take one more step."

"Where's Tina?" Walker blurted out, stalling for time and also hoping Cage would let his guard down. Curiously, he did.

Cage's lips twisted into a smirk and his eyes left his sights as he lowered his rifle an inch. Perhaps his macho sensibility had made him wish for a fairer fight, or, maybe, despite Walker's obvious lack of combat experience, Cage respected his attempt to avenge his father and rescue his girlfriend. In any case, Walker darted forward and got his strong hands on the weapon before Cage could pull the trigger, but that was the extent of his success. As the AK stitched the ceiling with automatic fire, Cage punched Walker in the throat again, following up with a series of brutal strikes to the younger man's jaw.

Cage's eyes fell on Walker's sprawled-out body, then shifted to the weapons on the floor. He started for them but paused midstep when he felt, then saw, out of the corner of his eye, Tony Park tracking him with a rifle.

"On the floor with your hands behind your head!" Park thundered.

Cage complied, but he did it with such agonizing slowness that Park was forced to kick him in the mouth with a steel-toe boot to hurry him along.

Cage glared hard as he spat out two bloody teeth. Then he flitted his gaze past Park for a second and finally submitted, putting his face on the floor and his hands on his head. Quite close to his ears. Almost covering them, in fact.

Walker fought with his balance before staggering to his feet. He and Park glanced at each other just as an ear-splitting series of detonations and ultra-bright flashes temporarily incapacitated every man in the vicinity who wasn't lying face down with his eyes squeezed shut and his hands over his ears.

***

Ten minutes earlier, under orders to remain upstairs, Daniels had been lying in bed when the first blast shook the grounds. He had no intention of cowering behind one injured limb when three were working just fine. Nor would he wallow in indecision. Not this time, and *certainly* not while his men were in mortal danger. He chewed up a painkiller and headed downstairs, joining his boss at the C-shaped desk, nodding to his guards as they stampeded out to fight. A few minutes later, when Cage hustled off to lead his team in one last victory, Daniels was left to watch the screens, provide intelligence, and stay ready with a pistol in his non-dominant hand.

A metallic boom echoed from below and Daniels wondered what it could have been. He knew Maria was down there, so he kept an eye on the basement door. When it eased open a crack, he caught a glimpse of someone looking out from behind it, so he turned away as if he hadn't seen anything. Two breaths later, he stood and followed a circuitous route to the door, around the room's perimeter, taking the most advantageous line in terms of concealment and shooting angle. Obviously the person on the other side was Walker's girlfriend, since Maria wouldn't be sneaking around, so he held his pistol at the ready as he approached. But before he got there, the door swung open and Tina stepped out, dropping into a low fighting stance with a key sticking out of her fist. The resemblance between her and Maria, with whom Daniels was in love, was astonishing. For that reason and also because he wasn't entirely loyal to Cage, who didn't treat him well, Daniels wasn't bent on hurting her (though he would if he had to, of course). They held each other's gazes as they passed each other, Tina moving toward the main doors and Daniels clomping downstairs to check on the woman of his dreams.

That morning, when Maria had shown up to work, she hadn't gone straight to the office. She'd stopped at the surveillance center, click-clacked up the stairs, and seen Daniels on the bed with his mangled elbow. Her face had fallen in dismay as she'd rushed to his side and comforted him for a moment. Then she'd marched downstairs and demanded Cage call a doctor, but the master smuggler had shaken his head with determination. It took her all morning to convince him to forgive Daniels for failing to pull the trigger at The East End.

Daniels was a good soldier, a trained sniper, qualified to lead the warehouse guards, yet for all his life he'd been held back by one major flaw: spotty self-confidence. As he headed down the stairs to see about Maria, he realized that the time had come to trust himself in every situation, without relying on Cage for encouragement or on Sergeant Miller to cover for him. So it was with new resolve that he pulled open the door to the holding cell, where he saw Maria slumped against the far wall, sitting on the floor and staring straight ahead. She didn't react to his presence until he knelt down beside her.

"Are you all right?" he asked as he helped her up.

"Yeah," she replied softly. God, she was gorgeous.

Unconsciously or otherwise, while supporting her weight, Daniels stepped closer and they slipped into an embrace. He couldn't decide whether her best feature was that curvy body pressed up against him or those dark, exotic eyes he was swimming in. With no further debate, he leaned in to kiss her for the very first time. "Stay here, okay?" he said after an unforgettable experience. "I won't leave without you."

She nodded.

He led her across the hall to the server room, where there was somewhere decent for her to sit and the air was cooler. Then he gave her his keys. "Lock yourself in," he said. "I'll be back."

As Daniels clomped up the stairs, an idea began to take shape in his mind, and after studying the monitors, it developed into a plan. No, he wasn't fond of his boss, but if he could save Maldonado while rescuing Maria and anyone else on his team who was still alive, then that's what he was going to do. He hustled to the weapons closet and stuffed four flashbangs into his pockets, then made for the warehouse.

Once inside, he threaded his way down the left flank and came to his former sergeant's corpse. He'd spotted Miller in the monitors, so it wasn't a surprise, but his first priority was to make sure his hero couldn't be saved. Then Daniels took off in a running crouch toward the center of the warehouse, where he'd seen Cage lying face down on the floor with a rifle trained on his back. He hid behind a forklift and peered around the rear of the machine. Exchanging a glance with his boss, he held up a flashbang. Cage pretended not to see anything, then put his head down and his hands near his ears. Acting purely on instinct with no time for insecurity, Daniels pulled the pins with his teeth and made four perfect left-handed tosses.

Five minutes later, Cage climbed into his blood-red muscle truck and roared out of the warehouse facility for the last time.

Maldonado followed him in one of the SRTs; Daniels in the other with Maria riding shotgun. The convoy headed for the Carlsbad boathouse, where they'd spend the night before driving down to Mazatlan in the morning.

***

Maldonado couldn't sleep. His revs were still high after the battle, and he had six hours to kill before the drive to Mexico, so he figured he'd help his boss and have some fun at the same time. The only problem was who to murder: Park, Goode, Taylor, Walker, or Tina? He hated Park for shooting two of his men and knocking him out in the warehouse, but he loathed Goode and Taylor for killing Miller, wished Walker dead out of respect for Cage, and despised Tina for slamming Maria's head into the detention door.

His decision made, the rangy killer stole down to the boathouse, found the tools he needed, and took one of the SRTs down to San Diego. He parked several blocks away from his destination. Staying out of the streetlights, he walked, then crawled to reach the motorcycle unseen. He had to unscrew six bolts to remove the plastic fairing before cutting the metal frame most of the way through on both sides with a hacksaw. That done, he bolted the fairing back on and retraced his steps with the same degree of caution as before. As he drove back up the coast, Maldonado switched on the stereo and sang along to the music. It hadn't been an easy decision between Tina Garcia's or Jeff Walker's bike. Tina's death would cause more suffering, but Walker's was more advantageous. In the end, he'd gone with his gut. *That's all you can do*, he thought. *Just go with what feels right and hope for the best.*

***

The next morning, Walker, Park, Goode, Tina, and Lieutenant Molloy took a seat across from Sergeant Taylor at his desk. There were reams of paperwork to fill out, next of kin to be notified, psychological assessments to undergo, statements to be given, and in Taylor's case, possible disciplinary action. No one looked ready for any of that.

While Taylor was busy on the phone, his visitors sat bleary-eyed and silent, sipping coffee until he hung up with a frown. Then he looked at them and said, "Cowgill told me two weeks but I'm guessing it'll be at least a month." The lawman went on to provide further details about the proposed joint effort involving Oceanside narcotics, the DEA, the Mexican authorities, and absolutely *no* civilians as Tina held Walker's hand and stroked it with her thumb.

Walker was still in shock. After this first taste of combat, he sharply regretted having questioned Park's ability to handle his stress disorder, so he tucked away a mental reminder to buy his buddy a beer and apologize properly. And now that the list of reasons why he hated Cage had grown even longer, he was flooded by the desire to straddle his bike and roar down to Mazatlan in a foolish single-handed attempt at revenge. Fortunately, "foolish" was something he no longer wanted to be. Having cheated death for the third time in so many months, Walker knew he needed further training if there was to be any possibility of a successful confrontation with his parents' killer. Tina had recommended her *shifu*, a Master Chang. She'd said he was tough and demanding; mean, even, but that sounded fine to Walker. As he swore to himself he wouldn't lose another fight to Cage, his body gave a sudden nervous jerk. Taylor stopped talking for a moment and everyone turned to look, but he didn't care. Walker was finally ready for anything.

20

TEACHERS AND BROTHERS

D avid Goode had risen early, meaning before nine. As he waited for his espresso machine to fill his cup, he gazed through the floor-to-ceiling windows at the quiet beach scene ten stories down. The marine layer had yet to dissipate, so he saw long rows of chilly waves cruising into shore under an endless canopy of thick gray clouds.

Goode would have preferred to be sharing this peaceful vista with his stunning new girlfriend. He smiled at the memory of the last time she'd come over; he'd made two cups instead of one and carried them out to the balcony, where the new couple had reveled in the rhythmic sounds of nature after a full night of explosive lovemaking. Now that he'd gotten to know that stunning new girlfriend, however, he feared it might never happen again.

He switched off the coffee machine with a discouraged flick of his finger. They hadn't seen each other for weeks, not since the battle at the warehouse. He grabbed his americano and headed out to the deck, alone, assuring himself she'd be more available after exams.

After breakfast, despite the clear message Lynn was sending, namely that she needed to be left alone, he came close to disturbing her with a call. His cell phone in his hand, he sat for thirty minutes debating whether or not to ask her on a special beach date he'd been planning. The idea was to pack a picnic, roll up a blanket, take the elevator down to the beach, and watch the sunset while sipping white wine. Yet according to his messaging app, three days had passed since he'd sent her a text, which she hadn't viewed, and four since his last call, which she hadn't picked up, so Goode's thumb merely hovered over her name as his passion waged war with cold, hard facts. In the end, he suppressed the impulse and settled into a lounge chair out on the balcony, cracking open a thriller novel as the cool morning gave way to another spectacular day in San Diego.

When lunchtime came, he stepped inside for a sandwich and a beer. After that it was back to the novel. But by five o'clock, having spent eight hours with printed-word action, he was lonely and much less interested in fictional exploits. He stuck it out for one more hour, hanging on for any trace of interest. Then at six, as the sky grew dark along with his mood, he grabbed his keys and blasted off in the Shelby.

*****

The evening air was still warm and sweet as Walker jogged to his try-out with Master Chang. Regrettably, the Mexican authorities had failed to offer any assistance with regard to the Cartel del Norte. According to Sergeant Taylor, this was because the crooks kept them on their payroll. Worse yet, when and if Taylor secured the cooperation of the DEA, Walker, Park, and Goode wouldn't be allowed to take part in the cross-border operation.

He slowed his pace as he came to his destination, a modest home with a patch of grass and a trampoline in the front yard. When he stooped to grab a rock and tap on a fence post, an Asian teenager came out to admit him, leading him down a long set of concrete stairs to an outdoor fighting ring and a grassy field. They continued along a paved walkway that wound around to a one-story building, a training hall with red padded dojo flooring. All kinds of punching and kicking bags hung down from the rafters and rose up from the floor.

To Walker's right, a diminutive Asian man hung upside down from what looked to be a squat rack in a weight room, but that's not what it was. The contraption turned out to be an inversion system, used to decompress the spine and increase cerebral circulation, and the inverted man turned out to be Master Chang, many of whose online videos Walker had viewed in preparation for that day's provisional session. His guess was that the master's millions of virtual students and subscribers kept him flush with money, since the man only taught a select number of students in person and at an absurdly low price.

Still hanging from his inverted position, Master Chang neatly executed a backflip with a half twist, landing on his feet facing Walker. He looked to be in his mid-thirties, but Walker had read his book; he was over fifty. Master Chang's introduction to violence had taken place on the street in Vietnam when he was five years old, and he hadn't stopped fighting since. A healthy diet and his rigorous training regimen had kept him looking young.

"How you doing man," Master Chang said, extending his hand with a pleasant smile, though his grip was not as friendly.

The first test was a wrestling match. No punches or kicks. Despite Walker's fifty- or sixty-pound advantage, the master took him down every time. It was like playing pool with Tony Park: if you slipped and made a mistake, the game was over. Walker hung his head.

"Up you go," the master said, helping him to his legs. "You got ten minutes to run the stairs twenty times. Up and down is one time. Go!"

Walker's legs whined like a child as they lugged his heavy body from bottom to top and back for the required number of repetitions. He counted seventy-four steps. Luckily, he was used to this kind of workout, but unluckily, it had been months since he'd done any kind of aerobic training. Once more he thought of Park, this time associating his struggling lungs with the pain his close friend must have endured in boot camp and BUD/S. And then there was the war.

"Nine minutes. Too slow," Master Chang announced, clicking a button on a stopwatch that hung on his neck and handing over a bottle of water. As Walker recovered, his hands on his knees with his head down, the master offered an assessment of his grappling skills. It was not a glowing report. Then they squared off again, this time in a full-contact sparring match using gloves, headgear, shin pads, and mouthguards. At each reset, Master Chang allowed Walker the initiative, but in a flash he'd switch from defense to attack and overwhelm his prospective student with a blur of practiced movements. He hit Walker hard and knocked him to the mat again and again. When Walker stayed down, Master Chang offered him a helping hand, then gestured toward a bench.

Walker took a seat and the master brought over a chair for himself. "Now we talk," the older man said. "You good fighter. Where you learn?"

"Mexico, on the street."

"Like me."

Walker nodded, still heaving for air.

"But why you need instructor?"

Recalling how he'd bored his boss at lifeguard headquarters, Walker told the story of his father's murder, his mother's passing, and his run-ins with Cage in the briefest possible manner.

Master Chang shook his head. "If you go down to Mexico, that's not self-defense. Hate poison your life," he said with a look in his eyes that hinted at a difficult personal experience. "Maybe you put in Mexican prison. Maybe die. Maybe someone *you love* die."

Walker hadn't thought of that.

"You agree? Stay in San Diego?"

Walker promised he would, then shook the offered hand of his new teacher.

"Now run the stairs again."

To Walker's surprise, he didn't pass out on the way home; in fact, he felt more energized than ever. While climbing the steps to his apartment, a cooling breeze on his skin felt like a reassuring message from the universe, whispering in his ear to tell him he wasn't fighting alone.

The next day, minutes before quitting time, it was a warming breeze that brushed over his tan features. Walker stood on the lifeguard tower scanning a sea of cool blue ripples, with the rays of the setting sun reflecting toward him like a glittering road that stretched back to the horizon line. As the waves rolled endlessly ashore, his thoughts trended to his plans for the night: in less than an hour, he'd be playing pool with his buddies, though that hadn't been the original plan. When he'd called to invite Tina, she'd been oddly dismissive.

"What are you doing tomorrow night?" he'd asked.

"I can't talk right now."

"You okay?"

"I'll call you back."

She hadn't called him back, and since Goode wasn't bringing Lynn Peters—nor Park Carla Reyes—to what had been conceived as a couples' night out, Walker had seen fit to invite Mark Thompson, the rookie who'd helped him pull the accountant aboard at Windansea and raced him across the bay to the main tower.

When quitting time came, Walker and his good colleague Slava smiled at each other and clasped palms in a heartfelt handshake. Slava had just worked his last day in California after landing a dream job back home in Uzbekistan.

Walker trekked up to the parking area, straddled his black sport bike, and savored the coastal air rushing past his body as he set off for the freeway. Accelerating up the on-ramp, he popped a quick wheelie before merging into traffic and leaving it behind.

"Culture" was the name of an upscale pool hall on Garnet Avenue, a wide main street in Pacific Beach. College-age customers packed the bar while many groups and couples occupied a sea of pristine felt-topped tables. Threading his way back to where his friends were already playing, Walker spotted Goode, who was sharply attired in black jeans and dress shoes but seemed out of sorts, unusually sullen. Thompson looked strong and lean, younger than the others, clad in a Nor-Cal sweatshirt and a baseball cap, while Park could have been a bodyguard or a police detective, with the telltale lump of a concealed firearm bulging out from under his sport coat.

In the first game, Walker played with Thompson against Park and Goode. Walker broke, slamming the cue ball into the racked object balls with all his power. With a piercing smack, the balls ricocheted and scattered about, three of them falling into pockets. While this represented almost half the balls they needed to sink to earn a shot at the eight ball, he and Thompson were still soundly defeated.

Park was the best pool shooter Walker had ever seen. His big Asian friend had played the game for a living before landing a spot on the lifeguard towers, but he never bragged or gloated. And he didn't always try to win. Like Goode performing on stage, Park's aim was to encourage and inspire his fellows, the important thing being that everyone should have a good time.

After several games, Thompson sidled up to Walker. "Hey, isn't that your bike outside with the dollar sign on it?" he asked.

Walker rested his cue stick in a corner. "It is," he replied with gusto, since Thompson had just broached his favorite subject. Lately Walker had been thinking about motorcycles quite a lot. On the one hand, with the insurance money from the Corolla, now was the perfect time to upgrade to a newer Ninja with a bigger engine. The one he had his eye on would be quicker off the line, with a higher top speed and better braking power. On the other hand, the black Kawasaki Ninja 500R up for sale was his pride and joy. He'd kept it in pristine condition ever since he bought it when he first came to the States. It represented everything he'd been through so far as a stranger in his parents' land: the search for Trent Bolton, Hillside Baptist, making rookie of the year, the hell of a spring break in Hawaii, and being invited to join the dive rescue team. His beautiful black ride meant all of that and more, but the decision had already been made; given the opportunity, Walker wasn't going to hang on to a bike that was smaller than his girlfriend's.

Thompson raised his glass to rattle an ice cube into his mouth and chewed it up. He'd been drinking water all night. "I need a bike that can take me up to Stockton," the rookie explained. "My two-fifty's not big enough."

If anyone was going to take ownership of his pride and joy, Walker mused, that person ought to be Mark Thompson, who reminded him of himself at eighteen, except the young man showed more talent in every respect. He was a newer, better model, just as Walker's next bike was going to be.

The foursome filed out the front doors and down the street to where Walker had parked his Ninja. The clean two-wheeler sported new tires and an aftermarket exhaust pipe that purred like a satisfied tiger. As the streetlights glanced off its glossy fairings, Thompson gave a low, appreciative whistle. Walker handed him a helmet and a key. Then the rookie started her up with an excited grin, his face growing serious as he pulled into traffic for a test drive.

For a few moments, Park, Goode, and Walker stood in a silent row, just breathing the cool night air as the cars drove past. Then Goode clapped Walker on the shoulder and said, "I don't fit into the Shelby."

Was Goode trying to sell him the car? No, Walker's generous friend would never do that. Then it hit him. "Absolutely not," Walker said sharply, shaking his head, folding his arms across his chest as Goode pressed a set of keys on him.

"You *know* I don' need the money, brotha," Goode insisted. "And I'm pickin' up a new Expedition tomorrow, so you can go ahead an' take it home."

After holding Goode's gaze for a long while, Walker finally broke into a smile and accepted the offered keys. He clasped his brotha's palm and pulled him into a joyful one-armed hug.

That's when Thompson rolled back up.

"Well? What do you think?" Walker asked.

"Incredible!" the rookie replied, grinning broadly as he took off the helmet and set the machine on its kickstand. "It belongs in a showroom, not on the road."

"That old thing? It's yours. Dave just gave me his Mustang, so I want to share that good fortune with you. Please."

Thompson's face lit up like stadium floodlights.

"I gotta *go*, y'all," Goode said unexpectedly, giving no further explanation. As the entertainer set off for his nearby condo, the rest of the guys went inside for a few more games.

Thompson turned his cap backwards to shoot, dropping four balls on his first turn. It was inspiring—a little scary, even, if Walker was being honest with himself—to see the rookie coming up so hot on his heels. But it was just one more reason for him to keep pushing himself. To keep fighting, quite literally for his life and for the people he loved.

21

A REASON TO KILL

They stood in Walker's kitchen, clad in colorful one-piece leather motorcycle suits. "Okay, love. See you then," Walker said into his cell, then clicked off and turned to Thompson. "We're going to have to take off without them, but they'll meet us for lunch and we'll ride back together."

"That's actually good news," the rookie said. His words came out garbled by bran muffin, which he swallowed before speaking again. "I want to see if I can keep up with you."

Walker put on a theatrically dejected expression; shaking his head, he replied, "You can try, bro, but in terms of horsepower, my Ninja beats yours by ... thirty-six percent."

Thompson laughed.

"Just kidding," Walker said. "To be honest, I don't want to race or do anything stupid."

"Agreed, but it's actually thirty-four percent," the rookie replied, reaching for an apple in a bowl. "Just double the difference between my fifty hp and your sixty-seven. Two times seventeen is thirty-four."

Walker did the math again and, sure enough, Thompson was correct. The rookie's mental quickness reminded him of Park, whom Thompson had recently defeated on the pool table. In only one out of several games, but still it was evidence of the young man's massive potential.

After breakfast, they inspected their bikes with a full walk-around, donned their helmets, zipped up their leathers, and sped away from the coast, taking the 54 up to I-8 east. Some thirty miles later, they leaned into a left turn, heading north on State Route 79 and following it to Lake Cuyamaca. True to his word, Walker rode slowly since he didn't know how well Thompson could ride. But after an hour, once he was sure the young man knew what he was doing, Walker gestured for Thompson to pull up next to him at the first of the lakeside curves. The rookie opened up his throttle to come alongside, and they held parallel position throughout the turn.

Walker's 650R was more than meeting his expectations. It was only three years newer than his old one, but the design was far more modern, so by comparison it seemed to have been built on another planet. Like the smaller Ninja, it was all black. Just twenty-two pounds heavier and one inch taller, the new-to-him speed machine could have been the 500R's big brother, much like Walker and Thompson themselves.

Walker delighted in the fresh country air and marveled at the tree-covered hills surrounding the lake. He slowed at the second curve to let Thompson catch up again, and they went into it just as before: neck and neck, both leaning right, gunning their engines as the centrifugal force locked them down, and on the way out they bumped gloved fists with their eyes on the road.

Behind them, a distant buzz flourished into a louder, high-pitched scream. It was Tina and her sister Dulce, coming up fast, and they blew right by on a single machine. The girls looked back and waved from afar, then slowed to let the boys catch up. Tina's leathers, helmet, and bike were black and white, chosen as a nod to the traditional Mexican colors of death. Dulce wore blue jeans, a black leather jacket, and a pink full-face helmet with a stylish design.

They rode in single-file formation for the last leg of the trip: a five-mile stretch of tree-lined mountain highway into the small town of Julian.

"Let me get this straight," Thompson said, a half hour later, between bites of fresh-baked apple pie and homemade vanilla ice cream. "You and Tony fought in a thirty-person battle where you came face to face with your father's killer?"

"True story," Walker said with a frown, trying to decide how best to change the subject.

"That's rad!"

"I'm not bragging," Walker retorted, a sharp edge to his voice. "Most of our men were killed in action and I'd be dead too if it weren't for Park."

Thompson nodded and studied his food.

As they dug in, three logs blazed and crackled in a fireplace nearby. Walker noticed Dulce and Thompson inching ever closer to each other so that they now sat shoulder to shoulder. Thompson kept stealing glances at her, grinning dumbly, and Walker couldn't blame him. If Tina was a knockout, her younger sister was a death blow. Dulce beamed back at the rookie, clearly thrilled at the way things were working out.

"So how did you guys meet?" Thompson asked Tina.

"We got set up on a blind date, just like you two," Tina replied, her features brightening into that dazzling smile of hers. "First we went to Sammy's, then to Dave's concert, and Jeff just told you the rest."

"Real romantic, right?" Walker kidded. "No way y'all's first date is going to end up worse than that."

"But it wasn't the first time we saw each other," Tina reminded him, her eyes narrowing semi-playfully. "You *do* remember, don't you?"

Walker had no idea. "Oh yeah! Wow! Yes, of course," he said.

Tina dropped her chin and hiked her eyebrows, her gaze hard and incredulous. "Really? Where did you see me, then?"

Walker looked to his wingman for help.

"She was driving the ambulance that day we brought in the shooting victim," Thompson said.

"Very good, Mark," Tina said with a giggle. "So what about *you*? Do you have a girlfriend?"

"Yeah, what's your story, man?" Walker asked. "I know you're from Stockton."

"No girlfriend at the moment," Thompson told Tina, then shifted back to Walker. "And you're right about my home town. Grew up with two brothers and a single mom."

"What about sports?" Tina asked.

"I played water polo in high school. We were good, won a bunch of tournaments."

Dulce pursed her lips and shook her head. "Water polo?"

"It's like soccer but in a swimming pool," Thompson explained. "You use your hands to pass the ball around."

"Oh, yeah," Dulce said, nodding. "I've seen it on TV in the Olympics."

"Oh, *yeah*!" Tina echoed, shooting her sister a wicked grin. "Big dudes in tiny see-through swimsuits." Then she turned back to the rookie. "So you're a great swimmer."

"Better than Jeff is," Thompson replied, at which Walker nearly leapt out of his chair before he realized his buddy was messing with him. When the rookie caught Walker's eye to show he was joking, the ensuing round of laughter warmed the rustic eatery even more than the fire.

"So what did you do after high school?" Tina persisted.

"That's when I came down to San Diego. Worked nights as a dishwasher while taking classes during the day: you know, CPR, first aid, water safety. Just got hired in September."

"We're lucky to have you," Walker said, and he meant it. Mark Thompson was the little brother he'd never had.

"I appreciate that, bro," Thompson said, and he meant it, "but I think we're focusing on the wrong person here. I'd like to know more about this sweet person sitting next to me. Like what do you do, Dulce?" he asked her. "Do you work, or study? How do you spend your days?"

Dulce favored the rookie with a heart-warming smile just for him. "Well," she replied with a twinkle in her eye, "It's funny you said 'sweet' since that's what my name means in Spanish, and I'm studying computer science at SDSU."

"Cool!" Thompson exclaimed. "So you're a hacker?"

A delightful peal of laughter escaped her lips. "Not quite, but maybe someday," she said.

The young'uns made eyes at each other while Walker and Tina exchanged a knowing smile. After Walker paid the check, they all zipped up their leathers and stepped out into the crisp mountain air. Popping on their helmets, they fired up the bikes and eased onto the road in single file. Walker took the lead, then Tina, then Thompson with Dulce's arms wrapped happily around him. As before, there was no dangerous play; they hit the curves at safe speeds and made sure to keep a healthy distance between each other.

That's when it happened. Over the whooshing of the trees whipping past, Walker caught the unmistakable sound of a motor vehicle accident occurring behind him. Ice water chilled his veins and the bottom dropped out of his stomach as he pulled a sharp one-eighty and raced back to where Thompson and Dulce lay motionless on the side of the road. Both halves of his old Ninja had come to rest in the middle of the highway.

Walker skidded to a stop and hurried to drag the broken bike off the road. Then he joined Tina, who was already kneeling beside Thompson's body. At first glance, the rookie's helmet appeared to have rotated around his nonmoving head, but then Walker saw that his little bro's eyes were still lined up with his visor and his neck was tilted at a sharp and unnatural angle. Nearby, Dulce gave a low moan and cried for help.

They flipped up Thompson's visor to reveal moving lips that couldn't make a sound. His brown eyes searched theirs in terror until the life drained out of them.

For the next thirty minutes, Dulce's heart-wrenching cries echoed through the mountains until the paramedics showed up with morphine. She would never walk again.

***

The funeral was held in Stockton, where Walker trudged up to the chapel after a seven-hour drive in the Mustang, and he stayed for a small reception at the Thompson residence. When he met Mark's mother and brothers, he told them it was all his fault, but they assured him that wasn't true. Walker's deep voice faltered as he spoke of Thompson's resourcefulness in the rescue at Windansea, his skills in the water, and how good he'd been at everything else. Then, when he handed them his own rookie of the year medal, a sob welled up inside him and burst out of his mouth. They all came together in a long embrace.

Walker declined Ms. Thompson's kind offer to stay the night, then said his goodbyes and fired up the Mustang with a roar, turning a seven-hour drive into a four-hour flight. When he charged into his apartment at three in the morning, he didn't sleep, shower, or even sit down. He snatched up a bag and threw in some clothes, Park's P226, and all the cash he had.

He'd seen the cuts in his old bike's frame, and there was no question as to who was responsible. Despite his promise to Master

Chang, Walker was headed down to Mazatlan to kill a man for the first time.

22

YOU ARE THIS CLOSE

Walker pretended to cast his gaze out to sea, while in reality it was a ploy; he was stealing sidelong glances at Tina's bronze-hued curvy body, her black bikini top supporting the most luscious pair of breasts he'd ever laid his eyes on. She turned to face him, her tender eyes and smile a reassurance that she was taking real delight in his company, unlike that other girl. He'd laughed when Tina told him how she'd tricked the stripper in the surveillance center basement.

Naturally, Walker hadn't forgotten about his vendetta against the smuggler who had caused him, his family, and his friends so much suffering, but that night after Mark Thompson's funeral, while driving down to Mazatlan, his rage had slowly begun to subside. Before crossing into Mexico, it had—luckily—occurred to him that the pistol might get him in trouble at the border, so he'd pulled over and tossed it aside. A few hours later, near Mexicali, Walker had realized how difficult it was going to be to search for someone in a city of half a million people. Cage would be well-protected, and that was assuming he was even there. In the cold light of day, he was clearly headed for trouble. The sun was just peeking over the dusty hills as he made the decision to turn around. To go back home, stay safe, and continue to improve his fighting skills. And the great sex with his girlfriend was another convincing, if shallow, reason to flip a U-turn.

So it was that the new lovers sat close together on the towels they'd laid side by side on the beach, eating lunch fifty yards from Sammy's Bar and Grill, where everyone was expected to meet for dinner later in memory of Mark Thompson. Dulce wouldn't be attending; she was still in the hospital, five days post-surgery and in stable condition.

"It's so pretty here," Walker said. "But the prettiest thing about it is you."

"Thank you, Jeffrey," Tina replied with an enticing grin, the rays of the baking sun hitting her just right. "But what about you? You could be on the cover of Men's Health magazine. I bet tons of girls wiggle up to your tower with that cheesy pick-up line about you giving them mouth-to-mouth."

After they'd finished their sandwiches, Tina knelt behind him and massaged sunscreen into his back, and he did the same for her. Then they strolled hand in hand down to Mission Beach, where he showed her the main tower and pointed across the bay to lifeguard headquarters. They played frisbee on the sand and splashed each other in the waves, cooling off with a quick dip in deeper water.

On the way back to their towels, Tina had to stop to take slow breaths. Before long, she was in severe respiratory and emotional distress.

"I'm so sorry," she lamented, trembling as she heaved for air. "But I can't go with you to dinner. I'm going to take a taxi." Tears streaming down her face, she slipped into her shorts, gathered her things, and ran across the sand toward the street. Walker watched the cab as it pulled away, following it with his eyes, looking that way long after she was gone.

***

Through his master bedroom window, David Goode watched the waves as they rolled reluctantly in to shore under a blanket of clouds lit golden-brown by the setting sun. When Lynn emerged from his walk-in closet, he stood up from the bed. It was time to tell her.

The law student looked appropriately somber in a dark-blue dress with a simple string of pearls around her neck. Lovely blond hair tumbled down to her shoulders and her blue eyes seemed able to read his secret thoughts.

He wanted to say he'd slept with his backup singers, but how? There wasn't an easy way. Flying seagulls squawked outside the open window, giving him an excuse to turn back to the beach, avoiding her innocent gaze for a few more seconds. He took a breath. His heart was pounding. If he didn't tell her now, he never would. Make a decision, man!

"Ready?" he asked, forcing a smile as he reached for her hand.

***

"Any news from Taylor?" Carla asked Park as they walked hand in hand to Sammy's. She wore a plain black dress that fell to her knees, Park a dress shirt with no tie and a sport coat.

"No. Why?" he replied, irritated not only by her daily questions about the proposed cross-border operation, but also by the heat of his jacket, which he had to wear to conceal his gun.

"I'm just worried about you, that's all." She brushed a few shining locks of curly hair out of her eyes, then stopped to meet his gaze and hold both of his hands. "No, that's not all," she admitted.

"I don't want you going down to Mexico. No matter how good of a friend Jeff is." She looked down at her rounded belly and rubbed it lovingly, reminding him in not such a subtle way that his new priority in life was supposed to be the baby.

Park frowned at the unnecessary visual aid. "He's not a friend. He's my brother."

Her eyes flashed. "He's not a relative!" she snapped, abruptly dropping his hands to turn away, gesticulating wildly as she shouted at the sky. "And I'm your *fiancée*!" Then she faced him again and stepped close, apparently calmer. "I don't care how tough you are, Tony," she said. "There's always someone tougher and I'm *not* going to raise our baby alone."

"You wouldn't understand." Park shook his head as they set off again, holding hands but not like before. Instead of filling his lungs with fresh air and gazing past the beach access at the sunset while feeling secure in his relationship, Park came close to wishing he'd never even met her. Nevertheless, he walked between her and the cars on the street and watched for trouble as they made their way to Sammy's. As he held the door for her and watched her storm inside, it occurred to him that he was going to need a cocktail. Or three.

***

"You all right, miss?" Tina's taxi driver asked. The older gentleman had glanced up at the rear-view mirror and seen her crying.

"Yes. Thank you," she replied, breathing easier now that she was headed home. For months, she'd been plagued by grisly nightmares, taken straight out of her thick mental scrapbook of accident victims. The worst one of all was Mark Thompson's death, the memory of his neck forced into a right angle and his frightened eyes searching hers as he suffocated.

She hadn't been sleeping much since the bad dreams began and that was only half the problem. The other half was that by going to the beach with Jeff and planning to attend the memorial dinner, she'd disobeyed her parents. Her fear of their reaction when she made it home was what had triggered the anxiety attack.

"We're just trying to protect you," her father had told her in Spanish that morning at breakfast. "You know I like Jeff, but that's not enough. I need you to be safe."

"You were kidnapped, honey!" her mother had insisted. "You can't imagine how I'd feel if something were to happen to you."

"We've decided you can't see him anymore," her father decreed. "Not for a while, at least."

Tina had pushed away her plate of eggs and stormed back to her room. She loved her parents more than anyone else in the world. She was close to them in a way most citizens of the so-called "first world" could never understand. But she had lived long enough in that world to see that there was another way. None of her friends lived with their parents, and at twenty-five, she was more than old enough to make her own decisions. Of course she wanted—and needed—their input. But orders? Not anymore. So she'd slipped on her black bikini and waited for Jeff to pick her up, but his charming company and the romantic beach walk hadn't been able to keep her stress level out of the red zone. As the taxi eased to a stop outside her house, she knew that the time had come to make a change in her life. It wouldn't be easy.

***

Walker proposed a toast, which was neither enthusiastic nor enthusiastically received. Tina's seat was empty, Goode's easy smile absent, Lynn seemed distant and lost in thought, Park's cocktails had failed to wipe the irritation off his face, and Carla kept shooting Walker dirty looks.

"What if we took a minute for each person to say something about Mark?" Walker suggested, looking hopefully around the circle. Some of his friends shook their heads sadly while others gazed down at the silverware. No one had anything to say. Not even when their fresh, piping-hot meals were set before them.

While waiting for the valet to bring his car around after everyone else was gone, Walker pulled out his phone and made a call. It went straight to voicemail.

"Hi! This is Tina. Leave me a message and I'll call you back. ¡Adios!"

"Hey," he said at the beep. "It's me. Are you okay? If there's anything I can do, like if you want me to come over or pick you up ... whatever you need. I love you."

It was the first time Walker had said those words to Tina or anyone else except his mother, but he was so discouraged that it didn't even occur to him that he could now check off the most important item on his bucket list.

Then the valet pulled up. With Thompson's death weighing so heavily on his heart, Walker took zero joy in the popping grumble of his brand-new race car as he merged into traffic and drove it home. When he stepped into his apartment and too-calmly eased the door shut, he wound up like a pitcher and hurled his keys into the TV screen, smashing it beyond repair, vowing never to ride a motorcycle again.

***

Twenty students aged fifteen to forty stood around Master Chang's outdoor fighting ring. Before the bouts began, the master took Walker aside. Holding his thumb and index finger closely together, he whispered, "You are *this* close to be great fighter."

Strapping on his headgear, Walker nodded and thanked his teacher. He slipped his hands into point-fighting gloves, bounded up a squat set of stairs, and stepped into the ring. Despite his racing heartbeat, he popped in a mouthguard and threw a few combinations in the air, drawing a cheer from his fellow students.

With a nod, Master Chang sent in one guy after another to fight Walker full contact until each of the opponents showed signs of fatigue. After four consecutive contests, Walker's arms were tremendously heavy and his body screamed at him to take a seat. Through his dizziness, he glanced outside the ring for help, but Master Chang shook his head, and with a concerned yet determined expression he nodded one more opponent into the ring.

Walker's visions of his proud parents and a scowling Jack Cage were the only thing keeping his leaden arms up, protecting his face, so when the fifth challenger strode forward, the guy opted to snap a brutal series of round kicks into Walker's legs. Jeff stumbled and swayed, but he didn't go down. With the last iota of fight he had left, he stepped in with a decent left hook, a great shot considering his condition. He and the other guy traded punches until one of those blows knocked him senseless. When he came to, twenty students had stormed the canvas, surrounding him. They cheered and patted him on his sweaty back, offering fist bumps as Master Chang passed him a bottle of water and his opponent helped him to his feet.

After several other students had taken their turns, Walker felt good enough to jog the five miles home. He strode up the stairs to his apartment but stopped halfway up, turning to survey the evening sky. Dark rumbling thunderclouds had gathered in the distance and a brisk wind made him shiver. Stepping inside, he told

himself that Cage was gone, that it was over, but he was quick to
lock the door.

23

BOCA NEGRA

One thousand miles south of San Diego, Jack Cage reclined on a lounge chair with a laptop on his thighs, yet the painful throbbing in his head made it hard to focus on his work. He'd only slept a couple of hours, then come down to the grassy cliffside terrace on which he now sat. The rays of the early morning sun glittered on the Pacific Ocean, which stretched out to infinity, and the balmy coastal air offered refreshment to every living being, but at the moment Cage could not have cared less about his environment. He was pissed off as usual. Besides his monumental hangover and the work he needed to get through, lately he'd been beset by delays in the construction of his home in Cairns, plus a broad array of complications related to the Cartel del Norte and the North County Kings. He was currently living in Mazatlan, Mexico, in the largest of three adjacent oceanfront homes, all surrounded by a single wall. The heavily protected complex was owned by the cartel, whose smuggling pipeline remained in place, all except for the abandoned warehouse. And the biker gang was handling everything Cage used to do. Trying to, anyway. At first, the so-called Kings' incompetence had resulted in multiple seizures of cash at the border, but with Cage's input and advice, the operation was gradually reclaiming its former efficiency.

His life south of the border would have been enjoyable if it hadn't been for the cartel. If it were just a vacation. On one side of Cage's sprawling mansion, Daniels and Maria were staying in a smaller but similar home, while Maldonado, his drinking buddy, had the house on the other side to himself. Sadly, it wasn't a vacation. The cartel was up to its usual tricks, forcing him to do their dirty work and monitoring his every move with hidden surveillance equipment.

In exasperation he gave up on the digital spreadsheets and encrypted emails he'd been trying to focus on, dropped his gaze to the pool deck, and eyed last night's second bottle. Or was it the third? He'd brought it down with him when he'd come outside. Now at the tail end of a week-long drinking binge, Cage had sunk into a depression out of which, he felt, it would be impossible to climb. At this point in the bender, the booze no longer improved his disposition, no matter how much he drank. So what could he do to feel well again? With so many drugs all around, he'd begun to fantasize about snorting white again, which he knew from experience was a terrible idea. His only hope was to escape to Cairns.

A yellow-green wave of nausea washed over him as his mind dragged him back through the years to the Christian boys' home where he'd lived from age three to fourteen. There, too, he'd found himself following the orders of perverse and violent criminals. His life had only improved once he'd had the courage to run away, and that's exactly what he intended to do now.

Cage's muddled thoughts then turned to yet another source of his frustration. He felt certain Jeff Walker would never stop chasing him, and he knew he wouldn't enjoy his retirement with that fear hanging over his head. He set aside his portable computer, reached for the bottle, and made his way past the pool to a low stone wall built at the edge of a fifty-foot drop. The waist-high barrier was topped by a rubber-coated chain threaded through rods placed every six feet or so, forming a succession of black arcs that looked like smiles. He peered down at the jagged rocks below, where a tall wave came crashing to an end, delivering salty spray all the way up to his face. Cage wiped it off and gazed out at the ocean, wondering what the hell he was going to do about Walker. He upended the bottle to guzzle down the remainder, then turned away from the sea and went back to the lounge chair. A plan began to take shape in his mind as his eyes fell closed and he drifted into drunken dreams.

***

Like a soldier on duty, Walker sat rigidly alert under the blue umbrella on the rock at Windansea Beach. Last night's storm had blown over, giving way to a bright and sunny day with extra-juicy surf. He looked at the children splashing each other in the swash; none of them were too far out, and plenty of parents stood nearby. Then he raised a pair of binoculars to watch the surfers out at the farthest break, where one of his friends pulled into a perfect barrel. The waves were going off! Next he swept his eyes over the gathering crowd of beachgoers: it was a lot of people for eleven a.m., or eleven hundred, as his father might have said. Nothing out of the ordinary there, either, but a lifeguard must always keep a careful watch as disaster can strike at any time.

For instance, a few days back, Walker had rescued three fishermen right there at Windansea. After his shift, he'd been up in the parking area, talking with a group of friends. Accustomed to scanning the sea for anything untoward, he spotted a capsized fishing boat out behind the north rocks. Its crew was struggling to survive in the water, all of them screaming for help. Walker peeled off his sweatshirt, hustled down the stairs, dove in, and fought his way past the break zone in the hazy twilight. It took him two trips to tow the men back to shore through the heavy surf, and once he'd saved the last of them, he dropped to his knees in the sand, choking and wheezing with waterlogged lungs. He finally coughed it out, then headed home and had no trouble sleeping—unlike Tina, who'd told him she'd been afraid to close her eyes for fear of a bloody nightmare. In the last week, she'd only texted him once to explain her anxiety attack and her parents' decision. That had been the extent of their recent communication.

The break guard arrived at noon. Walker chatted with her for a bit, then hopped off the rock and plucked his board from the sand. It was his favorite, a 6'9" Bushman Rocket. The hot sand cushioned his feet as he ran with the board under his arm, leapt, and landed in the water with a slap. He had to paddle hard, then duck-dive under an onrushing wall of water that would have held him down if he'd been hit by it. Popping up to the surface, he gazed in awe at the incoming rows of jade-colored breakers. After two more duck-dives he made it to the take-off zone, where he greeted a friendly group he'd known for years.

When it was his turn to take off, Walker put his fingers together to paddle strong and deep, and sprang to his feet when he felt the surge of the wave behind him. His board tipped forward and dropped into a gut-wrenching free fall before slapping the face of the wave and careening down. Grabbing the rail, he set his edge, looking down the line as a translucent sheet of seawater cast itself over his head to form a spinning cylinder. *If there's a heaven, this is it*, he mused, his four-second barrel stretching on for what seemed like minutes. Then it shot him out like a cannon, spitting so hard that it nearly blew him off his board. With nothing to be gained by riding farther away from the break point, he carved a turn and launched himself over the lip of the wave before dropping onto his belly again. His buddies howled like wolves and some flashed him the shaka sign as he made his way back. Comforted by the sun, the rush, and the sparkling waves, Walker managed to let go of his worries for an hour. Later that day, he felt so much better that he decided to go on a surf trip. He'd invite Park and Goode to Boca Negra.

***

Park's glittering view of the ocean was the saving grace of the awkward situation he found himself in. He and Carla were seated on a bench on the Coast Walk Trail, a mere ten yards from the edge of a hundred-and-forty-foot cliff. He gazed out at an aerial vista of the golden California coastline, which meandered forever northward until it faded into the distance.

"You're not sure where my loyalties lie?" he said suddenly, swiveling to face her. "I've been living at your place for a year. I've asked for your hand in marriage, and now we're about to have a baby! My priorities are clear."

"*I* am about to have a baby," she countered without turning to look at him. Gusty wind blew her curly hair everywhere. "You're so busy with your certificate courses, warrior retreats, workouts, and hanging with your buddies that we never get to be alone. Every time I start to think we're finally doing better, you have to run off and do something. Usually with Jeff, and I'm *so* sick of it!" she snapped, finally turning to stab him with the daggers in her eyes.

Silence hung in the air as Park collected his thoughts, then blew out a sigh. "Why don't you come with us, then?" he suggested half-heartedly. He really didn't think she'd be interested in a sandy camping trip with no bathroom facilities, but he was wrong.

"Fine. I will. *We* will. All the girls."

"Good," he said, shifting his attention to the edge of the cliff. He'd seen the famous 1898 photograph of "Professor" Horace Poole diving headfirst from that very spot, which used to be called "Dead Man's Leap" after a failed attempt made by the mayor's son in the same year. Under normal circumstances, it wouldn't have

occurred to Park to jump from that height, but at the moment he
felt tempted.

***

It's not uncommon for surfers to spend a week or more sleeping
under the stars at Boca Negra. The secluded surf spot sits
one hundred and twenty miles south of San Diego in Baja
California, Mexico, so it wasn't a long drive, nor uncomfortable
in Goode's royal-blue Ford Expedition Platinum MAX. The
generous entertainer had backed out at the last minute, but he'd
insisted they take his brand-new eighty-thousand-dollar SUV,
arguing that the Mustang wouldn't do well in the sand and that
Park's truck was too small for the whole group, despite Park's
vehement assertions that his was a big double-cab model and
would fit them fine. Walker wasn't sure what was going on with
Goode, but he did know how single-minded Lynn was in the
pursuit of her degree and how popular his buddy was with the
opposite sex. It wasn't a match made in heaven.

Park drove and Carla served as DJ, punching buttons on a
touchscreen to sift through the songs she'd uploaded into the
infotainment system. The sound of the Expedition's engine was
slightly softer than that of the Mustang, but the twin-turbo V6
did just fine. And Park had to admit that his massive frame
fit nicely into the multi-contour, massaging driver's seat, with
ample legroom for the entire crew. Behind him, Walker and Lynn
lounged regally in a pair of second-row captain's chairs, with an
impressive array of bags and gear piled high on the third-row bench
seat. As they cruised south on a Mexican highway, the deep bass
of reggae music pumped out of twenty high-end speakers all the
way to Ensenada. At that point, Carla turned down the music
so Walker could guide them through unmarked terrain to the

crescent-shaped quarter mile of coastline he'd been surfing since he was a teenager.

They crunched to a stop in a sandy clearing next to an old brown van. As Walker stepped out, he swept his gaze along a familiar and magnificently long row of sand dunes that ran parallel to the beach, sheltering a camping area half as large as a football field from the onshore winds. He and Park pitched the tents (though Lynn insisted on setting up her own) and they built a campfire but didn't light it. Then, with little daylight left, the two lifeguards set out for what they'd come to do, plodding over the sand dunes with surfboards under their arms. Together they paddled out to the smaller and closer of the two waves that broke at that particular spot.

The sun was sinking in slow motion as Walker waited for the next set to roll in. He thought of his mother and closed his eyes to reach back for the image of her face. She was happy for him. Rooting for him. She believed in him. His eyes welled up and a fat tear brimmed over to join its ancestors in the sea, but that was all; he drew a calming breath and put a lid on his self-pity, reminding himself that it was a blessing just to have enjoyed such a special connection with her in the first place, a privilege not everyone is fortunate enough to have.

Despite his mother's death, regardless of the threat posed by Cage, and forgetting for a moment the instability of his budding romance, Walker considered himself lucky to be alive. As he bobbed in the swell, watching the sky change colors next to one of his best friends, his heart slid back into the right place.

24

LYNN'S SECRET

While Park and Walker were out surfing, Carla and Lynn settled into folding chairs by the unlit campfire to soak up the last of the sun, their eyes shielded by dark sunglasses. The steady thumping of breaking waves could be heard but not seen over the long row of dunes as Carla pulled an ice-cold bottle of chardonnay out of a cooler placed next to her chair, then popped the cork and poured a generous measure into a plastic cup.

"Thank you," said her blond-haired companion, accepting the offered beverage with both hands. "So what made you want to come?"

"I just love getting out in nature. Helps me think," Carla answered truthfully, but that wasn't why she'd made the trip.

Lynn nodded as she turned her gaze forward to bask in the fading warmth, sipping the first of her white wine.

Carla wasn't yet well acquainted with Lynn, but she did need a friendly ear. Pulling out a bottle of water for herself and closing the cooler's lid, she said, "Okay, that's not really true. Actually, things have been rocky with Tony and me. I didn't know what to do about it, so I came along, hoping the time together would be good for us."

"I hear that," said the other, busying herself with most of the rest of her chardonnay.

The women drifted into separate thoughts for a moment while the sun dipped behind the dunes, shifting languidly from bright orange to dark red, infusing the scattered clouds with such colors. As Carla screwed the cap back on her water bottle, her gaze was drawn across the campground to the only other set of tents. She didn't see anyone there, and since Lynn hadn't taken the opportunity to explain why David Goode had canceled at the last minute, she changed the subject. "I hope the guys don't get hurt out there."

Lynn shook her head. "They won't. Not today, anyway. Jeff told me the beach break's an easy wave, that it's the reef break farther out that can send a surfer to the hospital. Or worse." They settled into silence for a bit, the crashing of waves the only sound. Then: "I assume you invited Tina."

Carla's lips curved into a tight smile. "I did. But she's having problems, too." She raised the wine bottle as well as her eyebrows. Lynn held out the empty plastic cup. "So how's law school?" Carla asked in mid-pour. "You're in your third year, no?"

"Second. But it's going well, thank you. I'll be working as an intern at the DA's Office this summer."

"Congratulations!" Carla shoved the wine bottle back into the ice and swung the top shut again.

"What about you? Are you going to take time off to raise the baby?"

"Good question. Yes, but I don't know how long."

Lynn raised her cup to propose a toast but her voice broke when she said, "Here's to you ... and the baby ... *Salud*."

"*Salud, amiga*," Carla returned, touching the offered cup with her water bottle. She was mystified by the tears rolling down Lynn's cheeks, but thought it better to wait for her friend to share what was wrong than to ask an invasive question.

Again the blonde law student gave no explanation, so the women turned west once more, gazing into the sun as it shrank imperceptibly, until it was but a glowing red blip at the top of a dune. And then it was gone.

***

The waves at the beach break were small but fun, a perfect warm-up for the outrageous surf Park and Walker would be facing the following morning. After the sun went down, they rode a wave all the way in and jogged up the beach, carrying their boards and chuckling all the way to camp. Walker saw two fires blazing: theirs and that of the unknown party on the other side of the clearing. He and Park ducked into separate tents and threw on jeans and T-shirts before coming out to join the gals. As dusk eased into night, the sky bloomed into a twinkling canopy of stars and the light of the crackling fire danced on all their faces.

"Thanks for inviting us, bro," Park said, raising a bottle of beer. "Don't worry. She'll come around."

Mirroring the gesture, Walker lifted an icy brew of his own, took a pull, and said, "Let's look at the upside. This is an opportunity for me to focus on the waves. I've gotten rusty."

As the night wore on, Carla was lively and entertaining, but Lynn hardly spoke at all. When they tried to include her, she came back with short, flat answers. Then, when the conversation turned to pregnancy and plans to marry, the straight-A student rose, bade them goodnight, and hurried off to her tent.

Carla followed her in and asked what was the matter.

"I got an abortion," Lynn explained between sobs, covering her face with her hands.

"Oh no!" Carla exclaimed. She took a seat beside her friend on a sleeping bag. "Did you tell Dave?"

Lynn cried harder at the question, but before long she regained her composure with a shaky breath and wiped her red, watery eyes. "Well, he knew I was pregnant. After the memorial dinner at Sammy's, we went back to his place and I told him. Right then and there he signed over his condo to me to show his support, but he also said he'd been seeing someone else. So I went ahead with the procedure." When she met Carla's gaze, her quivering lips fell into a pitiful frown, and then she hung her head.

Carla put a hand on Lynn's shuddering back and comforted her friend in silence as she wept for half an hour.

***

After a few more beers and a great many laughs, the hypnotic flicker and the warmth of the campfire had lulled Walker into a sleepy condition. He offered Park a knuckle smack and retired to his tent. Zipping himself in, he sorted himself out on his sleeping bag and interlaced his fingers behind his head. The next day's surf session was going to be gnarly. He was getting stoked! A picture kept popping into his mind, that of a twenty-foot drop as seen from the top of a monster wave. The trick was to outrun the charging wall of water without being pitched over the falls, pushed down, and pinballed through the reef. He told himself he'd be fine; after all, years earlier, he'd made the finals at Zicatela Beach, the Mexican version of Oahu's famous Banzai Pipeline.

Walker brought his arms to his side, closed his eyes, and drew air into the farthest reaches of his belly, then allowed it to slowly escape on its own. When his lungs were empty, he waited to breathe until his body asked for more. After several gentle cycles, his respiration grew so slow that a single repetition might have lasted thirty seconds.

Master Chang had taught him to let his thoughts go in meditation. To watch them float by like passing clouds. As his mind relaxed and his thoughts drifted farther and farther apart, breathing became the only focus. Each inhalation plunged him deeper into the shifting patterns of colors he saw through his third eye. At some point, even the task of breathing was taken over by an unseen force, freeing him to experience a timeless peace.

At sunrise, he and Park paddled out to the farthest break, where mountainous steel-blue breakers pounded the reef again and again. For hours they scored long, exhilarating rides up and down the rushing peaks. Time slowed and their bodies buzzed as they dropped into spinning blue rooms and got shot out like bullets.

Not surprisingly, the line for this particular attraction was a short one. The only other surfers in the water were the mystery campers: three guys from Hawaii named Sharky, Towney, and Davey. They said they had to leave later that day but had caught too many fish to eat by themselves, so they invited Park and Walker to join them for breakfast. It was easy to agree to fresh fish tacos after pushing their bodies to the limit for hours on end.

Charlie "Sharky" Cornell, of the same family that founded the university in New York, got busy flipping whole sea basses and yellowtail fillets on a portable grill he'd set over his campfire. Like Walker's, his hair was blond, but it was much longer, falling straight down to his shoulders. The only item of clothing he wore was a red pair of board shorts. The leathery texture of his deeply tanned skin and his strong, trim body hinted at how much time Sharky had spent in the water over his fifty years of age. His smile was infectious, his laugh contagious.

Park and Walker squeezed lime juice onto the steaming meat and salted it over a tortilla, devouring one scrumptious taco after another while Sharky regaled them with tales of his travels to famous waves all over the world. The seasoned surfer said that all those stories and more were compiled in his latest book, entitled *Surf Adventures*, and that he was also a musician and a record producer. If they were interested, his books and music would be easy to find online.

Once everyone had eaten their fill, Towney brought out his sax, Davey a set of bongo drums, and Sharky slipped a guitar strap over his head. Yet the guys from Hawaii weren't the first to offer a musical performance that morning—desert birds chirped, beetles buzzed, and a lone wild donkey brayed in the distance over the crashing waves—so, in fact, they were joining a work in progress when they kicked off a rocking groove called "Tropical Dreams." Towney belted out the lyrics and Sharky sang harmony while Davey pounded out the beat. Walker and Park clapped along, grinning and bobbing their heads to the tune.

The second number was a slower, hard-hitting blues entitled "Cruzin." As Sharky strummed the strings and Davey kept things moving, Towney warmed up his sax with his breath, clacking the keys with his fingers, waiting for his turn to take a solo. When the time came, he slipped the mouthpiece between his lips and launched into a fiery blend of passion and technical prowess. His improvisation led the tiny ensemble to dizzying heights. In Walker's opinion, the blazing solo was too long-winded, but when it finally came to an end, he high-fived the saxman while Sharky and Davey rocked on. Then, with a start, Walker realized the jam session had become a concert. Three women, not two, had walked across the clearing to join them.

Carla and Lynn had supposedly gone into town for supplies, but they'd been keeping a secret. Walker's gaze flitted from their excited faces to the third new arrival, who was beaming at him with a heart-stopping smile and those dark, exotic eyes. Tina had decided to trust him.

Sharky cast Walker a side-eye and smoothly transitioned into "Sexy Eyes," a slow, sultry ballad, as Walker and Tina stepped out of the circle to hug and kiss and whisper private words.

When the music stopped, the mood was one of celebration. Even Lynn was smiling and laughing. Backs were clapped, strong Hawaiian handshakes were exchanged, and well-wishes were spread all around.

Soon thereafter, Sharky, Towney, and Davey flashed the shaka sign and piled in to their brown van, beaming encouraging smiles as they disappeared over the hill. Walker and company headed back to their tents, expecting two more carefree days in the sun, with no problems of any kind.

25

MONSTER WAVES

Following unsuccessful chemotherapy, laparoscopy, and a last-resort total pancreatectomy, Christine Walker's cancer has been declared terminal. To make the most of her remaining time, she has discontinued all forms of treatment. Sixteen-year-old Jeff Walker takes her hand as they step onto the sand at Rosarito Beach. Shriveled by her disease and the failed treatment, the sixty-five-pound woman looks nothing like her former self. There is no sparkle in her sunken eyes; her emaciated frame and hollow cheeks are reminiscent of a desiccated corpse in a mummy museum.

She manages a hundred yards before saying she needs a rest. Walker steadies her as she gasps for air. After a few minutes, the alarm in her eyes fades and she attempts a smile, but there is so much suffering behind it that it looks like a grimace. Walker would later repress this ghastly facial expression so far back in his memory that he would only see it a few more times, and only when he was dreaming.

"Remember, Jeffrey," she croaks out. "Mommy loves you."

He wants to fall to his knees but watches for signs of fainting instead. "I love you too, Mom. You know I do."

She does know. Ever since she came home from the hospital, he's been managing her diet and medication and helping with everything from bathing to butt-wiping. He knows as much about pancreatic cancer as an oncologist.

Walker holds out his arms to offer his mom an embrace. When he wraps them around her scrawny back, a lump forms in his throat. Mother and son feel each other breathe for the last time as the final rays of sunlight drain out of the sky.

She makes it halfway back to the car before she has another episode, so he carries her the rest of the way; she's as light as a child. As he stoops to set her down in the passenger seat, he sees she's fallen asleep in his arms. On the way back home, he turns to check on her and she's still dozing. *One of these days,* he thinks, *she's going to look just like that but she won't be sleeping. She'll be dead.*

Walker's eyes shot open. Dark, unbearable emotions had seized him in their crushing grip and his heart was slamming against his ribcage. He pecked a sleeping Tina on her forehead and wriggled out of the double sleeping bag they'd made, then slipped on board shorts and stole out of the tent.

Every cell in Walker's body screamed at him to stop, to wait for Park before paddling out to the reef break, but he was past the point of no return. As night broke into day, he made his way out to the monster waves, desperate for a rush to ease his pain.

***

Tina stirred, blinked open her eyes, stretched her legs, and climbed out of the double sleeping bag. Jeff was probably out running or hiking, she figured, but when she emerged into the cool coastal air and counted the surfboards, an icy jolt of dread hit her like a freight train. She hurried over the dunes and down to the shore. The surf at the beach break was head high, bigger than the day before, so the swell at the reef would also have grown in size. She ran her gaze out half a mile, gaping at the sight of a wave as high as a castle wall.

Its crest began to slowly crumble, then faster and faster it curled, plummeting thirty-five feet down to the reef on which it exploded with a sound like thunder. She would have needed binoculars to know for sure whether Walker was out there, but where else could he be?

It was then that she swore to herself that she'd quit her job as a paramedic and enroll in beauty school, which she'd always wanted to do. Last on the list of things she wanted to see that day was another bloody vision, especially not her boyfriend's mangled corpse washing up onto shore.

***

Walker shook from the rush as he paddled back out to the reef for the sixth time. Wave after massive wave shoved him back toward the beach, but he muscled himself out past the break line once again. His heart was firing like heavy machine guns and his eyes were wild like those of a drug user. As a blue mountain loomed over him, he ignored the panic in his gut and pivoted, paddling and kicking with deep-rooted wrath. The sea lifted him high into the air and the tip of his board fell ninety degrees, so that he was staring down the highest vertical drop he had ever attempted. Walker charged it! Fear melted into elation as he reached fifty miles an hour, rushing toward the trough, the steep face snapping at his heels like a giant pack of wolves. With all that water sucking up to form the wave, the reef was closer to the surface than usual, some parts just inches below the trough. As he carved a hard right turn, the barrel began to throw itself over his head. This was going to be a great campfire story!

It might have been that awful dream creeping back into his mind that caused him to stumble, or just an unlucky ripple that knocked him off-track. In any case, Walker lost his balance and fell. The avalanche pounded him down and raked his body across the reef like soft cheese on a grater. In blinding pain, he tumbled and spun, with no idea which way was up. His lungs begged him to take a breath, but he forced himself to resist the urge and to think his way out of this predicament. The leash on his leg was being pulled toward the surface by the buoyancy of his board, so he swam in that direction until his head popped out of the churning whitewash. Walker gasped for air as his eyes climbed higher and higher up the face of a second killer wave that was about to drop on him like ten truckloads of wet concrete. He hastened to undo the ankle strap that shackled him to his board and tightly crossed his arms so his shoulders wouldn't be torn out of their sockets, then took as many breaths as he could before the mountain came crashing down.

Once more, Walker was held under water and dragged across the reef, but this time his ankle got caught in a crevice. Horrified, he tugged and jerked on it, tearing skin and muscle in a failed effort to free himself. The churn thrashed his body about like a flag in a hurricane as he burned through all the oxygen he had left, until finally his foot popped free! He scrambled to the surface, thinking ahead to what he'd find up there: a third wave and a fourth, and on and on until he swam clear of the danger zone, so when he hit the surface, he sucked in a breath and instantly set off on a course parallel to the beach. The monster waves held him down and choked him like a schoolyard bully, but he had nothing to lose and everything to gain; he was a champion swimmer swimming for his life.

Walker escaped to a safer spot, but by then he had breathed in too much water. Feeble and semiconscious as he veered toward the shore, he made it to the beach break, but that's where one more lungful caused him to—

***

A head-high wave tossed Walker's limp figure over the falls like a rag doll, plunging it deep under the water. As his lifeless body hovered halfway between the sea floor and the surface, Park ran down the beach, sprinted through the whitewater, dove in, and grabbed his bleeding buddy by the arms. He dragged Walker up through the swash onto dry sand, leaving a dark crimson trail behind him. Then Tina took over. She knelt beside her unconscious love with everyone huddled around. "He's not breathing, but he still has a pulse!" she reported, pinching his nose and tilting his chin to open the airway. She initiated rescue breathing, also called mouth-to-mouth. For an excruciatingly long minute, there was no reaction, but at last Walker's lungs took the hint. No cheers rose up from the worried circle of friends as Tina turned his body to one side and he coughed up and vomited a gallon of water.

She swept her practiced eyes over the deep lacerations all over his body, the worst of which was that shredded ankle. Thick flaps of bloody flesh hung down to expose the bone. Happily, the professional first aid supplies she'd brought included a suture kit. "Let's get him back to camp," she said.

Park hoisted his half-conscious brother over his shoulder and carried him over the dunes, just as Walker had carried his dying mother to the car.

***

A few days earlier, Maldonado and Daniels had stepped out of baggage claim onto the curb at San Diego International Airport, where the air was cooler and drier than it had been in Mazatlan.

They nodded to a pair of Harbor Police officers patrolling the pick-up zone, who returned the greeting and went on their unsuspecting way. Then they took a taxi to an automobile storage facility, where they reclaimed the one SRT they'd left behind. Maldonado drove them up the coast to the Carlsbad boathouse facility, where they ate, drank, geared up, and waited for nightfall.

Under the cover of darkness, they visited Walker's apartment complex, Tina's parents' house, Carla's cozy duplex unit, and David Goode's condo building, where they stuck tracking devices to the underside of everyone's vehicles, their orders being to find Walker and deliver him to Cage.

"JusdoasIfuckinsay," Cage had replied, his normally incisive mind clouded by his liquid diet, when Maldonado had asked why he shouldn't just kill the lifeguard on sight.

When most of the target vehicles had assembled at Carla's duplex and one of them drove down into Mexico, Cage's men had followed the signal to Boca Negra. Now, after watching the campground for a day, waiting for the optimal time to strike, their patience had finally been rewarded.

"It's not going to get any better than this," Maldonado hissed. He and Daniels lay on their bellies behind the crest of a distant sand dune as Park, Lynn, Tina, and Carla headed for the beach, leaving an injured Walker alone in his tent.

They ran to the camp in a crouch with pistols drawn. Within minutes, Walker was bound, gagged, and stuffed into a coffin-like hidden compartment under the SRT's second row of seats. His situation had gone from shit to bloody diarrhea.

Maldonado dropped the black armored vehicle into gear and raced away. Its precision engine purred with satisfaction all the way to La Paz, where he drove onto a ferry that would take them to Mazatlan.

26

BAD LUCK WITH COMPUTERS

The Australian sun toasted Jack Cage's back as he took his exercise. Gliding through the last four feet of his final lap in the pool, he stretched out his arm, touched the wall, planted his feet, and popped off his goggles to set them on his forehead. Practicing this or one of many other kinds of cardiovascular conditioning had been a daily habit for most of his life, though recently he'd been off and on. Today, however, Cage was "on" in every sense of the word: the other swimmers were smiling at him; not a single cloud marred the calm blue sky and an offshore breeze kept the heat at bay; down by the beach, endless rows of sparkling turquoise waves washed up onto the golden shore; his identity documents were now in his possession and the construction of his cliffside home all but complete. This day might well have been the best of all his life.

To celebrate, Cage was staying for a few extra days in a horribly expensive resort just a few blocks from his new house. Eating well and drinking less, he'd been strolling to the site every afternoon to supervise the final phase of construction. Today they'd be installing the jacuzzi.

Up on the deck, a cute young thing lay stretched out on a lounge chair, her miniature two-piece leaving little to the imagination.

This was the companion he'd hired for the duration of his stay. Her lovely face broke into a half-smile; she briefly waved, then returned to the magazine in her lap. Cage pulled his goggles back on and cooled off with a few more laps, then hauled himself up the ladder and headed for the lounge chair next to hers.

Without looking away from her reading material, she plucked a single French fry from a plate on the table beside her and bit into it daintily.

"Looking good, babe," he said as he toweled himself off. He was about to raise a hand to divert the attention of a passing waiter when his burner phone clamored for his own. The caller could only be Maldonado, he knew, so he reached for the device to take the call.

"D2 for D1."

"Go."

"Mission complete. We just drove aboard. ETA is thirteen hours."

"Copy. I'll be there in twenty-four." Cage performed a quick calculation. "Nineteen hundred your time tomorrow. Don't do anything until I arrive. Just stay alert, especially at night. Out."

***

At 0200 San Diego time, Park slid behind the wheel of his Toyota Tundra SR5 4x4, which was "displayed," as the dealerships like to say, in Nautical Blue Metallic. The brawny pickup was ten years old but still in showroom condition, with a beefy set of all-terrain tires, a 3.5-inch lift kit, a dual cat-back exhaust system, a cold air intake, and various other modifications that Walker had helped install to crank up its 5.7-liter V8's three hundred and eighty-one horses to well over four hundred. Once Goode had climbed in beside him, Park hit the accelerator with his steel-toe tactical boot and squealed up the ramp and out of Goode's parking garage onto the dark and rainy street. His ultra-bright LED headlights cut through the night as they barreled north on I-5 along a coast they couldn't see. Headed for Thunder Road, a biker bar in Oceanside owned by the North County Kings, they went over the plan as they traveled.

It wasn't long before Park and Goode came to a long one-story building with a purple neon sign and a handful of cruiser bikes lined up by the front door. Park drove on for two blocks and pulled over to watch the place, waiting for the neon sign to turn off and for all the motorcycles to grumble away, and then an extra fifteen minutes just in case.

They pulled on black full-face masks and hustled to the front of the bar. Careful not to crunch his boots on the gravel, Park made for the right side of the building with Goode behind him. Aided by the distant streetlights, he peered through his P320's sights and sliced the pie until he had an unobstructed view around the corner. "Clear," he said.

Goode hurried forward to the side window and smashed it in with a metal baseball bat, triggering a shrieking alarm. He knocked most of the remaining glass inside, making sure he cleared the lower edge, and stepped back as Park set one tactical-glove-covered hand on the windowsill and leapt inside, pistol up, panning left and right, scanning for any hidden threat among the dark stacks of tables. "Clear," he said again. Goode's boots hit the floor beside him.

The noisy alarm blared on as they sprinted behind the bar to a door they found locked and shoulder-smashed in on the count of three. Park rifled through the desk while Goode unplugged a desktop computer and tucked it under his arm like a football.

"Ready?" Park asked. "Let's go!"

They hustled back out through the stacks of tables, bounded over the windowsill, and flew down the block to the pickup. The

Tundra's engine grumbled to life at the turn of a key and Park took the corner hard, roaring down the boulevard back to the coastal highway.

Unlike Goode, Park wasn't religious, but his silent cry of hope that the computer might contain some clue as to Walker's whereabouts, which he cast into the infinite universe, desperately hoping to be heard by the source of his life, was just as fervent as any prayer that ever crossed the lips of the most passionate of believers.

***

Four cruiser bikes screamed back to the bar in single file. The Kings' new leader, a brown-skinned bruiser by the name of Chucky Matón, was the first to dismount. Crunching across the gravel to the busted side window, he dropped his gaze to the shattered glass on the ground. "Fuck!" he screamed. Matón stormed back to the front door, let himself in, killed the alarm, and threaded his way past the stacks of tables to his office. When he shoved the smashed-in door fully open and saw what was missing, a cold, sudden dread made him shiver. Maldonado was going to hurt him for this.

***

"I don't want to know how y'all got ahold of that computer," Sergeant Taylor said from behind his desk, "but you struck gold. We found him."

Seated before him in a row, Park and Goode bumped fists and grinned at each other while Tina let out an audible sigh. "As you know," Taylor continued, "I did manage to secure the cooperation of the DEA, meaning access to better surveillance and faster transportation, as you'll see in a minute."

The new leader of the narcotics task force had on a white long-sleeved shirt with the cuffs rolled up to his elbows, exposing thick, knotted forearms. He kept his hair shaved at the sides and short on top, not unlike Park's own semi-military cut. Park was counting on that connection since as civilians, he and his friends were expressly forbidden to participate in the rescue operation; he'd put his great brain to work and come up with a plan that hinged on Taylor's sense of loyalty to a fellow soldier.

Sean Choi trudged absentmindedly into the office. "Morning," he mumbled, then set his laptop on the desk. He failed to shake a single hand, but he did brush his unruly hair out of his face to look them in the eyes with an awkward smile. Then he pried open the portable machine so that everyone but Taylor could see the screen. Standing out of the way, beside his boss's desk with a presenter remote in hand, Choi straightened his shirt, cleared his throat, and then he was off. "The computer that somehow fell into your laps was one of the machines from the warehouse facility," he said. "From the surveillance center, to be exact. Its hard disk had been wiped clean, but not clean enough."

Park was reminded of the laptop they'd recovered at Big Rock. "Cage has been having bad luck with computers lately," he observed.

Sean Choi was the only person in the room who did not burst into laughter at the joke. Smiling grimly, he waited for silence like a schoolteacher before going on. "Among the data I was able to recover was a GPS tracking program, which Cage had been using to monitor a small fleet of tractor-trailers as well as the twin SRTs and his Shelby F-150." Choi's once-bleary eyes were now sharp and quick as he clicked a button to call up an aerial satellite image. "If you look at the time stamp," he told them, "you'll see that both black Jeeps and the F-150 are currently parked in a residential complex in Mazatlan. One of the SRTs just arrived. It rolled off a ferry a few hours ago and stopped at a restaurant, where this next image was collected. Take a look." Choi zoomed in on three men standing by the SRT. Two had dark hair; the other was blond with a bandage wrapped around his ankle.

"We *know* Cage considers Walker a risk," Goode pointed out. "So why go to the trouble of kidnappin' him? Why wouldn't he just order his men to kill him?"

"I don't know," Taylor replied. "It seems strange to me as well. My guess is Cage wants to take him out personally. Seeing-is-believing kind of thing."

"So this is a delivery," said Goode. "And we're too late. It'll take us half a day to get down there."

"Us?" Taylor retorted dryly.

"No, we're not too late," Choi interjected, clicking again to pull up a picture of a boarding pass. "Not yet, anyway. As we speak, Jack Cage is flying first-class from Australia to Mexico City on a seven forty-seven. He's fifteen hours away from Mazatlan."

"Thank you, Sean," Taylor said. "And in your case it *is* 'we.' I'm going to need you on this one."

Choi's eyes went wide, but he nodded meekly.

Taylor turned back to Park and Goode and held their gazes. "Here's the plan. I've got a DEA aircraft waiting for me and my team at the airport—"

"I'm in," Tina interrupted. "I've got a feeling someone's going to need a paramedic."

Taylor smiled but he shook his head. "You're out and you know it."

Park rose from his chair. Here goes. Fingers crossed. "I know how bad you want to nail this guy," he began, crossing his big arms over a bulging chest.

"You're not wrong," Taylor said. "My interest in this case is extremely personal. Big Don and I were working it together."

"And you know how much Walker means to us."

"You can stop right there, Park. You almost got me fired when you showed up at the warehouse with rifles and tactical gear."

Resisting the impulse to argue that he'd saved Taylor's life by showing up like that, Park stuck to his plan and dropped the bomb. "Did the DEA request and receive authorization from the Mexican Federal Prosecutor's Office?" he asked. "And will you be working with the Mexican Federal Police?"

Taylor's fallen features were answer enough. No and no. Just as Park had suspected.

"Because the Mexican Security Act establishes, and I quote in translation, that 'all enforcement of foreign laws or judgments shall be performed through bilateral cooperation with the Mexican Federal Police, subject to prior written authorization from the Federal Prosecutor.' I'd hate for your plane to be met on the ground and detained by the Mexican military. I don't want to place that call, but I will if I have to."

Taylor's face turned red and he flew out of his seat. "That law was just passed!" he thundered, stabbing a finger in the air.

"Come on, man," Park pressed in a softer tone of voice. "You're Special Forces. I was a SEAL. You know Dave can handle himself, and a medic's *always* good to have. We want to help, and it's not illegal for us to be there by chance and pitch in if we see someone in trouble. My Navy buddies are waiting to fly us down there right now."

Taylor fell silent. No one else spoke. Choi looked uncomfortable as the trio fixed the angry sergeant with pitifully hopeful expressions, like dogs under the dinner table.

Finally Taylor sank back into his chair and relented. "Fine. We're actually low on manpower at the moment. I'll text you the coordinates of the base camp."

27

WALKER'S LAST MEAL

The bitter cold made Walker shiver at the end of a long night in the SRT's secret compartment, which he'd spent breathing through his nose at the gap in the lid, but now the wait was over. Lying on his side in the dark, he heard and felt his captors drop into their seats and slam their doors. When the driver started the engine, fresh, warm air flowed into the coffin-like space, at last!

Some time later, the Jeep jerked to a halt to let someone out on the passenger side. Then it set off again, stopping after less than a minute. This time the driver got out, opened the rear door, and swung back the second row of seats. Walker groaned out loud. He could guess the identity of the man he was about to see, and he wasn't thrilled about it. Not with his hands and feet bound and a badly injured ankle.

Maldonado threw open the lid and smirked with amusement at Walker's piss-stained jeans, his bloody bandage, and the snot crusted all over his face.

"I need to use the bathroom," said Walker.

"Get out." The crook's mocking grin grew wider as his captive inched awkwardly out of the box like a man-sized centipede, worming his way out of the vehicle. Only then did Maldonado cut the duct tape around Walker's ankles with a knife. "Don't yell for help or do anything stupid," he said as he worked. "I won't think twice about breaking your leg."

Walker knew his captor's threat wasn't an empty one. The man was a trained killer and a sadist to boot, and since the lumpy scar that stretched across his face would be a permanent reminder of Walker and the failed attack at The East End, the mercenary would naturally be eager to make him suffer. And it really *was* a horrible scar; the knotted mark looked even worse than it had when it was fresh and pouring blood, if such a thing were possible.

Walker stayed in the SRT on the second-row bench seat, watching as Maldonado filled it up with gas. As Scarface returned the nozzle to its place, a look of self-conscious insecurity passed over his ruined features, but his arrogance was back in no time. "Enjoying your last day on Earth?" the man asked through the cracked-open window, then slid behind the wheel. "I'll take you to the bathroom," he went on, closing his door, "but not here at the gas station, since that might remind you of something tragic." He made a mocking pout with his lips while tracing a tear from his eye to his chin with his middle finger, then drove in reverse to the adjoining restaurant, his eyes alight with glee as he watched for an angry reaction.

Daniels stood waiting at the curb with bags of food in his hands.

"We'll be back in ten," Maldonado said, hopping out as Daniels slid in on the other side.

Walker fumed, his bound hands balling into fists as Scarface stepped back to the rear door and opened it.

"You go in first," Maldonado said. "Hide your wrists under your sweatshirt and remember what I told you."

Walker limped and hopped into the restaurant, favoring his good foot and resisting the urge to cry out in pain. Once he'd gone back to the bathroom and taken a seat in a stall, he called out to his captor, "A fair fight. That's all I want. Right here, right now."

Maldonado gave a derisive snort from the other side of the door.

A few minutes later, as Walker flushed and stepped out, a big overhand right caught him in the eye and knocked him back inside, where he slammed his head on the toilet. On the cold tile Walker stayed, stunned, and Maldonado stepped up to the commode to relieve himself.

"A fair fight?" the guard captain said, turning midstream to piss on Walker's face. "Nothing in life is fair. Get up or I'll hit you again," he commanded as he zipped up his fly.

Walker sat on the second-row bench seat as Maldonado drove into Mazatlan, steering through the city center into an affluent part of town, then winding his way to a massive solid-metal gate and braking to a halt. The towering portal appeared to be the only way in or out of a complex surrounded by a high white wall topped with concertina wire. A uniformed guard marched out of a nearby security station and rendered a salute, holding the formal gesture until Maldonado and Daniels returned it. Then he approached Walker's window, squinting to peer through the tinted polycarbonate. Satisfied, he looked back at the guard house, gave a nod, and the gate slid open to let them in.

The SRT lurched into motion and rolled up a circular driveway that served three stately homes standing in a row to the right. The first one they passed was large and modern, finished in white stucco, then a grander one in the middle, followed by a third that was identical to the first. As Walker hobbled up to the front door of this last house, shoved there and taunted all the while by you-know-who, he fixed his gaze past an open walkway that stretched between two of the homes. On the far side he saw a swimming pool, and past that, a low stone wall that ran along the cliffside edge of the property. A booming splash told him the waves down below were rough, but he couldn't see them from where he was.

The interior of the house was as elegant as one might have expected, but devoid of any signs of actual life. Maldonado grabbed Walker by his damp, stinky sweatshirt and help-dragged him to the top of the stairs. At the landing, Walker shrugged him off and they headed right, into a hallway where Maldonado stopped to enter a code on a keypad. "It won't be long now," the wiry sadist jeered, pulling open a door and nodding his captive inside. "Don't fuck with the tape on your wrists. I'll break your hands if you do."

Daniels caught the heavy door as Maldonado turned to leave. "He means it. I'll come for you at dinnertime and Cage'll be here shortly after that." Then his eyes went cold and he slammed the door shut.

Walker thought he'd seen a look of concern flash across Daniels' face, but he wasn't sure and he didn't care. He kicked off his only flip-flop and padded across white, deep-pile carpet to a large window in the center of the far wall that afforded him a spectacular view of the Pacific Ocean, yet he was neither soothed nor calmed; he was mortally afraid. By rapping his knuckles on the transparent portal, he learned it wasn't made of glass. And even if he did manage to break it, there'd be no way over or around the wide ribbon of jagged rocks at the base of the cliff. In his condition, the massive waves would grind him into sausage meat before he could pick his way through the boulders and slip into the sea.

Walker turned away and limped to the bathroom. The lights didn't work, but the faucet did. He splashed some water on his face and looked into the mirror at his sorry reflection: his right eye was black, blue, and swollen shut, a tender lump had formed at his temple, and the rest of his face was still covered in scratches from the surfing accident. Frowning, he made for the bed and laid himself gingerly down. The bare mattress offered no sheets or pillows, but it felt decadent after being trapped in the hidden compartment for such a long time. Before his tired thoughts melded into a subconscious jumble, he determined that he would palm a knife or fork at dinner, then use it to get his hands on a gun.

The pounding of a fist at the door jolted him awake. Outside, the sun had dipped halfway into the sea, so he'd been asleep for hours. Time was running out!

The door swung open. "After you," Daniels grunted, ordering Walker down the stairs with a flick of his pistol, his steely eyes a warning against any attempt at escape. The square-jawed mercenary was similar to Walker in height and build, but his brown hair was cut short like a soldier's, while Walker's was a long blond mop. Daniels trailed him down the stairs at a safe distance with his pistol trained on his back.

Two armed guards wearing olive-green uniforms and duty belts loaded with deadly equipment received them at the foot of the stairs. Daniels peeled off to a different part of the house as the guards led Walker to a dining room, where steaming platters of Mexican food had been set on a long, polished-wood dinner table. Maldonado and Daniels strode in together and the two guards snapped to attention.

"I'd eat up if I were you," Maldonado sneered, glancing at Walker's empty plate as he served himself. "This is literally your last meal. By the way, how's that eye? And what's that smell?" He cackled under his breath as he took a seat at the table.

Daniels cut the tape around Walker's wrists with a table knife, then picked up his plate to serve himself. Maldonado was busy with his food, so as Daniels loaded his own plate, Walker set his hand on the table as though he were supporting his weight and slipped the knife into his sleeve with the two guards watching his back.

After a silent meal, the guard captains stayed at the table to sip their coffee. At a nod from Maldonado, the guards in the corners ordered Walker to his feet. The time to act was now, while Cage was still in transit and before Walker was locked in his room again. He inched the tip of the knife toward the sleeve of his sweatshirt. It was a heavy piece of silverware, but it wasn't sharp or pointed, making for an extremely short list of target zones: left eye or right eye. His heart pumped with so much force that he felt the rushing blood in his hands, arms, and ears.

One guard started up the stairs with Walker behind him, and a second brought up the rear with a pistol aimed at Walker's back. When the first guy reached the top of the stairs, he turned right, paused at the keypad, and struggled to recall the correct sequence of digits. Now! Walker spun around and knocked the second guard's shooting hand aside with his left hand while burying the knife deep into the man's eye with his right; judging by the juicy thwock he heard and felt, his overhand stab had made it into the brain. Both guards went down: one for obvious reasons, and the other as a pair of bullets fired by his partner struck him in the chest.

The sound of heavy boots came clomping up the stairs. Walker dove for the smoking gun, got his hands around the grip, and rolled onto his back to fire, but Maldonado was on him before he could get his finger into the trigger guard. The scar-faced killer ripped the pistol out of Walker's grasp and jabbed its muzzle into his black eye. Walker cried out in pain, and Daniels put him back to sleep with a rock-hard right to the jaw.

When he came to, he was lying face down on the deep-pile carpet, the glow of the half-moon at the window the only light in the room. His ankle was killing him, his eye another source of pain, and now at the slightest movement of his head he saw fireworks, but not the festive kind. Walker didn't even try to stagger to his feet and hop over to the mattress. What would be the point? He'd have plenty of time to sleep when he was dead.

28

INFIL

C age's first-class flight from Sydney to Mexico City was an exercise in patience. Having dealt with most of the issues surrounding his transition to anonymous retirement, he was anxious to get back to Mazatlan and cross off the last few items on his list—principally Walker's interrogation and execution—which is why his long flight seemed even longer. He'd eaten, drunk, worked, read, slept, read again, worked again, slept again, and still had time to kill, so he composed a list of questions he'd ask Jeff Walker, such as the status of Oceanside PD's investigation into his illicit business activities, and what was known about Trent Bolton.

At last! Cage grumbled to himself as he stepped off the plane and bustled through the busiest airport in Latin America. He didn't need directions to his next gate, so as he towed his rolling suitcase through the concourse, his mind was free to recall a few challenges he'd overcome in the past, thus reassuring himself that he'd be similarly victorious in the present. Early in his career, while racing through the border tunnels, he'd outrun the Mexican Federal Police only to be greeted on the U.S. side by a fleet of DEA trucks that also failed to catch him. Years later, he was piloting a small jet full of cocaine into the U.S. when he'd been ordered to land and, upon his refusal, shot down by a Navy F-14. Before his jet was blown to pieces, he'd engaged the autopilot, sprinted back to the cargo door, and parachuted to safety, opening at a mere five hundred meters to maximize his chances of escape. That was a good one, he remembered with a grin of pride as he stepped onto an ascending escalator, but the next exploit was his most cherished memory: he'd been carrying a heavy load of drugs and guns in a speedboat from Mazatlan to San Diego when the U.S. Coast Guard intercepted him, took him aboard, and threw him in the brig. He picked the double lock on his handcuffs with the bobby pin hidden in his shoe (it pays to be prepared), tricked and disarmed his guard, murdered the entire ten-man crew, impersonated the captain by radio, thereby gaining safe passage to port, then called an associate while en route and slipped away with the full load of contraband. It was in appreciation of this extraordinary achievement that the Cartel del Norte had set him up with the warehouse facility, the house on the hill, the SRTs, and the supercharged Shelby F-150.

Cage chuckled out loud on his way to the gate, convinced he was about to claim the biggest and most important victory of all. As he settled into his seat for the short flight to Mazatlan, he graciously accepted a glass of champagne from a lovely young stewardess. There was practically nothing left for him to do but pack his bags and fly to the tropics, where he'd lap it up for the rest of his life. He deserved it.

***

Sergeant Taylor, his detectives, and a nervous Sean Choi climbed the built-in airstairs of a white Dassault Falcon. As they came to the cockpit, Taylor said, "I'd like y'all to meet DEA special agents Andy Stare and Lee Cowgill."

The pair of DEA pilots turned to shake hands with the new but not improved narcotics task force; after the massacre at the warehouse facility, Taylor's superiors had been reluctant to assign him any men at all, so there were only four new detectives, all of whom were male, each a veteran officer carrying a pistol in a hip holster, as their rifles and the rest of the gear had already been stored in the baggage compartment. Special Agent Stare, the copilot, was fair-haired, broad-shouldered, and mean-looking; Cowgill, the captain, was even more intimidating, with a dark beard and strong, rough hands.

Taylor and Choi settled into adjacent brown leather armchairs in the forward part of the cabin while the detectives took their seats in a plush six-seat cluster in the aft portion. Taylor was glad he'd allowed Walker's friends to meet him at the DEA base camp, but he was worried sick about the outcome of the mission. If things didn't go well this time around, he'd be hunting for a new job with no letter of recommendation. He and Choi spent the first hour studying satellite images of the oceanfront complex and ironing out the last remaining details. Then they headed aft and went over the plan with the team: instead of attempting a frontal breach of the guarded gate, Park, Taylor, and Stare would perform a night jump out of a darkened Cessna 182, landing on the pool terrace, which they expected to be dimly lit. When they hit the ground, the rest of the crew would already be in position near the front gate in a pair of DEA vans. From inside one of those vans, Choi would hack into the security system and provide remote assistance. Then, once the airborne team had freed Walker and was ready to exfiltrate, the breach force, i.e. Goode and the narcotics unit, would force the guards at the security station to open the gate. All the while, Tina would remain with Choi in the communications van, ready to provide emergency medical assistance.

The jet touched down at an unmarked airfield in the foothills close to El Tecomate. The landing strip was so short that Special Agent Cowgill had no choice but to sharply lower the nose, come in hot, make a hard landing, and apply maximum braking, producing in Taylor a surge of panic that would turn out to be the first of many surges of panic over the course of the current mission.

When Taylor gratefully disembarked down the airstairs, he walked past the only other aircraft parked on the taxiway, a red Cessna 182. It looked to be in good shape. In the hazy dusk, about half a klick away, two navy-blue vans were parked close to a cluster of shelter systems, some of which were small, others as big as a house.

"And this is our mobile command center," explained Special Agent Stare as they stepped into the largest of these tents.

"How about that landing?" Park jeered heartily, offering his hand to Taylor. Goode welcomed him in the same fashion, and Tina with a cheek-to-cheek greeting. After introductions were made and the gear was unloaded, everyone planted their backsides on folding chairs to review the tactical plan. When there were no further questions, Taylor said, "All right. I'm going to give y'all thirty minutes to gear up and do what you need to do. Choi, let's get you set up in the communications van."

*****

As everyone split up to prepare for the mission, Park led Tina aside. "Choi's a smart guy," he told her, "but one of you needs to be armed, and I think it should be you." He handed her a holstered Navy Sig as they came to a clearing with a hill behind it. "Jeff says you know how to use this."

"More or less," she replied, pulling her hair into a ponytail, then taking the offered pistol. At Park's nod, she leveled the weapon and squeezed the trigger, firing five rounds at a tree some twenty feet away, without missing.

"Good," Park said. "This time widen your stance and lock your elbows. Whenever you're ready."

Tina swiveled to target a different trunk and shot with better accuracy and precision until she ran dry. When she released the empty magazine, Park handed her a fresh one, which she seated with a proper push-pull motion.

A minute later, as Park threaded Tina's belt through the holster mounting system, he said, "I hope you don't need to fire it, but if you do, don't hesitate. The bad guys won't."

"Thanks, Tony."

"Don't get out of that van."

At the appointed time, everyone gathered in the command center, now clad in body armor, tactical helmets, boots, headsets, and eye protection. Taylor and Park stood facing the team.

Choi sat behind a computer monitor at a table off to one side. "Cage is forty minutes from landing at Mazatlan International," he reported.

"Good copy," Taylor replied. "Now listen up, y'all. As I said, breaching the gate at the right time is critical, and we'll have to coordinate it on the fly. So stay on your comms but keep the crosstalk to a minimum."

David Goode and the detectives nodded grimly.

Taylor looked to Park and asked, "Would you like to say anything?"

Park's gaze was hard, even as he eyed some of his closest friends. "Work as a team," he said. "Cover each other. Keep your eyes open and your head down. And good luck."

With that, Park, Taylor, Cowgill, and Stare double-timed it to the red Cessna, which Cowgill taxied to the runway, brought up to rotation speed, and lifted into the night sky.

As an ambulance driver, Tina was qualified to drive one of the vans, so she slid behind the wheel and followed the lead van fifteen miles to the coast. This freed up a detective to sit beside her, ready with an M4 carbine in case of any trouble. Choi sat in the back, at a communications bench mounted on the side wall, his fingers tapping away at a keyboard. When he initiated the comm check, everyone came back loud and clear.

There were eleven members of the rescue team: four in the Cessna and seven in the vans. If you'd asked them why they were racing toward danger, each would have given a different answer. Some were endeavoring to rescue a friend, others avenging a murder, and a significant number just doing their job, yet they all had one thing in common: they believed in what they were doing, and it was that conviction that would see them through the bloody showdown.

Most of them.

***

A battered Jeff Walker gazed out at the dark beauty of the sea, possibly, he knew, for the last time. The moon had taken cover behind a wispy patch of clouds, but it still lit up a fast-moving set of waves that met their fate on the rocks at the foot of the cliff. He'd long since scoured the room for poor workmanship, crumbling concrete, ventilation passageways, and anything else that might have led to a way out, but, of course, as he could have deduced from the heavy steel door and its high-security locking mechanism, he was trapped in a prison cell that offered no possibility of escape. Walker drew back his fist and punched the shatterproof window, then had to lie on the bed until the pain subsided. It was then that he finally admitted to himself that, just as Master Chang had said, hate had poisoned his life, in a gradual process that had begun in his teenage years and produced a long string of bad decisions made in anger. But things were different now that he was desperate to survive, with no energy to waste on Trent Bolton. Walker's only desire was to make it home to his exquisitely beautiful girlfriend and all his buddies.

It occurred to him that if he could somehow get up to the roof, he might be able to clear the rocks with a running headfirst dive, or at least make it into the swimming pool. So he started toward the door to pound on it and yell for help with a bogus emergency when, out of the corner of his eye, he detected movement down on the pool terrace. Walker rushed back to the window and gaped in disbelief as three paratroopers stepped out of their harnesses, hid their chutes, and drew their rifles from long bags strapped to their legs. It was Park, Taylor, and another man he didn't recognize.

Behind him, the security door's heavy bolts clicked into the unlocked position. Ready to fight for his freedom, he whirled around to face his nemesis, but no one came into the room. Walker stepped cautiously to the door, eased it open, and peered down into the dark, empty staircase. He waited. Still nothing. So he hurried back to the window and waved his arms to draw his friends' attention. Through a series of hand signals, it was agreed that they should wait for him by the pool.

***

If a person were standing on the circular driveway facing west, looking at the front side of the three stucco houses, Walker and the two guard captains were currently in the leftmost dwelling—the one at the south end, which Maldonado had quickly claimed on arrival one month earlier on account of the better view. Cage had chosen the middle mansion, of course, leaving Daniels with the north-side house, the least desirable of the three.

At the foot of the dark, empty staircase, there was a sitting room with black leather sofas, original oil paintings, and a chandelier hanging from the ceiling. It was there that Daniels and Maldonado sat facing each other at a polished-wood poker table, studying the cards in their hands. The game was five-card draw.

"Call," Daniels muttered gruffly, hoping his three aces would be strong enough to win the hand. He was sick of Maldonado's gloating and also down five hundred bones.

These two guard captains were staying close to their prisoner while waiting for Cage to arrive, which they expected to occur momentarily. Daniels was preparing to show his hand when he heard the whirring of a small airplane outside. He froze, straining his ears for any other sounds. He and Maldonado exchanged uncertain looks. Even though air traffic was an everyday occurrence, they rose, drew their pistols, and strode past the dark (but no longer empty) staircase toward the ocean side of the house, crossing the dining room to peer through the windows that overlooked the sprawling terrace. Outside, the lighting in the bushes provided some illumination, but the pool area was mostly dark. They scanned these rear grounds, staying alert for any sign of trouble. Especially at night, Cage had said.

Seeing nothing, they went back to the poker table where Daniels' three aces beat Maldonado's two pair. He won his money back and then some.

***

Tina watched through a pair of binoculars as the guards at the massive gate waved an airport taxi into the complex. The road she had parked on was poorly lit, but she could see that the neighborhood was an eclectic mixture of luxury homes, unfinished construction, and overgrown vacant lots. For reassurance, she patted her hip holster, knowing how it felt to save a life but wondering what it might do to her to take one.

The detective beside her keyed his headset mic and said, "Cage just passed through the gate."

Taylor's voice came back in a whisper. "Roger," he replied. "Choi, unlock the smart doors in the south house."

"Copy. Done."

"How's it going with the camera feeds?"

"Still working on it."

Then Park's voice, also hushed, came crackling over the radio waves. "There he is, up on the second floor!"

Tina drummed her fingers on the steering wheel as she listened to the airborne team making plans to wait for Walker in the shadows. Hope was not a strong enough word for how badly she wanted this operation to succeed. When it was all over, she decided, she would smother Jeff with hugs and kisses.

If both of them made it back alive, of course.

29

PAIN

Cage's airport taxi followed the sinuous drive past the rightmost house, also known as the north house or Daniels' place, and it eased to a halt at the middle mansion. The master smuggler tipped the driver moderately, then grabbed his bag and strode up the wide semicircular staircase, unlocked the immoderately massive Accoya wood door, and charged through ill-gotten luxury to the ocean side. Had he come to the kitchen during daylight hours, he'd have enjoyed a commanding view of the pool terrace and the Pacific Ocean behind it, but night had fallen, so he switched on the lights and removed a black pistol case from an overhead cabinet above the stove. After loading and cocking his trusty Ruger P90, the same pistol he'd shot Walker's father with, he marched through a pair of white French doors and out to the dimly lit terrace. The path to the south house, also known as Maldonado's place, Cage's current destination, was marked by a concrete walkway that wound its way left, but before stepping onto the path he dipped his finger into the jacuzzi. It was lukewarm. Promising himself a cigar and a long, relaxing soak once the deed was done, he switched on the hot tub as well as the pool lights. Now, in addition to the accent lighting in the bushes and trees, a bright turquoise glow emanated from the middle of the terrace.

Cage stopped and stood stock-still. He could have sworn he'd heard whispered voices. Willing his eyes and ears to sharper sensitivity and gripping his Ruger with both hands, he swiveled the weapon from left to right and back again. Aided by the pool lights, he could see clear to the low stone wall at the edge of the cliff, but he heard no further sounds and noted nothing amiss. Was he losing his mind? No. If there was one thing Cage had learned in all his years, it was to trust himself and his instincts. He knew he'd caught the sound of human voices, and his own men would not be hiding in the bushes. He hurried back into the kitchen and switched on the floodlights, illuminating every square inch of the complex, then grabbed his radio and ordered his guards to bring out the dogs.

***

Minutes earlier, as Walker had crept down the staircase from his room to the ground floor, his heartbeat was pulsing so powerfully in his ears that he feared the noise might expose him. Halfway down, he heard the sound of chairs scooting back and boots clomping closer, so he flattened himself against the wall and held his breath as Maldonado and Daniels hustled past the bottom of the stairs with their pistols drawn. Then he headed silently down and right, in the opposite direction of his captors. He slipped past a sitting room with cash on a card table, advancing toward a door he was certain he'd find locked, but it wasn't. He pushed it open and stepped out into the cool night air, quickly orienting himself. Straight ahead, a wall loomed high and white, marking the southern edge of the property. To his left, a small wrought-iron gate blocked the way to the front grounds, and to his right, he supposed, the concrete walkway he was standing on would take him to the pool terrace, so he limped off in that direction, his swift bare feet making little noise. Passing the dark waters of the pool, he made for the far left, or northwest, corner of the terrace. As he neared a cluster of bushes and trees, Taylor and Park stepped out to greet him with fist bumps. In a whisper, the third paratrooper introduced himself as Stare. All three surrounded Walker with their rifles at the low ready. "Hostage secured," Taylor hissed into his headset, then jerked his head east, away from the ocean, and in a cautious run they set off toward the front gate. All of a sudden, however, while hustling through a narrow corridor between two houses, the airborne team's night-vision scopes were rendered useless as night turned into day by the many floodlights set on tall poles all around the complex. Taylor and company continued to advance, but they hesitated when distant shouted orders and the barking of vicious dogs echoed throughout the grounds. A chill spread from the pit of Walker's stomach to his head and his toes when he felt the presence of an enemy behind him.

"Drop your weapons!" a booming voice commanded.

Park, Taylor, Walker, and Stare did as they were told.

"Now put your hands up and turn around!"

Again they complied, and there he was: grinning victoriously, Jack Cage stood flanked by Maldonado and Daniels, all three with rifles brought to bear. Worse yet, the vicious barking and shouted orders came closer until Walker knew without looking that, behind them, the path to the front gate was now blocked as well.

It was over. Walker and his would-be rescuers offered no resistance as Cage's men stripped them of their equipment and bound their wrists with flex cuffs. Two guards marched Taylor and Stare toward the north house, and a second pair took Park and Walker back to the upstairs confinement chamber in the south-side residence.

***

"How did Walker get out?" Maldonado asked as the prisoners were led away.

"Someone unlocked the door," Daniels answered.

"I know, dumbass, but who? And how?"

Daniels felt his face grow hot, but now was not the time to take any kind of action that might disrupt his plan. In a question of minutes, he'd be sliding behind the wheel of the late Sergeant Miller's SRT, never to lay eyes on the two assholes standing next to him for the rest of his life. The future he'd mapped out for himself, while it might not turn out to be bright, would certainly be a step up from the second-class status he'd been relegated to for the past ten years.

"I know you guys didn't unlock it," Cage said. "So the only way he could have escaped is if someone hacked into the security system. That means someone's helping them remotely. Get your asses to the security station and set the smart locks to manual. Then disable the cameras and send a team out to the road to search for surveillance vehicles. When you're done, meet me in the south house for the first interrogation."

***

Tina, Goode, and Taylor's men stood crowded around Choi in the communications van, all seven watching Cage's security camera feed, all seven troubled by the fact that Park and Walker as well as Taylor and Stare were being dragged to different rooms and shoved down into chairs. That's when the video transmission cut out. Choi's fingers flew over the keyboard in an effort to bring it back, but he shook his head after a minute. "They've deactivated the security system," Choi said. "There's nothing I can do from here."

"Why would they shut off their own camera system?" Tina asked.

After a pause for thought, Choi said gravely, "Because they know we're here."

No sooner had he said those words than the front gate slid open and a black 4x4 came barreling out. Through their front windshield they watched, horrified, as the two uniformed guards who were standing in the black pickup's cargo bed hopped down to the road and shot out the communication van's tires. Then the driver got out to join his comrades, and all three opened fire.

***

"Oh, you'll talk. You'll *sing*. The only question is how badly I'm going to get to hurt you before you do," Maldonado gloated as he showed Sergeant Taylor a hammer. The sadist's features glowed with anticipation like those of a boy at his own birthday party about to open the biggest present.

"Go ahead. Nothing's going to hurt me as much as looking at your disgusting face," Taylor retorted through fat, bloody lips. He and the chair he sat on were encircled by many revolutions of duct tape, and Agent Stare was in the same situation just a few feet away.

Daniels stood by the window with one guard next to him and another out in the hallway. This confinement chamber was a mirror image of the one in the south house, Walker's room, but it was to Walker's room that they'd been ordered to report, not here. After he and Maldonado had killed the camera feed and sent a search team out to the road, Maldonado had convinced Daniels to accompany him to the north house instead, so that they might "interrogate" Sergeant Taylor with no supervision. Daniels had only gone along with the idea because it suited his own plans.

The long, gnarled mark that cut across Maldonado's face wriggled and writhed like a worm as his lips twisted into something that must have felt like a smile to him. "Say that again, Taylor. I'm begging you."

"I said nothing you can do is going to hurt me as much as looking at your ugly fucking face." Taylor's eyes were hard and his chin held high.

Maldonado motioned for the guard to step forward and handed him a small piece of wood. "Slide this under his palm, if you would." This softly spoken request, if heard out of context, might have been mistaken for an instruction given by a bank manager. But Daniels knew better; the room was about to explode into bloody chaos. The guard did as he'd been told and then, in compliance with a second gentle direction, he secured Taylor's hand to the table with further revolutions of silver duct tape.

Maldonado's gaze brimmed with bloodlust. "For the last time," he said, his voice rising to a shriek, "which agency are you working with and who else is here?"

When Taylor locked eyes with his captor, pursed his lips, and shook his head, Maldonado raised the hammer and slammed it down. "Who else is here?" he demanded over Taylor's screams, hitting the back of Taylor's hand and his fingers, repeatedly, not stopping to let him talk. This wasn't an interrogation. This was pain for the sake of pain, hate in its purest form.

Stare shook and strained so vigorously against his bindings that he tipped over in his chair and hit his head on the floor.

Maldonado roared with laughter. "You'll get your turn."

"We'd better go," Daniels said.

Maldonado nodded. With a flick of his chin, he ordered the guard out first. Then he raised his eyebrows at Daniels, but the latter shook his head. "You first," said the man planning to pull a disappearing act of his own. "I'm going to take a piss."

Maldonado grunted and tromped down the stairs.

Daniels watched as Taylor moaned and hung his head. Stare lay sideways on the carpet, still lashed to his chair and still fighting mad. Instead of heading to the bathroom, Daniels spun on his heels and exited the room, not bothering to lock the door behind him. He hurried down to the garage and removed the tracking device from the underside of the SRT, then climbed into the driver's seat and brought the armored Jeep to life.

***

A noisy storm of rifle rounds riddled the armored body of the communications van, each booming impact echoing threateningly inside the vehicle. As the polycarbonate windows cracked and clouded up, its occupants glanced at each other in alarm. Goode and the detectives agreed that fighting back would be the smartest move, but Tina, only inches from the splitting windshield, slid behind the wheel to start the engine.

"What are you doin'?" Goode shouted over all the bullet noise.

"Backing away on the rims," she replied, but before she could do so, one of the guards set a rocket-propelled grenade launcher on his shoulder and squinted to take aim. Her eyes darted to Goode's and they grabbed each other's hands.

The lethal explosion they'd expected never occurred. The RPG operator was suddenly nailed to the side of his truck, with half his head missing and blood pouring out of the remainder. His corpse flopped to the ground. A second guard suffered the same fate. The third threw down his weapon and pleaded for his life with an approaching figure. It was Agent Cowgill! He'd come back for them after landing the Cessna at base camp.

The breach force had no trouble convincing the surviving guard to drive Cowgill and three of Taylor's men back through the gate as if they were his prisoners. Once inside the walls of the complex, the foursome took command of the security station, locked all the guards in a storage room, and opened the gate for the others. Then, when Choi reactivated the cameras, a bank of monitors on the desk blinked to life. One of them showed Park and Walker seated in chairs with their hands bound behind their backs. Cage was moving toward them, with Maldonado and two guards posted nearby. Park's lips moved unintelligibly, as the feed had no sound, but whatever he'd said appeared to be the cause of Cage punching him in the face.

On a second screen, Agent Stare was busy unwinding the duct tape from around Taylor's torso. Once free, Taylor rose from his chair and both men hurried off-screen.

"I'm counting four crooks," Choi reported. "Cage, Maldonado, and two guards."

Agent Cowgill moved closer to peer over Choi's shoulder. Then he turned to Tina, who, like Choi, had not been provided with any tactical gear since the plan had been for them to stay out of the gated complex. "You two get back to the other van and lock yourselves inside," Cowgill told them. Then he set off toward the south house as the point man in a formation that included Goode and the detectives.

Choi stood and started toward the front gate, but he stopped when he saw that Tina hadn't moved.

"You go ahead. I mean it," she said, drawing Park's Navy Sig and racking the slide with a metallic ker-chick. "But I'm not going to sit out there and wait to see what happens." She gave him a single nod and then hustled off in the same direction as the others.

30

TRAGEDY

Unable to hold back his grin, Maldonado entered the code to unlock the security door. So as not to interrupt the interrogation in progress, he told his two guards to stay quiet as he pulled it open and let them in. Crucially, in his excitement, he didn't push the door completely shut after he stepped inside. And when his guards took their places on either side of it, they failed to spot the security weakness.

"A word, D2," Cage growled, with a curt gesture toward a far corner. The master smuggler left Park and Walker in their chairs to lead his man away and berate him quietly.

Park and Walker eyed each other. They'd spotted Maldonado's blunder, but with their wrists still bound behind their backs and a pair of armed guards at the door, there was nothing they could do. Not yet, anyway; Park's hands were busy cutting his flex cuffs with a razor blade he'd hidden in his boot.

"Tina's here," Park said coolly, as though he weren't engaged in a frenzied attempt to free himself.

Walker let out a long groan, trying to appear more miserable than he really was.

"I know," Park went on, his features clouded with false dismay. "She felt guilty for leaving you alone in your tent and wouldn't take no for an answer."

"That sounds like Tina."

Cage strode back to his prisoners, leaving a red-faced Maldonado in the corner to compose himself. "Let's get this over with," he said.

Park turned to the smuggler and said, "Did you two make up?"

Cage punched Park in the face, then looked back at his right-hand man. "Shoot him if he says another word."

Park hung his head, seemingly fading in and out of consciousness while Cage asked a series of questions that Walker answered slowly and half-truthfully, stalling for time.

Frustrated by the absence of any useful information, Cage drew his Ruger from his waistband, but before he could raise it, Taylor and Stare exploded into the room.

Park's eyes flew open. His hands now free, he leapt to his feet and went for Cage's gun, which clattered to the floor in the resulting struggle. Then he charged forward and delivered a furious succession of rights and lefts that even the boxer couldn't dodge. Cage backed up, his head slamming into the wall again and again as Park went to work on his face.

While Stare and Taylor were permanently disabling the guards at the door, Walker jumped up to headbutt Maldonado, stunning him. "Let's go!" Walker shouted. Stare and Taylor flew down the stairs, but Walker stopped, turned to Park, and said, "Let's give them a chance to get away." He led Park up the stairs instead of down, taking them two at a time until they burst out onto the roof. The grounds were still lit up, giving them a clear view of the terrace below.

"The water's shallow," Walker said as they stepped to the corner to study their flight path and landing zone. "We're going to have to hit it just right." So they backed up, sprinted forward, and leapt off the roof in tandem, barely clearing the twenty-five feet of grass between them and the pool. Or so Walker had thought, after finding himself alone in midair. It was the old "we'll jump together" trick where one guy doesn't go.

His hands still bound behind his back and his body horizontal while plummeting toward the pool, Walker curled down his chin and chest, smacking the water hard in a near belly-flop so that his downward momentum was halted but his face and head were protected. As he set his feet on the bottom and popped his head out, gunfire cracked out from above and hot slugs fizzed into the water around him. He looked up at the roof. Maldonado and another guard were shooting at him, but when an angry Tony Park materialized behind them, they had to turn around and fight. Walker backed out of range, his eyes riveted on the rooftop action.

***

Park was not about to return to San Diego without his brother. He'd sooner die himself. Traumatized in the past by the decimation of his platoon, he was going to save Jeff Walker at any cost. That's why he'd run with Walker to the edge of the roof but stopped short, spinning on his heels to hustle back to the access door, positioning himself against the wall next to it. Seconds later, when the first guard came charging out but failed to clear the corner, Park swiftly disarmed him and shot him in the head with a smooth, practiced motion.

At the same time, Maldonado and the second guard burst through the door and sprinted to the edge of the roof. They fired at Walker down in the pool, likely with orders to consider him a priority target. Then, when Park shot the first guard, Maldonado whirled around with his pistol leveled, just as Park was staring down his sights at him. There followed a silent moment of hard gazes and itchy trigger fingers. In the midst of this mortal impasse, the second guard hurried back inside and down the stairs.

Without breaking eye contact, the two former soldiers set their pistols down and settled into fighting stances, then advanced like two fighters at the start of a cage match, though in this contest there would be no purse, no rules, and no tapping out. Park threw the first punch, catching his opponent on the forearms.

Having blocked Park's shot to his jaw, Maldonado stepped right with his left leg, crossing over in preparation for a spinning back kick, but Park anticipated the move and stopped it with a low kick to that front leg.

They collided in a painful blur of punches, kicks, elbows, and knees. Maldonado was faster and meaner, but Park was larger, and his heart was bigger. That's how he saw it, anyway, as his distress level crept from zero to tolerable to emergency situation. Fearing he might never see Carla again, the giant Asian lifeguard forced himself to relax and to trust his training. He ducked a punch and went for a double-leg takedown, the back of Maldonado's head smacking onto the concrete as he fell. Park crawled up into a mount and pounded the man's face with boulder-sized fists. At each rock-hard smack, Maldonado's efforts grew weaker until Park stepped away to pick up one of the pistols. The closest gun was his enemy's, an HK USP9. Dizzy and heaving for air, he gripped the pistol with two hands to line up the ugly man in his own sights. Park wavered between taking Maldonado's life or tying him up as the scar-faced sadist staggered to his feet near the edge of the roof. The look of resignation in the man's eyes was something Park knew he'd never forget. Maldonado showed no fear, no anger, nor any other strong emotion, as though he'd always known this would happen.

Park was mostly out of danger, but that wasn't true for everyone else on his team. He glanced down at the pool. Walker was just climbing out with Goode's help. *What a badass!* Had the massive singer started training at a younger age, Park thought, he could have been the most decorated soldier in the Western world.

Cage was still somewhere on the grounds, guarded by at least one other man, so Park needed to get down to the terrace with no delay. He shifted his gaze back to his swaying target and squeezed the trigger repeatedly, emptying the HK into every vital part of the sadist's body that wasn't shielded by body armor. At such close range and with a nonresistant enemy, it was an easy kill. Blood jetted through Maldonado's fingers as he explored his throat wounds. Then he toppled backwards and fell headfirst. Park stepped to the edge and looked down. A dark, clumpy blend of blood and brain matter was flowing out of a pile of dislocated limbs, spreading itself all over the concrete walkway.

As the adrenaline wore off, Park was hit by a familiar set of symptoms: tachycardia, facial flushing, worsening dizziness, and a roaring in his ears. He sat down immediately just before—

***

Walker's hands were still zip-tied behind his back, so he couldn't climb out of the pool by himself. He set his uninjured foot on a ladder rung as Goode reached down to help him up and out.

"You okay, brotha?" Goode asked, snapping open a knife to free Walker's wrists.

Walker nodded. Nearby, a burly bearded man whose vest, like Stare's, read DEA, was sweeping his rifle back and forth, as were four other guys wearing police badges around their necks. Taylor and Stare were also there, but they looked bruised and bloody, and Taylor could hardly stand; he looked like he was about to be sick. Walker's jaw fell slack when he spotted the sergeant's mangled hand, then the four narcotics detectives crowded around their leader and escorted him out the front gate.

"Name's Cowgill," grunted the bearded DEA agent, flicking his chin upwards in a reverse nod while panning his rifle from left to right.

"Walker," returned the sopping-wet lifeguard. "Appreciate you coming to get me." After peeling off his sweatshirt to improve his mobility, Walker turned back to Goode and held his gaze as the worry in his buddy's eyes gave way to relief.

At that instant, a door on the ground floor of the south house flew open and two men came charging out with rifles firing. It was Cage and his guard!

"Dave!" shouted Walker.

Goode reacted quickly, stepping in front of Walker to protect him. The massive entertainer brought his rifle into firing position, but before he could pull the trigger, his head exploded in a pink mist. Stare and Cowgill were hit as well.

As the violence unfolded in slow motion, Walker caught sight of another figure approaching from the opposite side of the complex. It was Tina! Heading straight for him, unprotected by body armor or any other gear. Just as their eyes met, sharp gunfire echoed from above and many rounds buried themselves in her chest. Still she staggered forward, her lovely gaze holding his, but when a final shot rang out, the bullet punched through her skull, jerking her head sideways as she tumbled to the grass in an untidy heap.

31

FINALE

C age's pulse raced with the excitement of war, for the last time, he reckoned, regardless of the final outcome: if he did make it to Australia, his anonymous retirement would not likely lead to any major gun battles, and if he didn't, well, this would be the last time his heart did any kind of beating. He and his guard had just gunned down Goode and the two DEA agents, and it seemed as though they'd also killed Tina. Either that or someone else had, Cage figured, so one or more of his guards might still be alive, in addition to the one at his side. Maybe it had been Daniels, the sniper, he thought. As Cage advanced, he stared down his rifle sights at Walker, fired, and missed, since both he and his target were on the move. Then sharp cracking gunfire issued from an unknown source and his guard stumbled and fell, groaning in pain, as further bullets drilled into the grass at Cage's feet. "God *dammit*!" he barked, with no choice but to lower his weapon and take cover behind the south house. Passing the bloody, disjointed pile of Maldonado, he fired three rounds over his shoulder, ran dry, and tossed his empty weapon aside.

***

Walker's frantic heart pounded against his ribcage as he fled across the terrace. Unarmed and barely in control of himself, he whipped his head around to watch Cage take aim and fire. Supersonic projectiles snapped so closely past Walker's body that it made him sick, but all of a sudden Cage stopped shooting and broke left, to Walker's right, retreating behind the south house amid a burst of small-arms fire coming from an unseen location. The smuggler chucked his rifle into the bushes as he ran, so Walker, in an instant, giving no thought to his injured foot nor to his earlier decision that revenge was ill-advised, set off in pursuit of his nemesis. He had often considered the possibility that when his father died, he'd perished while thinking of the son he'd never know. And it was a fact that his mother's body had eaten itself alive, probably due to the poisonous stress of raising him by herself in an inhospitable environment with a broken heart. As Walker pushed his body to the limit, hustling past Maldonado's bloody corpse, his thoughts turned to Park, Goode, and Tina, who had risked everything to save him, and now two of them were dead as a direct result of Cage's actions. Then came the tragic deaths of Mark Thompson and Big Don Roberts, which had either been perpetrated, orchestrated, or facilitated by the black-hearted smuggler. And the list went on to include other names, but as Walker flew around the corner and his eyes zeroed in on Cage at the wrought-iron gate, his mind shifted into animal mode and his hands curled into blunt force weapons.

The smuggler didn't startle or try to escape; he stopped what he was doing and turned to face the advancing Walker, fixing him with cold gray eyes and dropping into a boxing stance.

Walker drew a belly breath and let it slowly out as they collided.

The master smuggler struck first, connecting with a startling one-two-three combination, but Walker ignored the pain and countered with two successive overhand rights.

Cage covered up, slipped Walker's following punches, then stepped in with a tooth-rattling right uppercut and a left hook to the body. A liver shot! As Walker dropped helplessly to his knees, Cage pounced on his back, tightening steely arms around his neck in a suffocating grip.

Walker didn't know what was worse, that he couldn't breathe, or that he couldn't move his arms or legs. He'd been trained to escape a rear naked choke, so his brain was sending instructions as to how to wipe that God-damned smirk off his father's killer's face, but his body wasn't able to follow orders since the liver shot had short-circuited his nervous system. Suddenly Walker was tired of fighting, exhausted by the trials of a difficult life. Ready to throw in the towel. He wished for it all to end, and it would have been so easy to make that happen: all he had to do was nothing. Yet there was something in the back of his mind that made him reject that fantasy: the mental image of his young, healthy mother. She was two hundred yards away, perched on the sand, her legs curled under a yellow sundress, smiling and waving as he raced along the face of a wave on the board she'd given him. Many times she'd insisted the other kids were no better than he was, and the same was true in Mazatlan: Walker, now a grown man, knew he was just as tough as Jack Cage. He wiggled his fingers. His neurons were back online! With the last molecule of oxygen left in his body, and with all his strength, he reached back to crush Cage's testicles.

Cage howled like a wounded animal and released his grip. Walker straightened and spun around, smashing a backhanded fist into the smuggler's jaw, then a straight left to the throat. Choking, Cage ducked to cover his face and head, so Walker snapped a round kick into his knee.

As Cage stumbled backwards toward the low stone wall, Walker let out a roar. Bulling forward, he grabbed Cage by his ballistic vest and lifted him off his feet.

The smuggler's eyes went as white and wide as dinner plates; he grabbed desperately at the chain and at Walker's shirt as he went over the side, but the determined lifeguard blasted him in the head with a scything elbow, took control of the man's arms, and gave him a final shove.

As Cage plummeted to the foot of the cliff, he didn't glare hatefully up at Walker like one might expect. No, his final expression was one of ultimate self-disappointment as the rocks tore him into several twitching parts.

***

Five minutes earlier, Maria had been sitting on the side of her bed, her heart hammering, her body gripped by fear. Daniels had said he'd be waiting for her in the garage, but she couldn't bring herself to join him. Not yet. Not before she did something she should have done months before.

Maria had stayed behind to avenge the murder of her cousin, Paul Johanssen, but she'd waited too long already; it was now or not at all. She blew out a nervous breath and snapped open a fighting knife, then leapt to her feet and stormed across the pool terrace in search of that rat bastard Maldonado.

***

When Tina had left Choi at the security station, she'd hurried toward the houses but seen no sign of Goode, Cowgill, and the narcotics detectives. And the only gear she'd been given was a pistol, so she couldn't toggle any comms to ask them where they were.

Alert for any sudden movement, she came to a service ladder on the side wall of the middle mansion. Thinking she'd best be able to assist her team from high ground, she holstered and climbed up to the roof, taking cover behind a concrete structure. BLAM! A nearby gunshot startled her into action. She drew her weapon and peered around the corner, watching Park and Maldonado lower their guns and fight to the death on the adjacent housetop. At first it seemed that Maldonado had the upper hand, but Park managed to come out on top, scrambled for a gun, and shot Maldonado off the roof, the sadist's head exploding on the concrete below. Not far from that bloody walkway was the pool, where Jeff was climbing out with Goode's help and the detectives were surrounding Taylor to escort him back to the van.

Tina's relief turned to cold shock as Cage and his guard barreled out onto the terrace and fired automatic rifles at Goode, Walker, and the DEA guys, but she didn't hesitate, just as Park had instructed her. Tracking the crooks in her sights, she fired again and again, dropping the guard, but Cage slipped around the corner despite her careful aim. Just then, on the other side of the terrace, to her right, a female figure emerged from the next house over and charged toward Jeff with a knife in her hand. It was the stripper! Tina squeezed the trigger again, this time with relish as she nailed her lookalike to the ground. Then she cupped her hands to her mouth and stepped toward the edge to warn Jeff not to follow Cage. But she knew he wouldn't listen. In that case, shouting from the rooftop would only reveal her position.

Oh, shit! Distracted by her concern, she'd taken a false step off the side of the building and fallen into a tree, pinballing through the branches on her—

***

Walker allowed himself a final glance over the wall at his grisly dream come true. A crashing wave shifted Cage's broken corpse such that the smuggler's face turned to fix him with an eerie empty gaze. Walker had been aching for this moment ever since his mom had told him the truth about his father's death, yet now that it had come to pass, the feeling wasn't what he'd been hoping for. He wasn't glad to have taken a life, not Trent Bolton's, and not those of the guards after dinner at the top of the stairs.

He rubbed his windpipe. It hurt to breathe. Better put, everything hurt: his eye and his head from the damage done by Maldonado and Cage, his right side from the liver shot, and his shredded ankle from the surfing accident. All these injuries struck him behind the eyes with a collective bolt of lightning at every step as he hurried back to the pool terrace, dreading the sight of Tina's corpse. At least, he thought, he'd be able to take her home for a proper burial. But as he came closer, the physical differences between the two women began to leap out at him, each a little ray of hope. He turned her face up, and it wasn't her! It was Cage's secretary.

"I didn't shoot her to eliminate the competition, if that's what you're thinking," a heavenly voice called out from behind him. Walker rose and turned, drinking in a sight too beautiful for words. "That wasn't the only reason, anyway," Tina joked, rubbing her head from the fall. Walker hobbled forward to snatch her off her feet in a passionate embrace.

***

The detectives had no trouble getting Taylor to the van. Cowgill and Stare also made it back, saved by their ballistic vests. Before they all piled in and drove back to base camp, Tina made use of her paramedic equipment, one piece of which was a body bag.

As Walker helped the other guys load Goode's corpse into the van, he changed his mind. He'd thought that last look on Cage's face would haunt him for the rest of his life, but now he knew it wouldn't; he could forget about a weak-minded servant to the Mexican mafia, but he would never let go of the memory of David Goode.

When they'd first met at Hillside Baptist Church, Walker and Goode had been like oil and water, with fierce conflict breaking out at every possible point. But in the praise band they'd been forced to cooperate and work through their rivalry. Over the years, they'd ended up fighting on the same side at the community basketball court against other guys who'd brought too much aggression to the game, more than once. More recently, Goode had saved Walker and Park at The East End, helped to rescue Tina at the warehouse, and given Walker his Mustang. In the end, he'd paid the ultimate price for his generosity.

Tears splashed on Walker's shirt as he pushed Goode's body all the way into the van. Then he closed the doors, wishing it were him in that black bag instead of his brotha.

***

Cowgill and Stare went through their preflight routine as Taylor placed a call to his lieutenant, who authorized Park and Tina to board the Dassault Falcon under the circumstances. Then Dom Taylor felt a familiar surge of panic as Cowgill raced across the dangerously short runway to lift the jet over the trees just in time. He turned to Park, who was reclining beside him in a chair that matched his own. The former SEAL was staring out the window, probably to hide his tears.

Taylor was familiar with personal loss; he'd never forget his fellow Green Berets killed in the service of their country, nor Big Don Roberts, his close friend and mentor. However, now that Cage was out of the picture, North County would be a safer place to live, and Roberts' case could finally be closed. Taylor leaned back in his seat and shut his eyes. Before the painkiller he'd taken knocked him out, he saw Big Don smiling down on him, proud of the leader he'd become and warning him there'd be more work to do.

***

There wasn't much Tina could do for anyone as she made her rounds in the main cabin. For Taylor's mangled hand it had been immobilization, ice, and a narcotic analgesic, while Park had flatly refused any kind of care. Walker's treatment had included vital signs, wound cleaning, IV fluids, and a generous smothering of hugs and kisses.

"You don't know how glad I am you're okay," she said, brushing his hair out of his eyes as she settled in beside him.

Due to Walker's facial injuries, he couldn't clearly speak, but that was fine with him. It was a good thing, actually, because any attempt to communicate his jumbled feelings wouldn't have turned out well. His eyes welled up with tears as he lifted an aching arm, pulled Tina close, and kissed her with his busted lips. She rested her head on his chest and after a while she laid it down on his lap. Three hours later, she was still asleep. As the lights of Downtown San Diego glittered into view, Walker stroked her hair. He hadn't slept at all.

He wasn't sure he'd ever sleep again.

32

EPILOGUE

"You may now kiss the bride," pronounced a black-clad priest one month later. Standing on the altar before a sea of guests, Park lifted Carla's veil and leaned in to meet her soft, ample lips. When he pulled away, both newlyweds' faces lit up with contagious excitement and the cathedral exploded into applause.

To an even greater extent than she normally did, Carla looked stunning in a white bridal gown with a long, flowing train. Her elaborate hairstyle had been a wedding gift from Alvaro from the beauty salon, her makeup expertly applied by her own hand. At her side, sharply dressed in a black tuxedo, Park gazed out at all the beaming faces. His and Carla's relatives sat in the front rows with Tina and Walker, while Lynn Peters and Sergeant Taylor sat together a few pews back. Notably absent was any member of David Goode's family.

Carla brightened the sanctuary with her best smile, and when Park turned back to her, he knew he'd never forget her lovely image, both because of his perfect memory and also since he saved it with the utmost care in the best-guarded reaches of his mental vaults as he drank in the love he saw in her liquid brown eyes. Then, when the organist launched into the recessional march, he gave her one last smooch and led her down the aisle, past the cheering guests and out through the doors. The grand departure was a sham, however;

Park and Carla then circled back into the church and stayed for a photography session that lasted forever.

The reception was held at The Marine Room, an award-winning venue built on the sand at the south end of La Jolla Shores Beach. As Park and Carla entered the main section of the dining room to another heartfelt round of applause, they peered through a fortified wall of windows at the panoramic view of the cove and the towering cliffs above it. At certain times of the year, Park knew, giant waves would dash themselves against those windows, thrilling diners who'd paid for that experience, but not on this, his wedding day. A good distance away, baby waves washed up on the shore, and as the sun dipped into the ocean at the horizon line, casting its rays in their direction, it seemed to offer them its warmest wishes for a shared life teeming with special moments such as this.

They floated across the dining room to a different section, where a short white staircase led up to a raised platform. They joined their families at a long table, which, like all the others, had been set with white linen, fresh floral centerpieces, and spotless crystal glasses. From the same stage-like space, on either side of the stairs, two balustraded balconies extended out into the main dining area, on which a few smaller tables had been placed, and it was there that Tina, Walker, Lynn, and Taylor sat chatting with each other and with several other VIPs. Beyond the platform of honor, a second wall of windows looked north, up the coast, at an infinite procession of glittering turquoise waves.

Park draped an arm over Carla's shoulders and sipped from a glass of champagne, the newly married couple glowing under the unrelenting attention of their families. Park's clan peppered him with questions about his decision to become a police officer. Some of them applauded his sense of duty while others warned of the risks, but all parties agreed that it was an honorable choice and wished him the best of luck. Carla's family began to chant "*Be-SO, be-SO, be-SO*" and they were joined by the rest of the two hundred people in attendance, obliging the love-drunk newlyweds to kiss again, which they were more than glad to do.

Walker clapped absently, his mind focused on his own bride-to-be. Beside him, Tina's dress spilled over her curvy figure to just above her knees. It was the same shade as Carla's gown but cut in a slightly less formal style. Her spectacular bright-white smile contrasted appealingly with her creamy bronze-hued skin, and her flowing black hair was done half-up in an ornate design.

"How was your first day at beauty school?" he asked.

"Like a dream," Tina replied. "I made lots of friends, and I'm sleeping better, too."

Walker was glad to hear that, although he wished *he* were sleeping better. "You know, you have a real talent for it. Look at you, so beautiful with your perfect hair and makeup. You look great!"

She waved his words away. "Thanks, but the important thing is that I *feel* great. Healthier and happier, you know what I mean?" He nodded. "How about you?" she asked in return. "How was your interview?"

"Chief Downing is no joke."

"Neither are you, Jeff Walker," she said. "I always thought I wanted a nice guy, but you're even better than that. You're a good man."

At that, he reached into his jacket pocket for a black velvet box. "I got you something," he said, dropping into the traditional position. Holding her exotic gaze, he snapped open the box and offered her a ring that had cost him half his savings. "Tina Garcia, will you make me the happiest man in the world?"

Her features lit up at once. "You know I will, honey," she said. When he rose, she threw her arms around him, planted a tender kiss on his lips, and they held each other close as tears of joy streamed down their cheeks.

"May I have your attention!" boomed a voice from down in the main dining room. Forks clinked on glasses, the chatter died down, and every guest focused on a burly Black man standing in the center of the crowd. It was Lieutenant Molloy, looking quite distinguished in a black suit and tie with a carefully folded white handkerchief peeking out of his pocket.

"Thank you," Molloy began. He was the only member of Hillside Baptist who had agreed to attend, so while the focus of the celebration was naturally and rightly on Carla and Park, for the guests who knew what had happened down in Mexico, the sight of this man and his family brought with it the stabbing pain of loss. And, in Walker's case, overwhelming feelings of guilt.

Lieutenant Molloy proceeded with a smile. "Ever since I hired Tony Park, he's shown himself to be an exemplary human being, so it's no surprise to me or anyone else in the lifeguard service that he's movin' on to bigger and better things." The gentleman lifted his gaze to the table of honor, speaking directly to the groom. "We'll miss ya at headquarters, buddy, but I *know* you and Walker are gonna be even more valuable to the Harbor Police. I'm as proud as I can be, and I wish y'all a wonderful marriage. To Park and Carla!" he roared as he raised his glass.

For a long moment, Park held his drink and his chin high as he met his boss's gaze, amid a wild cacophony of cheering and applause.

Lively conversation flowed over soft jazz played by a quartet on a bandstand as the meal was served, consisting of hot and sour soup, roast duck, Szechuan chicken, Mongolian beef, honey prawns, and chow mein, while a gorgeous three-tiered wedding cake waited in a corner for the plates to be cleared away.

After dinner, the bandleader stepped forward to pull the mic out of the stand and raise it to his lips. His dark skin was the same color as David Goode's, and his features held more than a little resemblance. With deep and stirring professionalism, the charismatic entertainer intoned, "Ladies and gentlemen, would you please turn your attention to the dance floor, where Tony and Carla will have their first dance as husband and wife."

Everyone rose as Park accompanied Carla down the stairs, and as he did, he broke into the widest, most elated grin that Walker had ever seen on his buddy's face. In the silence before the music started, Park gave her a twirl. They'd been practicing. Then the rhythm section kicked off a slow groove, to which the singer snapped his fingers and swung his hips. He began to hum as Park and Carla held each other tight. They moved well together. The well-dressed vocalist offered a subdued rendition of "Misty," and after two verses, he invited all the guests to join the happy couple.

Walker felt a warm shiver run up and down his spine as he and Tina made their way to the dance floor. The sensation assured him that his brotha would always be with him, that Goode's greatest gift hadn't been handed over begrudgingly. Quite the opposite: Walker was sure that Goode had freely and knowingly sacrificed his life, and he swore to himself he would never take that for granted, for it was only through that final act of love that Walker had survived, so that now he might slip his arm around the waist of the woman of his dreams, hold her slender hand shoulder high, and rock her back and forth in his embrace.

"I love you," Tina said, her generous lips curling into that heart-stopping smile of hers.

"I love you more," Walker returned as he pulled her close, their lips meeting in something much more significant than a kiss. It was a promise.

READERS CLUB

Dear reader, I sincerely hope that you have enjoyed this first installment of The Park and Walker Action Thriller Series. If you did, I'd appreciate it if you left me a review on the website(s) of your choice. It would help me as well as other readers. Just a line or two is fine.

Now, would you like to receive—for free—an award-winning Park and Walker prequel short story? You can do so by signing up for my readers club, members of which receive a monthly email that announces any discounts or promotions I'm currently running, contains personal book recommendations, often showcases the work of one of my author colleagues, and shares advance material or news about the next Park and Walker book in the series. You can unsubscribe at any time and I won't ever sell or disclose your email address. Just visit my website at patrickweill.com to download the short murder mystery described below:

A Hell of a Spring Break: A Prequel Story to The Park and Walker Action Thriller Series
In this award-winning short story, beach lifeguards Jeff Walker and Tony Park are sent on a week-long exchange program to the North Shore of Oahu, where a serial killer strikes twice. Are they to be the next victims? And which of their colleagues is the North Shore Thrill Killer? There's only one way to find out!

ABOUT THE AUTHOR

Patrick Weill first made his living as a professional musician, then as a licensed teacher, next as a commercial and literary translator, and now as a thriller writer. You can follow him on Facebook at facebook.com/PatrickWeillAuthor, and his website is www.patrickweill.com.

Weill is proud to be included in the bullpen of A.C.E. Thrillers: The place for Action, Crime, and Espionage books, keeping you up-to-date on what your favorite thriller authors and characters are up to.

THE LONG JOURNEY NORTH: Chapter One of Bad Traffic

BOOK II IN THE PARK AND WALKER ACTION THRILLER SERIES

A s Nayeli Sanchez labored in her family's cornfield, the Mexican sun beat down on her back with relentless cruelty. Fortunately, her body was conditioned to and adapted for such treatment. Unfortunately, the girl's tolerance for emotional distress was not developed enough to endure the mental suffering that had been weighing so heavily upon her for such an unnaturally long period of time. In other words, Nayeli was about to snap.

"You can do it, sister. Another half hour and we'll eat," her older brother Murci said in Spanish. He had just returned from the United States with jagged, knotted scars on his hands and face and had thus far refused to tell her how he'd gotten them, nor would he share any other details about his two-year stay. In the end, it didn't matter. Nayeli was beyond glad for his return, even if it meant a serious problem for her and the rest of the family.

Murci drove his digging stick into the drought-hardened soil so it stood up on its own, left it there, and came up behind her to knead out the tension in her neck and shoulders. Nayeli was relieved by the back rub, but her brother's pep talk had been of little consolation. She didn't need him to tell her she could handle another half hour of work. After all, she alone had tended to the small, heavily mortgaged plot of land for as long as he'd been gone! And at the moment, she was too upset to care about lunch.

As soon as Nayeli got back to work, her approach to soil loosening went from reluctantly slow to desperately fast. Plunging her tool harder and harder into the crusty earth, she advanced along her designated row with wild abandon until she no longer could. Tears welled in her eyes as she took a knee and heaved for air.

Murci sat down beside her and pulled her into a hug. "Don't give up," he said, then let her go, and they sat for a while, in silence mostly, save for a few bird calls now and then. When Nayeli was ready, he helped her up and walked her home.

As she trudged along the dusty dirt road, Nayeli resolved—for the millionth time—to do as her brother had told her: not to give in to the overwhelming temptation to fall down the slippery slope of despair, which, ironically, was even steeper now that he was no longer sending dollars home. Don't give up, he'd said, but isn't that what *he* had done? *If it had been me*, she thought, *I'd have stayed under any circumstances until I'd earned enough money to make a difference*. A small, secret part of her wished he hadn't come back.

They hiked past the old farmhouse, the one their father had built before they were born. The one in which they'd lived all their lives until only recently. Neither one turned to look at it. From that point to their current residence, Nayeli counted ten semi-feral dogs roaming the streets, anxiously searching for anything edible; without exception, the animals' ribs were jutting out from under their skin like those of starving concentration camp prisoners.

***

"I went to the butcher shop today to see about some chicken, but Pablo had raised his prices *again*," said Mamá at the main meal of the day, setting a cloth napkin folded around hot tortillas in the center of the table.

"It's not the butcher's fault," replied Papá, whom Nayeli had helped from his bed to the wooden table. He had dark, sickly circles around his eyes and his voice came out in a breathless whisper. "It's the...heartless...companies that control everything."

"Everything including the government," Murci added, rolling a tortilla in his palm and biting off a third of it. "Just like in the United States."

"Just like everywhere," said Nayeli. "I wish money had never been invented. What this planet needs is another meteor shower."

"Did you go to the police station today, son?" Papá asked, as if he hadn't heard her.

"Yes sir. Boot camp starts on Monday."

"Good." The farmer's eyes came alive with pride.

Nayeli wished her father would look at *her* like that, and she wondered why her parents were about to spend the last of their money on Murci's uniform, given the offensively low odds of his being selected for a paying job from among the vast ranks of volunteer officers.

"And *you*, honey?" Mamá asked, finally taking a seat after she had served everyone else. "How's school?"

As Nayeli reached for another tortilla, she refused to wish that the diced cactus paddles she was about to scoop into it were rich and savory chunks of meat. Her gaze darted around their rented lodgings, falling on the dirt floor and the rusty iron sheets that served as a roof. "Everything's fine, Mamá," she replied, saying nothing of her overcrowded classroom, the absence of textbooks, the lack of running water at that state-sponsored institution, and—crucially—the risky appointment she'd scheduled for later that evening.

***

One good thing about Murci's return to Mexico was that it allowed Nayeli to devote more of her energy to her studies. Just that morning, she'd found herself with free time between classes, so she'd strolled over to an announcement board and scanned the notices stapled there. In Spanish, one of them read as follows:

> Seeking female students to work in the U.S. as housekeepers or nannies. Nine dollars per hour with free room and board. Study for your GED at night. College scholarships available.

College in the United States of America? From the little she'd learned in school and expanded upon through independent study on the internet, her English was passable already. A swift mental calculation told her nine dollars an hour with no expenses, over one or two years, would literally lift her family out of the mire. As Nayeli mulled over the pros and cons of this enticing opportunity, her thoughts trended back to a recent conversation in the cornfield.

"Gringolandia's just not a good place," Murci had snapped, squinting in the sun as he whirled around to face her. "It's a rotten apple that only looks good from the outside."

"Right," she'd replied. "A rotten country where they pay twenty times what they do here."

Her brother's features hardened. "You don't understand. It's a dangerous place for people like us."

"I'm almost fifteen. I understand more than you think I do."

"Well, I've been there and you haven't. End of discussion."

Nayeli had turned her back on her brother, sure that hard manual labor or some other form of torture was the future that awaited her. *Life in the U.S. can't be as bad as Murci always says it is*, she'd thought. In her view, he just wanted her to stay home so he could boss her around.

As she came out of her musings, the alluring flyer returned to front and center. She tore it off the announcement board, stuffed it in her bag, and strode off to find a phone.

***

The next day, when Murci awoke before dawn as usual, he looked across the room to see Nayeli's bed still made, but he wasn't worried. As far as he knew, she'd slept over at a friend's house. Yet as the morning wore on, with no news from the family's brightest star, Mamá grew so alarmed that she took the bus to Nayeli's friend's house and learned that she'd been lied to.

On his mother's return, Murci searched Nayeli's belongings for any clue to her whereabouts and found the flyer in her backpack. That's when it dawned on him that his sister had gone in search of the money he was no longer sending home, and his fear and guilt emptied the contents of his stomach onto the floor.

His parents wanted to wait a day or two before contacting the police. Maybe the job offer was legitimate, they'd said. Maybe Nayeli would call or come back after changing her mind. But Murci knew better. He immediately called the number on the flyer and was told he'd dialed the wrong number, so then he asked a female friend to feign interest in the ad. She was given an appointment and directions to a house on a hill not far from where Murci lived. He knew which one it was. As a boy, he'd often gone up to "Beltran Manor," usually on a dare to knock on the door to what was reputedly a haunted house.

As he came up the crest, the massive home loomed majestic, but on closer inspection, its peeling paint, rotting fences, and overgrown garden told a different story. After being invited in, Murci thrust the flyer in the Beltrans' faces. "My sister's missing, and I found this in her things!" he exclaimed. "Have you seen her?"

"No, we haven't," Mrs. Beltran replied, looking baffled as she read the advertisement, seemingly for the first time. "We haven't had a visitor in a month."

"Is that your phone number?"

"No," Mr. Beltran broke in. "It's Diego Lopez's. He's a friend of my cousin's who needed a place to stay."

Murci eyed Mrs. Beltran with suspicion. "No visitors except for Diego Lopez, you mean. I had a friend call that number. She was told to show up right here, right now. This Lopez wouldn't be hiding in the next room, by any chance, would he?"

"I don't know what else to tell you," said Mr. Beltran. "He left a few hours ago. If you leave me your number, I'll have him call you when he gets back."

"Bullshit," retorted Murci, strong and loud. His pulse leapt into overdrive as he held his neighbor's gaze.

Mr. Beltran was not a small man. He stepped forward until their noses were an inch apart. "Get out of my house, boy!" he roared.

But Murci was not a boy. He whipped out a revolver from under his shirt and jabbed its muzzle into the fat man's gut. "Back up, *cabrón*," he hissed through clenched teeth. "Tell me where my sister is or I'll shoot you right now."

"They took her to San Diego," Beltran whimpered. "That's all I know, I swear to God."

Minutes later, Murci was securing a duffel bag to the back of his motorcycle. Single-focused. Furious. Imagining how terrified Nayeli must have been at that very moment and all the things they might be doing to her. After inspecting his ride and topping it off with the gas can, he stalked into the house and headed for his parents' room, where his father struggled to sit up in bed.

"I'll bring her back, Papá. I swear."

"I know you will, son. I believe in you."

Murci placed his hand on his father's shoulder, bowed his head, and begged God to keep his dad alive until he returned. *If* he returned. Then he stomped back outside to where his mother stood waiting beside his bike with open arms. She pulled him close, told him she loved him, gave him every peso in the family's possession, and blessed his trip with the sign of the cross.

Murci swung a leg over the machine and fired it up. "I love you, too, Mamá," he said over the grumbling engine. At her somber nod, he gave the throttle an aggressive twist and the two-wheeler leapt forward, roaring and snarling, matching his own rage as day turned into night on the long journey north. *Whoever did this is going to hell*, Murci vowed. *And I'm going to send them there.*

SEASONING: CHAPTER TWO OF BAD TRAFFIC

The previous evening, as Nayeli made the uphill trek to Beltran Manor, her mind was filled with mixed emotions, chiefly fear. Fear of acting against the objections her family certainly would have made, had she mentioned the alluring flyer, and fear that the ad itself might have been a trick. Yet, she thought, the latter was a remote possibility. Nayeli couldn't think of a reason why anyone would lie about a lowly service job. For all she knew, people in the USA were so rich that such employment was widely available. *And I'll take it!* she told herself as she came up the crest, feeling more confident with every step. If there was one thing Nayeli had learned in her fourteen years, it was that freedom lies in doing what one is afraid of, not in turning back once you've made up your mind. A second emotion that kept her pulse pounding as she neared the "haunted" house was excitement. The idea of saving her family made her feel important for a change. And, if she was being honest with herself, the thought of traveling to a clean and shiny world where money grew on trees was absolutely thrilling. So, when she came to the front door, she knocked without hesitation, and was admitted by a middle-aged woman who held in her hand what was decidedly not her first drink of the night.

"Hellodear! You mus' be Nayeli. ImissusBeltran. Comeonin," is how Nayeli was greeted at the door in Spanish. As she stepped inside, she saw two friendly-looking men seated at a table on the far side of the room.

"Nice to meet you, Nayeli. I'm Samuel Beltran," one of them said, hefting his bulky frame up and out of a chair to shake her hand. He nodded to the other man. "This is Diego Lopez, who runs the work-study program you called about."

Lopez rose. His eyes were sharper than those of the other two.

"Hello, Mr. Lopez," said Nayeli, sticking out her hand. "It's nice to meet you."

"The pleasure's all mine, Nayeli," Lopez replied with a reassuring smile. "Please, have a seat while I get you an information packet."

Mrs. Beltran came in from the kitchen to set a plate of quesadillas and a glass of lemonade on the table in front of her unsuspecting visitor. "Hereyagohoney," she said. "Illgetyasomenapkins."

Ironically, Nayeli would later remember thinking, as her hostess wobbled off, that it might have been better for the woman to drink some of her own lemonade instead of pouring herself another alcoholic beverage. But after the dusty uphill walk, her throat was parched, so without any further consideration, she gulped down half the contents of the glass. Not long after that, Nayeli's experience of the visit became a disjointed blur of events, in which the only thing she'd clearly recall was that Lopez came back for her, but not with any papers.

The next thing she knew, she was in the back of a car. Lopez pulled open the door to her left, admitting a blast of cool air that sharpened her senses for a moment. He held it open for another girl about her age, who scooted in beside her.

"Hi! My name's Marcela," said the newcomer. Her eyes gleamed with nervous excitement. Like Nayeli, she was petite, her skin the color of coffee and cream, with straight black hair flowing past her shoulders. As Nayeli sank back into a sleeping position and nodded off again, Lopez shut Marcela's door, got in front, slid behind the wheel, and turned to offer Marcela a bottle of lemonade.

Nayeli's next recollection took place in the darkest hours of the night, in a remote and deserted parking lot, where Lopez pulled to a stop next to a van. He stepped out to meet a tall and handsome Latino, who handed him a fat wad of cash, and the men carried the girls to the van, dumped them in the back, and slid the door shut. At some later point, that van jerked to a halt, rousing Nayeli once more. The only indication as to how much time had passed was that the sun was high and hot. The side door slid open and, with the assistance of two others, the tall and handsome Latino help-dragged the girls into a pink mansion. Once they were inside, he locked the front door with a key and said, "Listen up, ladies. My name's Martinez, and I'm going to help you get settled in." His words bordered on polite and they had been spoken in the girls' own language, but his grin was alarmingly dark and eager. As the three men herded her and Marcela up a wide marble staircase, Nayeli steadied herself on a dusty wooden handrail. By then she knew she'd made a terrible mistake.

On the second floor, they came to a hallway with several doors. Martinez opened the nearest one and gestured for Marcela to enter. "I'll be back for you," he said.

Before he shut Marcela in, the girls exchanged a look of panic. Then his goons positioned themselves on either side of the door and he headed for the next one, opened it, and motioned for Nayeli to go in. As she did, she saw a completely unfurnished space except for a queen-size bed centered along the right-hand wall. A folded blanket lay at the foot end and no pillows had been provided.

"You'll be staying here for a few weeks before we leave for the United States," Martinez said, easing the door closed. "I'll be taking care of you until then."

As he stepped closer, cold dread seemed to pour out from his eyes into Nayeli's and flood her with such terror that her only thought was to run. *Now!* Her eyes flitted to the door and he slapped her, hard.

"Your trip north is going to cost us a lot of money," Martinez went on calmly. "So you're going to work off that debt starting right now. Your job will be to keep me happy." He then recited her home address and her parents' full names, saying he'd kill them if she didn't unzip his trousers and manipulate him to orgasm. Before that day, she'd never even kissed a boy.

"Not bad," he said matter-of-factly when it was done. "But you'll have to learn to do it better. Sexier, if you know what I mean. Don't worry, I'll show you how."

After he'd gone, Nayeli slid down the wall to the floor and wrapped her arms around her knees, staring straight ahead. A sharp cry escaped her lips, and she burst into tears. *Murci was right all along.*

Over the following weeks, Martinez forced Nayeli, Marcela, and three other girls to perform unspeakable acts. If they refused, he'd hit them, and if they didn't do it in a pleasing manner or showed any other kind of resistance, they'd go without food and water for as long as it took to adjust their attitude.

One evening, all the new recruits were sitting in a common room watching a movie, curled up on couches and covered by blankets. At a lull in the on-screen action, Marcela spoke up. "At least he hasn't gone all the way," she said. "I wonder why not."

"It's because he's not all bad," another girl answered. "Today he gave me a twenty-dollar bill."

Nayeli tilted her recliner forward, set her feet on the floor, and shook her head. "I hate to be the one to tell y'all this, but it's not because he's nice. I bet he gets paid more to deliver virgins. Think about it. They can charge a lot more for your first time."

Marcela visibly tensed. She and Nayeli had grown close, often talking for hours late into the night, so Nayeli knew her friend was fragile, both in body and spirit.

"Good evening," said Martinez, sweeping into the room through an open archway and stopping beside the television with three unknown men behind him. Clad in a crisply pressed gray suit that matched his businesslike demeanor, he dominated the girls with his gaze and announced, "Tonight y'all are going to do something different. By now you know I'm not the only man you'll have to service, so let's get it over with." He nodded to his colleagues, who stepped forward in a row. Their greedy eyes made Nayeli sick. One of them pointed straight to her, but Martinez shook his head. "She's off-limits." Then Martinez jerked his chin in Marcela's direction. "And *she's* not ready."

This left three young teenagers for three middle-aged men, who made their choices like captains picking teams in the schoolyard.

"Do you want to stay up for a while?" Martinez asked Nayeli and Marcela once the other girls had led their visitors upstairs, by the hand, just as they'd been trained to do.

Nayeli couldn't tell whether Martinez was just being nice or if he had some other motive, but she couldn't afford to waste the opportunity in any case. She nodded, and so did Marcela.

"Okay. But you'd better be in your rooms by eleven."

After he'd gone, Nayeli hurried to sit on the couch beside Marcela, whom she looked dead in the eye. "This is our only chance," she whispered. "Once we're over the border, it'll be much harder to get back home."

"I'm not sure," Marcela replied, also in hushed tones. "What if he catches us?"

"He probably will. But I'd rather die than keep on doing what he's making us do."

It took Marcela some time to make her decision, but at last she nodded with determination. Nayeli took her by the hand and led her into the darkness of the kitchen. "I've already had a look around," Nayeli said, as quietly as she could. "Every door is always locked. All the windows too, except for that little one." She pointed to a small pane of glass above the sink, which, she figured, might have been forgotten when the house was refitted for malicious purposes. "I'll go first," Nayeli said, climbing onto the counter to push open the window. No alarm went off and nothing else occurred, so she squeezed herself through and dropped down to the dimly lit back yard. A quick glance in all directions showed no signs of life. She spun back around to grab Marcela's dangling legs, but as she did, something hard slammed into the side of her head and that was the last—

***

"That's why you said I was off-limits," Nayeli groaned, addressing Martinez. She didn't sit up in her bed or turn to look at him because the resulting headache would have made her throw up again. "Last night was a test."

"Correct," Martinez replied from a kneeling position. Still clad in gray slacks and the white dress shirt from the night before, but with no jacket and his sleeves rolled up, he was busy scooping up her vomit with a plastic dustpan and knocking it into a trash can. "I knew you were smart, and now I know you're brave. Too brave for your own good, in fact. We're leaving for the border tomorrow, and I didn't want anything bad to happen to you up there."

"So you taught me a lesson."

"Something like that." For the third time, Martinez glanced remorsefully at the massive goose egg on the side of her head.

This display of concern was confusing. *First the bastard kidnaps and abuses me*, Nayeli thought. *Now he cares, but not enough to let me go?* Involuntarily, her stomach clenched and her throat widened, so she leaned over the bed toward the floor.

Martinez heard her gag and looked up just as a second quart of putrid sludge poured out of her mouth and hit him in the face. He froze for a moment, as though resisting the urge to strangle her, but then he simply pulled out a handkerchief and wiped himself clean. "You won't eat or drink until we get to California," he said.

Nayeli rolled over to face the wall.

***

It took two horribly uncomfortable days to reach the border in the van, during which time the five girls were kept bound and gagged in the hot and stuffy rear cargo area. There would be no work visa, of course, so before the vehicle rolled to a stop at the checkpoint, Martinez turned and warned them not to make any noise. Despite this, just as he reached the front of the line, two of them kicked the walls and gave muffled cries for help. There were no windows back there, so Nayeli couldn't see the border guards' reaction, but they must have heard the commotion and waved Martinez forward anyway. Thus, as the van left the barren land and ruined streets of Mexico for the irrigated greenery and the wide, perfect roads of San Diego, she came to the frightening realization that she was caught up in a criminal operation with a budget big enough to bribe its way past the U.S. authorities.

Martinez dropped off the other girls before driving Nayeli and Marcela to a place known as Western Nail Spa, where a heavy-set older woman, maybe fifty years of age, met them at the front door and watched them like a hawk as they trudged inside. As she passed the reception counter, Nayeli saw something she'd only seen in movies and magazines: pedicure and manicure stations.

"Follow me," said the older woman, whose breathing grew heavy as she led them to an office that reeked of stale cigarette smoke. "Sit over there," she said in English, then plopped herself into a chair behind a desk. "You may call me Mama." The woman's coarse and curly hair was dyed brown to hide the gray, and her bright-red lipstick and floral dress stood in stark contrast to the lifelessness in her eyes. She might have been beautiful once, but not anymore. As the scowling madam reached for a pack of cigarettes and fired one up, Nayeli considered making a run for it, but Mama tossed the smokes to a young Latino blocking the open doorway. It was a good throw and a better catch. The young man's forehead, cheeks, neck, arms, and knuckles were covered in crude tattoos, and his body language sent a clear message: he was not to be crossed.

"I'm the manager here," Mama explained. "And this is Beto, my assistant. We'll be in charge of you from now on."

Beto cupped his hands as he lit up, then drew deeply and held it in before blowing out a toxic cloud. "Come with me," he told the girls in Spanish, with an accent Nayeli couldn't place. She and Marcela followed him up a staircase. At the top, he unlocked a door that opened onto a carpeted hallway with many doors on either side, like in a hotel but with less wall space between each one.

"This is where you will sleep and work," Beto said, opening two doors to tiny rooms that looked like prison cells. Each contained a massage table, a sink, a mirror, and little else. "The bathroom's down the hall. To show you my heart's in the right place, I'll give you the afternoon off, but you'll start tomorrow morning. Questions."

Marcela raised a shaky hand. "Will we have to...to...do everything?"

"Oh, right," their inked-up handler returned. "No, only what you're already accustomed to. When your big day comes, I'll be sure to let you know." Then he headed back down to the ground floor, locking the door at the top of the stairs with a heavy click that echoed like the end of the world.

A painful lump formed in Nayeli's throat. *What would Mamá, Papá, and Murci think of me now?* Marcela reached out her arms, and Nayeli stepped into the offered embrace, holding on for dear life as both girls burst into tears.

Made in the USA
Las Vegas, NV
09 March 2024

86952290R00163